It Always Works
Sometimes

It Always Works Sometimes

A novel by:

Joel F. Pullen

Dedicated to:

Everyone in particular.

No one in general …..

Forward

A Paradox:
Something seemingly contrary
to common sense or absurd
and yet possibly true.
An enigma or mystery.

An Enigma:
Something obscure or hard to understand.
A paradox or mystery.

A Mystery:
Something not understood.
A paradox or enigma.

Axiom:
It Always Works Sometimes. . . .

Wisdom:
"Them's the conditions that prevail."
James Francis Durante

IT WAS 23 April 1979 about eleven in the morning. I was late and the last members of the funeral gathering were leaving the small cemetery just as I arrived. It was better this way. I really didn't know any of them anyway. Two distant cousins I knew existed but never met. The other five people were evidently relatives or friends of the deceased, a step-mother I never really knew. I can't bring myself to even think of her as a step-mother since I never lived with her or the man purported to be my father. I only saw him two times my whole life and each time was an unpleasant experience. He died suddenly almost two years ago and was buried before I found out about it. I met her once.

I guess it's okay to finally admit that neither of these people buried next to each other in this miserable little excuse for a town mean very much to me. Stone View, Arkansas, needs to at least be considered as a candidate for the anal orifice of this old world. Why anyone with any thought toward civility or any cultural aspect of life would wish to be buried here, much less live here, is beyond my understanding.This was my first trip back to the "old country", as my brother calls Arkansas, since I was eight years old. I had never been in this part of the state. I had only been in Little Rock, where I was born in 1932, and Black Springs, when I traveled with my mother and brother in a 1934 Chevy owned by a male friend of the family, when my great grandfather was buried in 1937. We traveled west later on.

There have been several times in my life when I have found myself in a particular setting asking myself why or how did I get here and what purpose have I for being here. I guess all thinking folk have at one time or another experienced this strange detached feeling. The feeling of hovering above or beside a setting but not really being a part of it—when I was a kid I had these wonderful realistic Technicolor dreams of free flying through the air from place to place—the trouble was that every kid knew—for certain—if you fell during one of these dreams you would die. How and why am I here? I truly have no idea why I decided to come at the last minute. I could have put this closure in the hands of a local attorney and never looked back, but something drew me here. Some deep and gnawing need to know something, anything. The first and most rational curiosity has always been the name change thing. The subject had, at one time, been broached and denied without discussion. The question of why he never aspired beyond primitive moral baseness and meager cognition remains unanswered as does the curiosity about how he survived financially. Never in my 46 years was any understandable means of support exhibited.

I have almost total recall of places and things I have seen or read and also of conversations which have taken place since I was about 3 years old, and this stuff is on some type of storage tapes waiting to be projected like a movie on the inside of my eyelids, or sometimes a voice within my mind which seems to read aloud these things I wish to recall. The only change is the size factor. The actual streets are never really as wide or distances as great when reviewed as an adult, but nevertheless the picture and the voice over is very accurate. I have never been here before and will never return.

1 926 MUST HAVE been an exciting year. Silent Calvin Coolidge was President of the United States, the Volstead Act, commonly called prohibition, had been in full swing for about eight years, Doctors Macleod and Banting had learned to manufacture insulin, Gertrude Ederle swam the English Channel, Theodore Dreiser had written his eight hundred forty page "An American Tragedy", Ernest Hemingway finally sold his first novel called "The Sun Also Rises", the 1925 silent movie "The Big Parade" was still showing, Oliver Wendell Holmes was 85 years old and my big brother was born right on the kitchen table in downtown Little Rock with a midwife attending.

The marriage had taken place about 9 months earlier and from all I have heard it was legit. The marriage that is. Mom could not have been happier. She and Charlie had been engaged for three whole months before the marriage. She was now Mrs. C.C. Lubeck. Mrs. Charlie Clyde Lubeck to be exact. Not Charles. Charlie! They had known each other in Caddo Gap as kids, but Charlie dropped out of school and ran away to God only knows. Mom went on to finish high school and moved away to Little Rock, when she was eighteen. She ran into Charlie one night at a dance and although she didn't know it at the time things began to go down hill from there.

Mom should have known from the beginning that Charlie was less than what he said he was but she took most people at their word because when she told you something was the truth, you could bank on it. On the other hand, Mom never was free, as I recall, with answers about things. The answers always came with a price. "You don't have any need to know about that" became a well worn phrase throughout my life. She always has had a second sense about people telling the truth. That is everyone except Charlie.

I guess Charlie Clyde Lubeck told more lies per day throughout his entire life than any other human in history. The biggest lie he told to Ada—Ada was Ada Laura Slewter which was my mother's maiden name—was that he loved and cherished her and would care forever—or some such bull shit and that he would work night and day to give her all of the things a dutiful husband could and should give to his new bride.

The only problem with this night and day story was that he got confused. He had apparently forgotten to mention that during the courtship with Ada he was also courting Beatrice and Beryl. There is also no doubt that he failed to mention to Beatrice or Beryl his courtship of, let alone marriage to Ada. I suppose that he could have been forgiven by Ada for this failure, except that he didn't cease and desist with the B & B courtship after the marriage.

No one knows how long Charlie actually refrained from seeing B & B after he married Ada but the odds are it wasn't for very long. Beatrice soon found something else to do with her evenings and dropped out of the picture sometime in 1927. Not so with Beryl. Beryl had an itch to become a Nurses Aide.

Charlie wasn't "fairly shiftless", he was "really shiftless" and was only able to find odd jobs until he ran into a friend who got him on as a construction helper building the Colonial Bakery at Markham and Cross in Little Rock. When the construction work was completed, Charlie applied for and got a job as a helper in the Bakery. He never managed to keep enough money on pay day to move Ada and my brother into a house or even an apartment. The best Charlie could do was a rooming house on Barber Street. The three of them shared one room. Nine others shared the rooming house and the one bathroom. An evening meal was included in the weekly price and was served family style in a small dining room on the first floor.

Charlie, if nothing else, could do some talking even though it always came out in what could be described as nasal or adenoidal. His actual use of the English Language was corrupted with an Ozark "twang"—he couldn't say "things"—he said "thangs" and "jest" instead of "just"— and "ah reckon" was also a standard. He was about 6 feet tall, thin as string and walked and carried himself much like Walter Mathieu but somewhat resembled a young Henry Fonda in the face. I guess he cut quiet a path with the ladies in spite of this language barrier. I forgot to mention one of Charlie's other problems, an unquestionable problem with hooch. I also guess Charlie spent most of his entire life in a state of denial about a lot of things, this one especially.

Being the good talker that he was, Charlie finally convinced the owner of the bakery, an honorable and trusting man, or Charlie would have already been run down the road, that he, Charlie, could run a bread route better than anyone and was finally given the opportunity to make his mark in this world.

He now got a small salary plus a commission on all of the bakery goods he could sell over and above a set number of units. It wasn't long before the bakery expanded its domain to some of the rural towns and one of these towns just happened to be Hot Springs. Beryl was also spending some time there and I don't even need to tell you what took place. Now Charlie hardly ever got back to the boarding house until the wee hours, if at all.

THE YEAR WAS 1930 and Ada had had just about all she could take. She had been working part time cleaning rooms at the Albert Pike Hotel which was within walking distance of another boarding house, the fourth or fifth or maybe the eighth since the wedding. It was strange how the same boarders seemed to drift to the next boarding house kind of like a family unit but only after they had worn out their welcome which always seemed to equate with running out of resources.

Helen Stewart was the lady who managed but didn't own the first boarding house Ada and Charlie and my brother lived in and was now running this one. Ada and Helen would remain lifelong friends.

Helen was fairly stable and was married to a brakeman on the Missouri Pacific Railroad. For some unknown reason, the Stewarts never owned a home and were content with living in boarding houses. Mack, Helen's husband, was killed in a rail accident in 1933 and Helen received a lifelong railroad pension. But, that's getting away from my story.

Needless to say, Helen didn't like anything about Charlie from the first moment she laid eyes on him. I don't guess Charlie had much good to say about Helen either since she pretty much told it like it was and had great influence over Ada. Helen convinced Ada that things could not be or get any worse without Charlie since he spent so little time with his family anyway.

About this time in Ada's life a "good news—bad news" thing happened. The bad news was that her mother became a widow for the second time and decided to move to Little Rock.

Now Miss Laura, as Ada's mother was known, was a true American epic. She had been born in The Indian Territory in 1878 and by now was approaching 52 years of age. She had intelligence beyond that which comes from graduating from a small country town high school like Caddo Gap Academy. Her father was from an old German family with principles and work ethics not clearly understood today. He had graduated from an Arkansas Trade Tech in Fayetteville, which would later become the University of Arkansas, and became a Master Surveyor. Surveyors were in great demand in the Indian Territory, getting things all laid out in one hundred-sixty acre plots for the great land rush which led to the state of Oklahoma.

Now you know how Miss Laura happened to have been born in The Indian Territory. Well, be that as it may, straight and rigid, hard shelled Baptist, tougher than an Indian bow string, teetotaler, bible thumping, hymn singing, praise the lord Miss Laura showed up one day and Charlie, after being gone most of the week, showed up that night. Woe be unto Charlie!!! Hell had no fury like a Baptist with a cause.

The good news part was that Charlie departed that rooming house just ahead of Miss Laura's belt. Helen threw what few belongings he had into the middle of North Street and Charlie was lucky she didn't throw them in the middle

17

of the water works pond which was right next door.

Miss Laura and Ada never really got "right" with each other from that night on. Not because of Charlie, but because by this time in her life Ada had rediscovered that she was a very attractive twenty four year old woman who—had it already been the nineteen forties—could pass for a Barbara Stanwyck double and had just devoted the past years of her life to a real loser. She unleashed at least four years of pent up anger, regret, scorn, resentment and just plain old every day hate.

Ada raised more hell around the Little Rock nightlife scene by accident in the next year and a half than most people did on purpose. Men flocked around and there was always a speakeasy nearby. Ada always pretended as if she would give it all. That is all except her body and her love. No man would ever again. . . . my brother was now four and a half years old.

The bottom—to use the most famous cliché—had fallen out of the economy and things were beginning to go to hell in a hand basket. Miss Laura managed to find jobs in millinery stores and as a seamstress so there was always survival money and Helen was pretty generous with food— after all, she only managed the place she didn't own it—so Ada, Miss Laura and my brother survived. Even though she raised hell at night while Miss Laura took care of my brother, Ada always managed to find her way on time to whatever job she was presently doing. I guess she was a very good worker because she managed to find work all through the great depression.

Good old Charlie continued to stumble his way through his bread route and Beryl had finished her training as a Nurses Aide and returned to Little Rock. The two of them hooked up in a loose alliance and Beryl found a job at the

Missouri Pacific Hospital doing what Nurses Aides did best. Charlie continued to do what Charlie did best. That is to say he drank a lot, told one lie after another and cavorted with Beryl and just about anybody else with a skirt or some money to spend or lose. I'm not sure how much cavorting Beryl did but it is my belief that she could cavort, drink and tell lies almost as well as Charlie. Not a dime was contributed to the family during this entire time.

This arrangement went on for about a year or so when for some unknown reason Beryl decided to move to Kansas City, Missouri. Charlie always maintained that he was kept in the dark about the reason or reasons. No one knows much about Beryl's cavorting sessions during her detachment to Kansas City, but it is believed that Beryl managed to become—in a loose—perhaps name only sense—married.

A LL OF THE antics of which Charlie managed to partake brought the world almost through 1931. Christmas of that year and my brother was five years and three months old. The three of them— Ada, Miss Laura and my brother—were now living in a tiny house next door to the old boarding house on Barber Street. No one remembers just how they acquired this luxury of house living but never the less, it at least had some privacy. Two bedrooms, a tiny parlor, a kitchen and a "private bathroom." The Star Spangled Banner became the National Anthem, W.H. Carothers created panty hose— well that's not true—actually he invented nylon and Chester Gould created Dick Tracy.

One industry which managed to thrive during the ugly years of the depression was the insurance business. I don't know how long the so called "dime policies" had already been in effect and popular with the ordinary folk in America, but I do know that in 1926 Ada had taken out a life insurance policy on Charlie. The salesman sold these policies in increments of ten cents per some unit of return. It was the custom for the salesman—more commonly known as "collectors"—to show up at the same time each month—God knows how they managed to track down the constant tide like surging movements of most of these "clients" during these depression days—but they did. The "collector" would write down the date and amount of the monthly payment in a small receipt book kept by the "client" and also record it on his "master record."

The collectors eventually came to know lots of things about lots of folks. Who was doing what to whom and so forth. At any rate the policy Ada had started in 1926 was for six hundred dollars. Not so much then but by Christmas 1931 it seemed like a fortune. Don't know how she managed, but she never missed a payment in all those years. Almost too good to be true, but in four more years the policy would be paid up for life.

The insurance company actuaries never figured on an Ada when they factored in the attrition rate. If she had nothing else, not even a divorce, she had that policy and one day, by her reckoning, "that Charlie son of a bitch Lubeck" would get himself killed or die from alcohol poisoning—she didn't much care which—and she would collect on that policy.

I have never been able to figure out certain inevitable datum in life's trek. For example: why women never seem able to get air in a low tire or filling the fuel tank before the little yellow light has been on for eighty miles or turning the thermostat up to eighty five so it will get warm faster or never taking a sweater when going on an evening outing in early spring. I could go on and on but you get the picture.

Well! How in hell or in the name of anything even closely related to good common sense Ada let herself be talked into a reconciliation by Charlie rates as one of life's great mysteries never to be solved. The fact is that it was inevitable because that's how those things work and no amount of scientific study or prayer can change the teeming inward stupidity that can come about during situations such as this. Plainly put, there is no way to account for it. Charlie was back just in time for Christmas. Everything was going to be just like a beautiful new dream and Ada bought it. She had been struck dumb and Charlie was flying high.

"Spectator, this machine, you see here wound up to the full in such a way that the spring will slowly unwind the whole length of a human life, is one of the most perfect constructed by the infernal gods for the mathematical destruction of a mortal" so said Jean Cocteau in the prologue of his stage play version of Oedipus.

It is a true inviolate fact that I have never had an Oedipus complex. It is also a true inviolate fact that "I became"—in September of 1932.

I guess that if that machine hadn't been properly unwinding just like the plans called for I would be residue somewhere and you wouldn't be reading this. There are many with whom I have crossed paths during my years as a "fact" who would opt—could they change history—for the residue arrangement—but if nothing else I have always been tenacious.

MISS LAURA WENT back to Caddo Gap shortly after the reunion in order, she said later, to keep from maiming Charlie. She was, after all, a God fearing woman and didn't believe in killings only "maimings." Miss Laura wanted to disable, damage and otherwise impair Charlie because she knew that Ada was destined to become—My Mother.

Before Miss Laura even had time to reach Caddo Gap Charlie was on the prowl once again. Ada was too embarrassed to admit that she had made two horrible mistakes. Number one letting Charlie back into her life and number two letting me keep mine. I don't to this day, even for an instant, believe Ada had any qualms about abortion. I instead choose to believe in destiny—a predetermined course of events much like Caucteau's machine and perhaps Ada had these same thoughts. We can never know.

Charlie, at some time during his employment with the bakery, had learned how to skim and pocket money from the daily sales. He had never been a very good employee at any time during these past several years and was always the first to be laid off during slack times but somehow also managed to talk his way back. I believe that at this particular time he was only working part time and perhaps on another probation period at that. At any rate Mr Jones, the owner, was pretty used up and very suspicious about his profits on the day that Charlie decided to make his "big move." Keep in mind that Charlie was never as bright as Charlie thought he was.

The plan was scheduled for the 19th of August. Charlie thought he did everything right that early morning. He ordered up almost a double load of baked goods for the day's service and took off toward Hot Springs. He must have actually worked pretty hard that day or had prearranged sales at a discount because he accounted for, according to the police reports, one hundred and twenty seven dollars when his truck was forced off of Arch Street Pike just north of 65th street in the outskirts of Little Rock about 7:00 pm returning to The Colonial Bakery.

The sheriffs reports noted: *"Lubeck stated that two masked men pulled him from the bread truck, hit him with a black jack on his chin and on the back of his head, leaving him stunned and helpless and took all of the day's sales collections."* Charlie was taken to the County Hospital in Little Rock in the Sheriff's car and pronounced in good physical condition after an exam. The absence of any bruising or edema where the trauma from the blackjack was supposed to have been applied was noted. However, the medical report did describe several lesions which appeared to be fingernail scratches on his neck and under his torn undershirt.

Charlie's scratches were cleansed and dressed and he was released from the hospital. Ada had been contacted by this time and came to the hospital to take him to her place in a borrowed car. I doubt much sympathy was discharged during the convalescent period which didn't last beyond the next afternoon. In any event, my brother, being six years old by this time, still remembers the events of the next two days.

The next day Charlie left the house late in the afternoon not to return until the next morning at which time Ada let loose all over him verbally. He had returned with a car he said he had borrowed from a friend.

That day just before noon—Ada had gone to work early and had instructed him on how to care for my brother—Charlie loaded my brother into the car and drove across town to a location still unremembered. On the way they stopped for something to eat and my brother remembers he had some chocolate milk with his sandwich.

After reaching his destination, which seemed to be a boarding house, Charlie instructed my brother to sit in the car and wait because he had to attend to some important business. Twenty minutes for a five year old can be like a day but after some long amount of time a "police car" pulled up in front of the car in which my brother was lounging and one behind. Police officers of some brand emerged from both cars and disappeared into the building. More time elapsed and finally one of the police officers came to my brothers "hiding place" and told him that he was going to take him home to his mother and that Charlie would not be coming with them.

Things get slightly more muddled about this time since the only account of the fiasco comes from two almost identical articles written in the Arkansas Democrat newspaper and in the Gazette. The first stories were taken from the police report and covered what had been reported to have happened during the "robbery" and reached the readers the next day. The day after the arrest, both newspapers filed stories indicating that Charlie Clyde Lubeck had been brought in for questioning and further investigation was taking place.

I don't know how long Charlie squirmed or how many times the police brought him back for questions but I think it is fair to say that it was more than several. This was a serious crime and so far, Charlie was their best suspect.

Certainly no one in our family knows the name of the person or persons Charlie was visiting in that apartment. One would have to suspect that the sheriff considered some hanky-panky had taken place right from the first contact. Charlie was probably under surveillance and followed when he left the house with my brother.

When Charlie was released and given a warning that the investigation would continue he had every right to be worried. However, I guess the sheriff couldn't come up with enough solid evidence to bring him up for trial and he was released. No bail nor bond was requested. Charlie hauled ass for Kansas City. No one knew where he was and frankly, most who knew him could care less even if he was.

Great suspicion with little or no evidence makes for a poor court case and all charges were actually dropped but Charlie could not have known this clear up in Kansas City.

It turns out that this was not his first time in Kansas City, nor even his second. It seems that he had made his way there first as a teen after he left school and before he met Ada at the dance. In fact he had lived there for about a year then drifted for a spell learning many survival skills which now served him well playing the "I'm sure a warrant is out for my arrest in Little Rock" game in the local gin mill. Whether he had any help during this bread route robbery is unknown and if he did what his cut amounted to could only be supposition but however it worked out it probably served him for a couple of months. At least some amount of justice was served because he did run scared.

When September 1932 finally got around to being, I got around to being—on the elevator at the County General Hospital in Little Rock, Arkansas. *Birth Certificate—out of sepsis and male by examination—Mother—Ada Laura Lubeck—Married—White—611 W. 6th St.—Amer. Citz.— Age 25 Occupation—HsWf.—Father—Charlie Clyde Lubeck—White—Add.Unkn.—Amer Citz.—Age 26 Occupation—Salesman.*

I didn't tell you about Trixie yet because the story already is fairly complex and I have liked uncomplicated things all my life. However, I need to take a few minutes and tell you about Ada's younger sister who was born to Miss Laura about five years after Ada and fathered by my grandfather—whom I never knew because he died in 1913—when Ada was just six.

George Washington Slewter must have been a hell of a man because when he died at the age of 32 he was licensed to practice law, teach secondary school, was the editor of the Caddo Gap Sentinel newspaper, had a license to sell insurance, was a member of International I.O.O.F., had taught Miss Laura in high school, married her after her graduation and fathered Ada and Trixie. The fact is that I really love this man even today and never ever knew him. He always called my grandmother Miss Laura.

Ok, back to Trixie. Trixie had been more or less raised by the great grandfather I told you about at the very beginning. The one who was a surveyor who's funeral I attended in 1937. He was Trixie's Maternal Grandfather. Well, Miss Laura and George evidently could really throw some genes together because if Ada was as beautiful as Barbara Stanwyck, Trixie looked like a red headed Doris Day. Ada was the smarter of the two but Trixie could get things done.

Trixie was married to Louie Benabenuto better known on the professional wrestling circuit as Louie Benuto. He was as tough and profane as he looked. Six foot even, with a thick chest, huge shoulders, a thick neck which seemed to be just a continuation of a massive head which had features consisting of large cauliflower ears, a mashed over nose and teeth and jaws which could crack black walnuts. Other than that, he looked quiet normal.

Trixie and Uncle Louie traveled throughout the country like all professional wrestling folks did but always called Little Rock their home base even though they never owned a home or even had a permanent address. Uncle Louie was also part owner of a speakeasy roadhouse called the Venetian out on Arch Street Pike which was not far from where Charlie was "robbed." He was connected with the bootleg mob in some capacity and had pull with the sheriff's department since their road house never got raided before a "get da hooch out fast" call reached the front office of the inn.

He had been World Heavy Weight Wrestling Champion in 1915-16 and 18. Those were the days before when men were men.

It so happened that in September of 1932 Trixie and Uncle Louie had just returned from a very successful wrestling tour and life had been financially rewarding. In fact very rewarding. He drove a rather substantial 1930 Cadillac Fleetwood. Trixie arrived at the hospital shortly after I arrived at the hospital. I suspect the folks at the Pulaski County Hospital didn't see a lot of deliveries in their elevator or chauffeur driven Cadillacs at their front door. You know what? My Aunt Trixie never ever learned to drive a car and I went home in that very same chauffeur driven Cadillac three days later.

My Aunt Trixie thought I was hers and took the privilege of naming me, mainly because Ada had decided not to name me anything. As I write this today, believe me when I tell you that had it not been for my Aunt Trixie my name would be No Name Lubeck. instead of L. H. Lubeck.

Actually it is Laurel Hardy Lubeck because Trixie loved movies and had earlier in the evening gone to the Arkansas Theater to see the first run comedy film "Pack Up Your Troubles" starring "Stan Laurel and Oliver Hardy" .

I remain forever grateful that she had not decided to stay in the hotel and read Erskine Caldwell's just published best seller "Tobacco Road." . . . Good God—Jeter Lester Lubeck ?

Ada by this time had moved out of the little house on Barber Street and was once again living in a boarding house with her guardian angel Helen. She was in a world of hurt. Two kids and nothing else.

It apparently is not a well known fact that the great depression didn't much affect the very wealthy, the already very poor city dwellers, what we moderns call "street people" and the poor dirt farmer—who didn't even know he was poor and who's life had always consisted of boiled vegetables during season, canned vegetables out of season, eggs from a few layers who could scratch bugs and once in a while fried chicken, but mostly black eyed peas and some hog parts. Since every thing in this world is, whether you choose to believe it or not, relative, the above mentioned segment of society carried out life as usual and without much change.

For Ada the struggle was forever. She finally convinced Miss Laura that she should return to Little Rock to take care of Laurel and Magnis. Oh! I hadn't told you yet— Magnis Caravle Lubeck that's really my brothers name.

Charlie had named him and I suppose he had the word Magnum on his mind though I doubt he ever drank from anything larger than half a pint.

Charlie liked to talk about old sailing ships—although he had never seen one—and was probably trying for the old 15th century Spanish Caravel to round out my brother's launching. You don't often find either one of these names in print.

Christmas 1932 found Ada, Miss Laura, Magnis and me pretty much without. And would you believe that audacious hoax Charlie Clyde Lubeck just happened to drop in on Christmas day acting as if nothing had taken place over the past year.

He told Ada that he had been working right there in Little Rock but everyone believed he was lying. Ada didn't know that he had been in Kansas City and truth is, didn't care.

He brought Magnis a little toy truck. He didn't bring me anything. Ada tried to be civil but the hurt was deep. Miss Laura just walked out of the boarding house and went to church, telling Ada on her way out that she didn't want to find Charlie there when she returned. I didn't much care one way or the other, I was only four months old.

Well, Charlie did leave the boarding house shortly after Miss Laura, but not before he made a pass at Ada. Magnis remembers her laying a "right hay maker" along the left side of Charlies face. This one stunned him and while he was recovering Ada made a lunge for a thick gnarled stick which tapered much like a baseball bat and which always leaned against the door frame and was designed to serve as a deterrent for intruders. Charlie saw what was coming and made it through the door as the club swished the air and just missed his least vulnerable part—his head—by inches.

A deadly serious life taking attempt.

That was the last Ada, Miss Laura or Magnis or anyone else saw or heard of Charlie Clyde Lubeck for almost two years.

1934 found Trixie and Uncle Louie headed for Kansas City on a wrestling tour which was well advertised. Magnis had been attending Kramer Grammar School and was on vacation and that was about the most exciting thing going on in the world except that Al Capp first produced Li'l Abner in the funny papers. Actually there were so many things going on world wide that you would get all swirly headed if I started mentioning them so I won't. You know, the old tag about "those who—or is it whom—fail to study history are bound to repeat it"—or something like that—falls on deaf ears with the young generation of today.

Trixie decided that it would be fun to have him along. Magnis had never been any place. Uncle Louie drove the Cadillac and they stopped often to see things along the way and eat at "fancy places."

I don't believe "Living well is the best revenge" had been coined at that time but it was certainly apropos. Several days into the wrestling tournament Trixie had a message at the hotel Muhlbach, where she and Uncle Louie were staying, which was from Charlie. The message said that he would like to see Magnis if it was alright with her. Of course Trixie had no idea that Charlie was even still alive much less in Kansas City. The note revealed a phone number where he could be reached. She was, the voice said, just a friend and a message could be left for Charlie.

Trixie arranged for him to have a free pass to the wrestling arena that night and left instructions on where she and Magnis would be sitting and he showed up right on time. They spoke civilly for a while and Charlie asked if

Magnis could spend the next evening with him at his place. Trixie conferred with Uncle Louie before deciding that it would be okay but not before Uncle Louie confronted and admonished Charlie about what would become of him if any harm or sadness came upon Magnis. I certainly don't believe Magnis was in any danger. I believe Charlie simply had one of the few guilt sessions with his conscience he ever had in his life and probably just wanted to "show off" Magnis to whom ever.

I have a feeling that the "significant other"—another phrase coined much later—with whom Charlie was co-habitating was not so thrilled as was he because Magnis remembers after having a hot dog and a soda, that they went to a city park where some band music was going on and then sleeping on a blanket all night. This was kind of fun for Magnis but Charlie was quick to tell him the next day that the "camp out" was to be their secret and not to tell his Aunt Trixie where they had spent the night.

Magnis was returned to the hotel in good condition and true to his word, he didn't tell.

MY OLDEST SYNAPSE dates back to age three and a half and the year of 1936. I guess it must have been in the spring because I was barefooted and we were allowed to go barefooted sometimes in the spring because it wasn't yet hot enough for hook worms to be active.

Miss Laura had now assumed complete control over raising Magnis and me and there were certain things one just did not do and one of these things which one just did not do was to "act uncivilized." However, occasionally it was okay but I never did figure out when the occasions were to be so I pretty much did as I was told. At three and a half one didn't do much arguing with Miss Laura. Nor at twenty-nine and a half for that matter—which was now Ada's age.

Another modern day myth which seems to be constantly bantered about by the baby boomer crowd is that somehow there is safety in numbers and that if a whole lot of people can't make their mortgage payments, because they lost their jobs—or whatever reason—that the banks just can't take every one's house away because where would all of the people live: etc. . . .

Ada had a job making card board boxes at the Scott

Paper Box Company working 60 hours and cleared a little more than twelve dollars each week. She worked mostly at night so she was at home sleeping and caring for me during the day. Magnis didn't need much supervision since he was in school most of the day. Miss Laura had managed to get a day job cleaning offices.

She came home late in the afternoon and made cottage industry women's hats for some outfit downtown. She got fifty cents per hat. The store furnished all of the material. Apparently she was pretty good at this since we occasionally saw newspaper ads featuring these hats. I believe she could make almost two hats each day and still have time to go to her bible classes and in the evening to the "Hard Shelled Baptist" services from which no day of the week was exempt.

She would drag Magnis and me along when she couldn't find a neighbor to look in on us. These trips to the fire and brimstone temple in my early days did much to drive me into becoming an Agnostic. Until I was 10 years old I remained subject to these forays and my olfactory system still remembers and I wince with the thought of old fashioned 1930's women's face powder which always clung to the one-half stick of chewing gum I might receive from Miss Laura's purse for not doing what ever it was that I was doing under the pew. To this day I resent it when my wife offers me a half stick of gum. If I can't have a whole stick I don't want any at all.

But I stray. I started to tell you about being three and a half and having my first conscious synapse. My very first memory is of walking down the street about a block and a half from home along side Miss Laura and holding for dear life a large bottle of something cold inside a paper bag. I don't even remember one second before this and have not a clue from where we had come or how we got whatever it was that I was carrying. Right back to square one—I didn't know how and why I was there. Nothing existed before that instant. It was as if the world just appeared.

Baby boomers—trust me when I tell you that bankers did foreclose on people for not making mortgage payments. Hundreds of thousands of them throughout the country and probably thousands of them in and around Little Rock. Ada, don't forget to remember, was pretty and bright. She found out about repossessed houses that were empty. Lending institutions would not like for them to be empty because of vandalism.

They would make a contract with an Ada which allowed that person to live in the repossessed house for a very nominal monthly fee. The catch was that you were subject to moving almost without notice if the house resold or could be rented for a higher price. Some Gypsies had it better.

This present domicile was on the corner of 14th and Oak Street. I remember coming down a slightly sloped street. Cater-cornered from this little house was a two story wooden structure which housed a mom and pop grocery store downstairs and upstairs housed mom and pop. Wonder of wonders, I experienced my very first taste of an ice cold drink of Par-T-Pak Cola, the contents of that bag. I knew we got the Par-T-Pak someplace distant and I remember wondering why we had not just gone across the street to get this cola. I ask Magnis about this a few years ago and he told me that we probably had run out of credit with mom and pop and needed to extend our foraging circle.

I have several other significant memories of this house and time period. I confirmed these with Ada in my adult years and my memory and timing is right on target. I remember being really sick but don't remember going to the hospital for a reduction of this problem. I suspect a home remedy was used—seems to have worked.

I remember Magnis playing with the boy next door. The two of them must have had terrible bouts of enuresis because they practiced pyromania daily in the back yard. Building little miniature huts, which resembled south sea island grass shacks, out of pine needles. They ignited them by crashing little cast iron toy trucks with flaming matches tied to the front bumper. Another of Miss Laura's patent "words from the wise folk" discussed the wetting of one's bed after having played with fire. And boys heard not.

Magnis told me just recently that they found hundreds of beautiful crystals over this entire neighborhood. He said you couldn't dig a hole without finding one. Fortunately none were diamonds and all without value since I have no idea what we would have done with anything of value. He also told me about the mom and pop grocery. His friend lived there above the store with his grand parents. This boy had an electric train but wasn't allowed to play with it so I guess it lasted a long time.

I had my first experience with a female and a teeter totter in the same instant. The little girl I loved jumped off while I was toward the high end—what you would call the dependent position. My first fall from love you might say.

The other vivid happening revolved around fear. I slept on a cot on a screened porch which also housed an ice box. I guess we had acquired a few things along the way. I was awakened by a tearing sound which later proved to be a slashed screen door and the rattle of the hook. A huge man made for the ice box and grabbed what he could carry then ran. I guess I was much too frightened to holler so I just

36

watched. Now looking back it's hard to imagine someone being so hard up as to need to steal from the likes of us. Poor devil must have really been hungry.

My last memory of 14th and Oak Street is of several friends of my mother's gathered around some social event and me saying to a rather rotund lady "you sure have gotten a lot fatter since I saw you last." So much for relativity. I believe Ada and Miss Laura might have had some words to say to me soon after the guests left.

W E MOVED FROM 14th and Oak, shortly after the icebox incident, to a great big brick house on the corner of 22nd and Cedar. Lots of things happened while we were living in this house. We had a large front yard filled with clover and the four leaf anomalies in abundance. The street was very wide and cars were frequent.

I had a friend who lived across the street. I remember all of his distinguishing features and his family name was Are so some one named him Aye. I believe his dad had been in the navy. We were able to lay on our stomachs under the front porch and watch the world go by and if I remember right we could lay on our backs and play with ourselves handily. It apparently was a good hiding place. The large front yard is where I first learned from the older kids how to do a "Summerset." I was sixteen before I realized they were somersaults and well over forty before finding out that the big brick house was about twenty feet wide and maybe thirty five feet deep arranged on a thirty by sixty foot lot with a ten foot wide solid dirt lawn and Cedar is not wide enough to be anything but a one-way street.

Lee Grammar School was the closest to both the 14th

Street house and the "big brick house" so Magnis continued his classes uninterrupted. I, on the other hand, managed to get the insurance "collector" chewed up by Boomer, a rather substantial German Shepherd, owned by Trixie but temporarily boarded with us, and to get my self chewed up by a Bentley, which also was substantial but not German . This Bentley was British built and driven by an elegant and wealthy lady and I doubt it was her fault. I believe I was doing what everyone believed I was doing most of the time—running around like a butterfly with the hiccups.

Well—back to the hospital and again without a thought to remember. Ada told me in later years that it really rang my bell and the nice lady paid all the medical bills, spent long hours of each of the six or seven days in the room with me, brought me goodies and the best "Tonka" type dump truck money could buy. I had that truck for years—what a nice lady—she meant no harm. Our courts today would have given that nice lady to Ada.

FALL OF 1936 and we moved to a little house about   half a block from the boarding house on North Street where Ada, Miss Laura and Magnis were living in 1930. You remember—the boarding house next door to the water works.

I remember spending Christmas in that house. Also it was the first time I heard Fred Allen on radio. I don't know who owned the radio but I doubt it was the Family Lubeck. North Street was a curious little street. It ran East and West—a slight elevation overlooking the river if you looked out the back door—with railroad tracks paralleling between the river and the back of the houses. It began from a westerly direction and was anchored there with a huge and magnificent—at least in my four year old mind—brown brick building which contained a child's paradise of wonderful excitement called a streetcar round house and repair shop and ended only one or two blocks easterly with a dead end into the other splendid curiosity called the city water works. I have no idea from where the drinking water, which flowed into this odd assortment of culverts, pipes, valves, concrete lined ditches and pools came. I do know that you were not supposed to mess with the water so I did.

The streetcar barn was every boy's dream come true.

No one ever seemed to find it necessary to tell me to get out or go home. Just these mechanics and workers, all very busy, but with a kind answer to my many questions. They just seemed to know me and perhaps some did. Maybe one of them lived next door. They probably didn't even know I was poor. Ada or Miss Laura, but probably more often Magnis, could find me at one end of the street or the other.

It is now 1937 and even though time just dragged along in Little Rock it was a little faster in a lot of other places in this world. How could anyone this day and age forget just who—or is it whom—Stanley Baldwin was or is ?. . . . Tolken wrote Hobbit, Steinbeck wrote Of Mice And Men, Amelia Earhart got herself killed in some fashion over the pacific, the Golden Gate Bridge officially opened, Joe Louis became the Champ and some lady named Wally married some guy in England.

Kansas City, however, had Charlie Clyde Lubeck who—or is it whom—I will never be able to get it straight—occasionally used the name Clyde C. Dodge. Years later he told people that he had changed his name to prevent Ada from finding him and making it hard to keep a job by calling his employers about money. This is patently untrue. Ada knew about him being in Kansas City through Trixie—but, she had no desire to contact him or even recognize his existence. She knew they were still married and this fact only served to keep her life simple with any man friend seeking more than an evening out since she could declare "I'm a married woman and can't get involved." She may have secretly hoped that Charlie would be dumb enough to marry someone else without getting a divorce from her thus marking him a bigamist and she could really charge him with something serious. She never attempted to contact Charlie Clyde—or Clyde C.—or

41

anyone else in Kansas City before many years went by. She also did not know nor care about Beryl being in Kansas City or any place else. Ada hated but didn't snoop.

Stanley Baldwin, for those of you still worrying, was the Prime Minister of Britain before Neville Chamberlain and everyone knows Chamberlain lost Europe to Hitler at a later date, but who—or is it whom—remembers Baldwin?

S HOW BUSINESS IS a fickle consort—timing is everything—and the timing was perfect for Trixie and Uncle Louie. They had just finished a tour on the wrestling circuit and they found themselves in Missoula, Montana. Trixie loved to fly fish for trout and Uncle Louie liked to eat all she could catch. She had been taught by the hands of a master as a child—the old surveyor—her grandfather—and would wet her line at any opportunity. They had found Lolo Creek driving south out of Missoula and were charmed by the whole of Lolo Valley. The wrestling season was over and they had some free time. They went back to Missoula to buy a small travel trailer, stocked with all the gadgets and appliances available, in those days, for civilized and genteel camping.

They drove up Lolo Valley and offered a rancher some money to allow them to camp alongside Lolo Creek, which ran through his property. Four weeks later Uncle Louie had grown a substantial beard because of sheer laziness and being on vacation, and had sprouted an idea from sheer creativeness. The two of them were having wonderful fun living like "hillbillies"—she in old dresses and Levis—he with bib overalls and his beard.

Another trip to Missoula shortly after the creative

session and off went telegrams to four good wrestling friends with requests to meet immediately in Ogden, Utah, to discuss an exciting business adventure. All four responded promptly and the meeting, from which came the "Arkansas Scufflers", took place.

Uncle Louie had hit on an idea that would be even more financially rewarding than any in the past.

The Walt Disney animated movie "Snow White" had just been released and Trixie just loved it—from this they took the names—"Grumpy"—"Doc"—"Sleepy"—and "Dopey"—Uncle Louie adapted the name "Pappy" and Trixie was called "Sis."

The plan was that all of these wonderfully conditioned athletes would come to Lolo Valley, lease a small resort camp called Lolo Hot Springs which was available for a pittance, and spend the rest of the summer getting ready. Getting ready meant growing beards, long hair and acquiring costumes, consisting mostly of bib overalls and denim shirts. They built a wrestling ring and worked out daily, teaching and learning from each other. Two of them brought their families to Lolo and everyone loved this happy camp.

All of this was accomplished by up front money from Uncle Louie. He was the boss and his and Trixie's share would be 28 percent and the other four 18 percent each.

Sometime shortly after the turn into the twentieth century someone named Mitchell tried his hand at producing an automobile. I don't think he was in Detroit. I think he may have been in Iowa—but who cares. He built some handsome automobiles I tell you. Indeed, I saw one just recently in a "Horseless Carriage" parade. Well, back to the story. It seems that Mr Mitchell didn't believe in assembly before shipping. Something about saving assembly and transportation costs. At any rate, dealerships were set up and the automobiles were shipped unassembled in large crates. A widow in Missoula still had one left from her dead husband's dealership days. This was a 1912 model still in the crate and Uncle Louie bought it and had it assembled. A brand new, just out of the box, 1912 Mitchell in 1937! This is analogous to finding a brand spanking new 1946 Lincoln Continental just off the assembly line in 1976.

They then had a semi trailer constructed that would accommodate the Mitchell and all of their props.

Uncle Louie was also busy scheduling and ballyhooing this newest grappling showmanship oddity. They headed for California where they instantly became the best thing that had happened to wrestling since folks started getting paid to do it.

They took on the best that the promoters in each scheduled city could find. Single matches and then, "tag team" matches for the "main event." They were good and their opponents knew they were good because they had all met at one time or another. They were now supposedly "incognito" with the beards but I doubt that they fooled the real fan of the sport. They had a great time and the money rolled in and in and in. The following summer found them in Little Rock and I was supposed to go with them into Tennessee and Mississippi but got to get chicken pox instead.

Outside the scheduled city limits, they went into their act. The Mitchell came off the semi and all piled into it for an unscheduled trip through town. The men in full dress bib overalls, "Sis" in the most colorful old fashioned high neck dress, high top button shoes and topped off with a bonnet. Waving and acting just like "Arkansas Hillbillies." My

God! Did they attract the people!

They simply took over a town. By the next day, the newspapers were filled with them and I have to tell you the people loved it. By the way, they were always the "good guys" inside and outside the ring.

1938 found Charlie and Beryl living together most of the time. They also wrestled—but with existence—and fought a lot yet always seemed to have that affinity for temporary reconciliation that so often comes when two dysfunctional people grope around with binging and purging. Beryl continued a part time job at the Kansas City Tuberculosis Sanitarium and Charlie bounced from here to there. He worked occasionally as a stable hand across the state line in Kansas City, Kansas at the huge Gamble Estate—it seems that he had worked in this same place in the same capacity as a teen when he ran away from Caddo Gap in 1919. He infrequently drove a truck for a junk collector, rarely delivered produce for a farmer near Independence and we have every reason to believe that he also was involved in a few shady activities. Not much progress for this guy. Beryl was supposedly married to someone but nothing much is known about this part of her life. Charlie was still married but no one cared. And he was still about as handy as a monkey screwing a football.

THE "ARKANSAS SCUFFLERS" had had their heyday and in 1939 Trixie and Uncle Louie had found their way to Las Vegas, Nevada. Uncle Louie bought the promoting rights for professional wrestling and boxing and bought a gift—curio shop across the street from the train station for Trixie. There was no "strip" at that time. Bugsy Siegel was still running amuck back east and Las Vegas was one of the cleanest and safest towns in America. Boulder Dam had been completed in 1936 and was a candidate for one of the wonders of the world. It wasn't until 1947 that it was renamed Hoover Dam in honor of the ex president . Gambling was all downtown on Fremont Street and each train brought lots of visitors even then. When a group of passengers would cross the street she would invite them into the "totally air-conditioned" shop. People would just need to get inside out of that hot sun and they would buy anything. Given enough time and Trixie would have come up with the present day printed tee-shirt craze. People actually bought fake desert jack rabbit crap in a jar, plaster Indian dolls made in Romania, feathered headbands made in China and beaded Indian moccasins made in Tunisia.

Uncle Louie converted a small building behind what is

now the Silver Dollar Hotel into a business office, ticket sales, dressing room combination , built an open air wrestling—boxing arena and promoted bouts until later in the year when the really big time opportunity opened up in Los Angeles. They bought the promoting franchise for all of the South and East of Los Angeles. They settled down in Stanford Park, the place they would call home for the next ten years.

It was at this time that Charlie—I should say Clyde—and Beryl began using the name Dodge full time. Remember, Charlie had used this name from time to time but mostly in covert ways.

No one knew how Clyde got the money but some way or other they always had adequate cash to do as they pleased and he also managed to acquire an apartment house. Six one bedroom apartments. This was the big time. Both tried to give up drinking periodically and would succeed for months on end. Beryl seemed to be best at this. She continued part time at the sanitarium. No one ever really knew what Clyde did or didn't do. Mostly he hung around drinking and smoking the Bull Durham cigarettes he carried in a brass case. He had one of those little cigarette making roller machines he kept at the apartment. This would make him look like he smoked "ready made's."

Clyde also became several years older during this time. That is to say he told people he was older than he really was.

Many of the little communities in and around Montgomery County, Arkansas, had obtained rural electrical districts and were grateful for it. In Kansas City, housewives had been using electric washing machines long enough that there were now used ones on the market. Clyde acquired a stake truck and filled it with used washing machines and headed for Mt Ida, Arkansas, which is the Montgomery County Seat. He had a half brother living nearby who was almost as good at drinking as was he. I forgot to tell you, prohibition had been rescinded in 1933 . The washing machines would be unloaded at Brother Billie's place and bartered with locals for wean'er pigs.

Pigs on the truck and back to Kansas City where they would be sold at auction. Pretty clever! This went well, but Clyde just could never sustain—couldn't carry success very far so after two runs he petered out.

No one in Little Rock knew of these transactions but I believe he must have had the eidolon of things past trailing him each time he crossed the state border into Arkansas and his nerves were never great even during the best of times.

Had not Clyde been the braggart bull shit artist he was and had he been able to sustain at any of his undertakings, he might have been successful. I believe the poet e.e.cummings must have used Clyde for his model when he wrote "nobody loses all the time." I would like to quote this delightful tribute to a looser, because Clyde wore it so well, but the publisher Harcourt Brace Jovanovich, Inc in New York probably wouldn't like it so you will have to seek it out for your own enjoyment.

WHEN 1939 CAME over the horizon for us in Little Rock I was six years and some change and already in the third grade and John Steinbeck, who is my favorite of all writers, did get Grapes of Wrath published in March. It wasn't until last year at a high school reunion, all these years later that I discovered why I was the only freshman who didn't have pubic hair. I am at least a year and a half younger than my classmates. I had never realized it but my friends had actually known it and didn't care.

It seems that my being in the third grade came about back in 1937 because Ada and Miss Laura somehow managed to get me enrolled in the first grade at Garland Street School when we lived on 21st and Abigail Street when I am just barely five years old. Two weeks later some lady comes into the first grade class room and tells me to come with her. I think" boy am I gon'na get it now—I'm probably not even supposed to be in this school." She took me down a hall and into the second grade class room. Well, I didn't know whether I was "afoot or horseback" in the first grade and here I am in the second grade. You talk about being "screwed up like Ned in the Third Reader"— Wow!! I don't know to this day what happened.

About this time we had to move again—clear across town to a little house on Riverside Drive—always a little house—which could have been an extension of North Street but wasn't. It was on a hill not far from the Missouri Pacific Hospital and about a mile from the Colonial Bakery where I caught the street car for the cross town trip to Garland Street School everyday for some months or until we moved again—across the world. Actually across the river—the Arkansas River.

Riverside Drive has now been completely obliterated from the face of the earth and replaced by some company headquarters. But, in 1939, it was an exceptionally good place for a kid to be. This would not be our only stay on Riverside Drive.

This short street ran obliquely up a slight hill from Cantrell Road, which we called Pulaski Highway for some unknown reason, turned west and went downhill then up a slightly higher hill then down this hill to end in the middle of an abandoned rock and gravel operation.

Besides several old rusted metal tanks, an even rustier metal conveyor and other broken machinery which made wonderful climbing and hiding places, there also remained "old scum pond." This was not really a pond but us poor city kids didn't know the difference. It was actually a rectangular shaped above ground concrete water tank with six inches of green oozing "yuck" floating over the surface. It could have been three or thirty feet deep and I wouldn't have known.

I never needed to get wet badly enough to jump in that ugly thing but my buddy, Mernon, did. I don't know what ever happened to Mernon but have often wondered if he grew extra digits or developed alopecia universalis or maybe an extensive case of vitiligo or lost his toe nails or if he lived long enough did he father children with these or other problems ?

Baring Cross School in North Little Rock is in my memory bank because I experienced chocolate milk for the first time, saw a man don a huge diving suit, with the big brass screw on helmet, and then he was dropped into a large glass tank which was on a truck bed. I always wondered how this exhibit came about and why.

It was also during this time that I was told that it would be better if I just rested my head while the other children practiced their "up-and-downs" and "O-loops" which is how we did penmanship practice in those days. It seems that I was so awkward and uncoordinated at this that it was just wasted paper, pencil and motion without any accomplishment whatsoever and that I probably should not plan any part of my life around anything involving hand writing. I have to level with you—my penmanship went down hill from there.

Magnis had joined the Little Rock Boys Club the previous year. It cost fifteen cents a year and was the best buy in the world. A kid could attend cultural events, play basketball, swim in the basement pool, see free movies on Friday evenings and have access to a marvelous library. I wasn't old enough to join but Magnis could take me as a guest to the gymnasium on Friday nights to watch a free movie. That is as long as I didn't aggravate him along the way.

Magnis sold the Arkansas Democrat Newspaper downtown Little Rock and while we lived in North Little Rock the two of us—I'm almost seven and Magnis is thirteen—walked across the Missouri Pacific Railroad trestle bridge daily and into downtown Little Rock where we captured all four corners of Capital Avenue and Center

Street. Magnis ran three corners and I ran the fourth which was in front of the Sterling Five & Dime. We got a one-half cent commission for each sale. Life was good.

Sometimes we would be half way across—do you know how far it is from the center of the railroad bridge spanning the Arkansas River to the south bank for a seven year old kid looking down through the ties, seeing the water flow past and expecting a train at any second ?—when Magnis would unearth one of those degenerate states of mind which overcame him occasionally and begin to run and leave me behind yelling "Run for your life Dumbo here comes a train."

Hell, I didn't even have long pants on—my feet were shorter than the distance between the rail ties and my legs weren't long enough to stretch two at a time so there I would be—not a second smarter than the last time he pulled this on me—crying, peeing down my leg into my sock and swearing in general that some day I was gon'na make him pee down his leg, and besides that I couldn't swim because Ada always said that I couldn't go near the water until I learned how to swim and trying to run and hitting each of the four million railroad ties to the bank where I would find Magnis leaning against the fence rail laughing his "silly ass head off." Besides that, he already had pubic hair and I could just barely find my "whizzer."

Ada and Miss Laura were never prejudiced. They both seemed to pretty much accept people for what and who they were. I don't ever recall either of them using the term "nigger" and the first of only two slaps to the face I ever got from Ada came one day when I was about five. I tried to be a "smart mouth"—as Miss Laura used to say—and decided to repeat something the "big guys at school" said which included "nigger man"—splat !! a quick forehand across my mouth that I didn't even see coming "We don't speak like that in this family. Would you care to rephrase it?" That little sortie captured my attention for a lifetime.

Ada had a good friend who lived in a small neat and trim bungalow off of an alley on W. 6th Street only a couple of blocks from our newspaper corner. She had met and worked with Pansy when she was cleaning at the Albert Pike Hotel. Pansy was a very dear person and her skin color happened to be rather dark brown and we called her a Negro Lady—when I think about it I don't believe Pansy ever referred to my mother as a Caucasian Lady. I think she just called her Ada—maybe we were prejudiced and didn't even know it—we called her Miss Pansy. Well, be that as it may, I was always instructed—if I had any trouble downtown—to run for Miss Pansy's' place because my mom trusted her. She also made great cookies as I recall.

One day out there selling papers, in front of the Sterling Five and Dime, I went into the store for some water from the fountain. I've always had a thing about drinking from a fountain with just a trickle of water coming out . Some "miserable squint faced old bird stuffer woman" saw me drink from the brown water fountain, which gave out a good stream, and she went ballistic and tried to—"take me out"—verbally as well as whacking me with her sack. I dropped my papers and headed out for West Sixth Street and the comfort of Miss Pansy and will always remember that lady holding me against her huge bosom while I cried and shook.

I am sorry, I got lost again telling about "some things" when I should have been telling you about "other things."

Back tracking to 1936—which is only three years in real time—we lived on 22nd and Maple Street. I don't know why I think this needs to be told but something must have seemed important when I started this paragraph. I was four and already had my own picture of life. It consisted mostly of waiting for someone else to make some kind of decision about, or for me that would affect me for the next few minutes or days. This must have been in the fall because I remember large piles of leaves being raked into piles and being set on fire. I wondered why grown people didn't wet their beds or did they? Or maybe I should caution them, or maybe I should just keep quiet and let them find out the hard way.

I was still into afternoon naps and dreamed about flying—this, incidentally, before Superman Comics—I also nap dreamed, night dreamed and day dreamed about Knickerbockers. Magnis got to wear "Knickers" as we were fond of calling the britches worn by the school boys of those days. Long knee socks went with the outfit and since Magnis always had one sock down around his ankles, I always assumed that this was how they were supposed to be worn and it bothered me a lot. Well any way, my fervent prayer was getting into school so I could wear these "Knickers."

Until first grade, kids wore short pants winter and summer. I guess no one ever wondered or worried about those mini-legs getting cold. Girls all wore dresses but they had legs made out of different stuff and didn't get cold— now I remember—as luck would have it "Knickers" went out of style the year I started school.

My mind has always been diabolical but in a pragmatic, rascal fashion rather than the fiendish, evil definition. Miss Laura and Ada both climbed my frame—as skinny as I was, it didn't take a lot of climbing so perhaps "soured up my day" would be more appropriate—about something and for the first time in a long time I wasn't guilty "Honest Injun and cross my heart"—but that didn't seem to matter. When pronounced guilty by Ada, the first portion of your sentence was going to the nearest hedge and cutting your own capital punishment machine—the thing about selecting your own switch is that you never want to just select a twig because then your mother will go out and select her own and we all know what would happen after that.

You then had to cry even before the first blow. It was better if you committed your crime at home because if you were down the street, you got hit every step of the way home and sometimes that could be half a block.

It sure is good that the government run goodie two shoes, piss ant Child Protection Agency social doctors, with their present day constant incessant urge to meddle in other peoples business, didn't exist in those days, because Ada would also have beaten the crap out of them had they gotten in her way. Well, you get the picture. Needless to say, I walked the gauntlet and was sent to the back steps to think about things.

I wasn't sure what it was I was supposed to think about so I thought about other things. I knew that "From Little Acorns, Mighty Oak Trees Come" and my eyes seized upon an acorn lying not far from either me or its mother. I didn't know how long it would take to make a big one from a little one but I dug the hole anyway—right next to the foundation and definitely under the roof line—so as to catch the roof and tip it over when it got big. I watered that acorn daily for several weeks with secret excitement knowing that someday revenge would be mine. I still wonder if it grew at all because we moved again shortly after. Magnis has made some trips to Little Rock over the past years and says that there is a vacant lot where that house used to be. Naw!!!

BY THE END of 1939 I was into my seventh year as a person, in the third grade and, as I recall, I believed I was a whole lot dumber than most people thought I was. I was matriculating at Peabody School, which was as close to downtown Little Rock as you could get. This school was two stories high and covered the entire block between Capital and 4th and fronted Gaines Street. Actually the building didn't cover the entire block but the grounds did. Solid dirt and without one blade of grass. We had been living someplace close but I don't remember where and neither does Magnis. Maybe with Helen who by this time was living in a rental next door to Miss Pansy on 6th Street. At any rate, we were shortly on our way to another stint in the vicinity of 21st and Abigail which was almost at the end of everything. The streetcar went only a couple of blocks further and made a loop in the middle of a field and started back into town. I didn't know what the poor farm was or what people did at the asylum but was told often that both were just a few blocks away and I was sure to end up in one of them if I didn't do exactly what it was I was supposed to do.

The Italians had invaded Albania and I knew the whole alphabet forward and could blow a bubble out of my right eye by holding my nose and pressurizing my cheeks. Miss Laura was still my guiding light and I was apparently the summation of all the goodness that could happen to her. I "should'a" been able to figure it out but when one is still struggling with all the stuff one needs to struggle with, "hard stuff ain't easy"—or something like that. What I'm getting at is Ada never believed a word I said but believed everything Magnis said and Miss Laura was the converse since she mostly believed me.

It is my understanding that Ada never stepped foot inside any church except the Catholic Church for the entire length of her life after graduating from the Caddo Gap Academy but never became a Catholic or anything else. Miss Laura had no use for Catholics and was certain that all were headed for hell in a hand basket.

Sometimes Ada would grab me by the hand and drag me off to a Catholic Mass just to aggravate Miss Laura. I understood a Catholic Mass slightly less than Ada—but not much less than the public fits conjured up at the nightly Baptist disturbances. I never got the hang of any of that stuff.

I really thought the guy in the dress was saying something about playing dominoes. I couldn't even play checkers.

It was very strange this yin and yang between mother and her daughter. I believe now that Miss Laura was by this time already in the early prodromal stages of what was later believed to be multiple sclerosis but wasn't and just didn't feel well much of the time. I believe she also managed to get some of the tonics that were still in vogue in many parts of the country. These snake oil tonic holdovers from earlier days were still loaded with opiates, alcohol—usually 30%—and or codeine and usually purchased from one of the deacons wives. You could still buy Cheracol syrup over-the-counter in 1959. People stayed loaded and didn't even know it.

I don't know why Ada was so angry with Miss Laura. I guess she just needed anger to keep her going. Projection—call it what you will.

Ada could not hold her alcohol even a little bit. Obnoxious after two glasses of beer! Miss Laura could not tolerate nor sanction the use of these "evil concentrates" nor would she have been able to mitigate her own habits had she been cognizant of them.

Miss Laura taught me more during the short time we spent together on earth than can be understood from just reading this.

The greatest lesson was to think for myself—although it was many years to fruition. She did this in a subtle fashion. I would be allowed to carry on dialog with her as she read to me from books she got from the library. It is strange for me to understand even now, but she never preached to me, as one understands preaching even though she was totally intolerant of those not believing that the Bible was all knowing .

I don't believe that anyone can be taught judgment in this life. Everyone has judgment—unfortunately, so much of it is poor. She seemed to lead me around situations, probing and directing—giving me options or choices—all of which when thought of later in life were good—and leaving me to believe that I had chosen the best one. I still marvel at how this lady from the back woods of Arkansas knew all of the things she knew. She taught me protocol, convention, custom, decorum, formality, manners—in general, all of the things listed under the term etiquette. I didn't know until many years later that I had been taught. I spoke to Magnis about this not long back and he didn't remember Miss Laura doing this for him. He remembers her being kind but distant. Perhaps she knew something no one else knew about me and felt the need to supplement my ramble through life. Maybe she just thought that I would epitomize one of her sayings which was "well, he's dumber in the head than a hog is in the tail", and would need all the help I could get.

Most of the places where we lived had the utilities turned off. Ada became very adept at bypassing meters with the special "cheat wires and hoses" which many poor folks managed to acquire and carry with them from place to place.

I will never be able to understand the rationalization that must have taken place in Miss Laura's mind, relative to this "by-passing the meter" trick, since she perceived lying or stealing to be almost mortal sin. Survival is a powerful plea.

Ada on the other hand thought it was just fine since the Arkansas Power and Light Company got the electricity free by plugging up the rivers which belonged to all the folks anyway, the same for the household water and I'm not sure how she explained away the gas.

All this having been said, one thing was for certain, you didn't get under Miss Laura's quilts if you weren't clean. We were poor but we were clean. No—I never heard her say anything about "godliness and cleanliness."

IN AND AROUND Kansas City things l
looked great to Clyde depending on the
time of day the question about his well being was inquired
upon. Clyde did like to deliberate when presented with any
question. He had a way of looking at the ground, scratching
with his shoe what ever the covering happened to be and
"shucking" his cheek in a manner which allowed one to
believe he was actually thinking through whatever it was
that had been passed on to him. Most of the time he simply
was not tuned in to much of anything being said to him,
which required any thought, and passed the time of day
contemplating things like what would be happening at the
gin mill in the evening after finishing his stint as aide-de-
camp at the pony ride at Shope park which was presently
his station in life.

Here is a guy who had made an art of saying: "let me
study on that" when asked something like "do you walk to
work or carry your lunch."

Clyde could display a nasty temper when faced down
with a question or situation he called "hi—fa—lutin" and
for which he had no answer or hunch. He talked about
"them edge-a-caded fools without a lick ah sense." I do
believe he knew better but was embarrassed about his own

lack of education. The only reading he ever did in those days was an occasional newspaper and pulp magazines about the old west or old sailing ships.

Beryl had by this time been promoted to full time on the midnight shift at the TB Sanitarium. This was the low end of the totem pole but at least she was on the pole unlike so many others in the world.

Another miracle took place just as 1940 rounded the bend. Clyde bought a four-plex just off First Street and Vine in Kansas City. The apartment house was still in his possession so Clyde C. Dodge was a rather noteworthy landlord considering the times. Remember, 1939 was a horrible and terrifying fragment of the depression.

If ever there was anyone in this world who could "screw up the arrangements for a two car funeral" it was Clyde.

He managed to buy all of the ponies at the pony ride by "putting one over" on his boss one evening at the gin mill when he thought the boss was too sloshed to reason. He never figured that the boss wasn't as wasted as was he.

He now needed to hire out the ponies. But, he failed to remember that the concession contract agreement belonged to the boss. There he was, a commodity without an outlet. He ended up making another deal. He would hire the boss to feed and stable the ponies and the boss would then pay rent on the ponies based on a percentage of the net profit each pony generated. He never did figure out subtracting overhead from the gross in order to obtain the net.

It's at this time that another one of the " ole boys" from Clyde's past showed up with an idea to get rich quick. They would buy watermelons "real cheap" in Arkansas and haul them to Kansas City to sell to the "mom and pop" grocery stores. Clyde sold his ponies back to the boss—for a loss of course—and recovered some of the cash he had now begun to realize was flowing in the wrong direction.

Off to Arkansas, where Elmo had a guaranteed deal to "corner the market" on watermelons, to pick up the load. Mind you, Clyde hadn't seen Elmo in over two years and didn't even know his last name. He was just one of the "ner-do-wells" with which Clyde sopped up the booze in the days gone by. They had borrowed a truck from another friend of Clyde's with the understanding that the owner would receive a piece of the action.

It was on the return trip approaching Joplin, Missouri, when Elmo showed his colors. Late at night and he asked Clyde to pull into a rest area where the "hi-jack" took place. A friend of Elmo's' was waiting and Clyde was left standing, never to see Elmo, his watermelons or the truck again. You're right, the truck owner was not the least bit understanding and after holding Clyde for ransom until Beryl brought enough money to cover the truck beat the crap out of Clyde right in front of her.

Why anyone would want to "hi-jack" watermelons or plan a robbery around watermelons is utterly beyond my understanding. Actually it is fairly incomprehensible why any one would even think to drive all the way from Kansas City to Arkansas and back for watermelons. Why didn't Elmo just knock the crud out of Clyde at the onset and steal his money and the truck? And besides that, some of the best watermelons in the country could be found within thirty miles of Kansas City. Some things are just unknowable.

DURING THE TIME Clyde was going through this last learning curve I told you about, we, Ada, Miss Laura, Magnis and I, were still in the house on 21st Street just off Abigail close to the other house we had been in during one of our prior lives.

Magnis is now in West Junior High School and had a paper route delivering the Democrat. I am catching a street car several blocks away and riding four hundred miles into down town to attend Peabody Grammar School which is where I was going when we lived the first time on Riverside. God, I never could remember where I was supposed go after school.

One day, coming home from Peabody, I was the only kid on that streetcar right downtown on Main Street when in mid block the driver stopped and all the grown folks bailed out and ran into a department store. Nobody told me what was going on so I just sat there. I probably thought they were having a sale or something. That tornado went right past the streetcar to the next corner and headed east on 4th Street. I was probably the only one in town who got a good close look at it. Should this happen today I would be on national television three days running: "Simple-minded child rides out tornado." No one even asked me about it or for that matter even asked me about me. When I told my story that night Ada didn't believe me and sure was pissed off and acted like I probably caused it if there really was a tornado and to not ever do it again or I was really gon'na get it.

Miss Laura had already gone to one of her evening paroxysms so I found no succor until the next morning. By then, of course, I had managed to parley my story into congressional record size and Magnis egged me on and then even Miss Laura didn't believe me and remember, she believed everything I told her. That night however I was sanctioned when a story came out in the newspaper. Not that I was mentioned. I told you that was 1940 and Little Rock didn't become Oz until election day 1978.

Remember I told you that maybe Miss Laura knew something about me? I always feel like I have this aegis protecting me and am constantly grateful to who—or is it whom—ever out there is in charge or looks out over this sort of thing. I can get up in the morning and think of someone I haven't seen for months and that person will contact me that day. Deja vu is a constant.

When we were still living on Riverside, at the top of the second hill before the street ended down the hill at the "old scum pond", I experienced something that few in this world have seen. The only person I told was Miss Laura and she actually knew what I was talking about. She let me know that most people to whom I would tell this story would not believe me or be too ignorant to care. She also related a story about my Grandfather having experienced the same thing before they first met. George Washington Slewter, the Grandfather I never knew and the Father Ada and Trixie never really got to know, came into this world about two minutes before Thomas Jefferson Slewter. Twin boys born in 1878 in the little valley community of Shiloh, Cleburne County, Arkansas, to Robert Washington Slewter and Sara Bone Slewter who was Robert W's second wife. The Romulus and Remus of their part of the world. These twin boys devoured knowledge and were competitors in any "I can read and quote" verbatim encounter.

Unfortunately, Robert W. was not at any time in his life wealthy and could not afford any higher education for the twins and in those days and in this part of the world, no young boys ever got ahead just on brain power. Well, be that as it may, some combination of genes on the DNA strands took place and these two talents reaped the rewards of being superior intellects. That is, the rewards of Shiloh such as they were.

These two, as could be imagined, were inseparable and were planning their assault on the world of academia when, in 1894, Thomas Jefferson developed a mild case of cholera.

Cholera in young adults in those days took two forms, both caused by the then unknown endotoxin producing vibrio comma bacterium. Both forms are caused by the same organism giving symptoms of diarrhea, vomiting and abdominal cramping to name a few, but one form is more virulent and progresses to death while the less virulent form creates a self limiting disease. There is a wonderful adage in medicine: "you never say never but you never say always."

Well, in the good old days of the past, some well meaning holder of the caduceus concocted a compound known as "10 and 10" which was a combination of 10 parts calomel, which contained a massive amount of mercury chloride and an extract from a plant known as ipomacaeu Jalopa. This "10 and 10" was advertised to stop diarrhea, cramping abdominal pain and vomiting, and, Mercury chloride will cause all of these. I would be willing to bet that half of the young people buried in the rural areas of this country, and maybe even in the urban areas, who had cholera as a cause of death on their death certificates actually died from mercury chloride poisoning since the greater the symptoms, the more calomel and or "10 and 10" they got and the vicious circle was formed and not broken until death. I guess it's a wonder anyone lived through that "the cure was worse than the ill" period of medicine.

I again apologize for becoming pedantic. I don't seem able to overcome this awful characteristic but I needed to explain the most probable cause of Thomas Jefferson Slewter's death at the early age of sixteen even though it has little if anything to do with my story.

Should you be curious enough to try finding Shiloh, Cleburne County, Arkansas, don't bother. Greers Ferry Lake flooded that part of my heritage in 1962 with the completion of a dam.

Damn if I didn't almost forget the point of my story. I was sitting on the front porch steps one afternoon at that house on the second hill on Riverside and it started to pour down rain. In a very few moments lightening and thunder began to rip across that hilltop. The walls and porch of this house were made of wood as were the three steps which led to a concrete sidewalk and ended at the street about fifteen feet away. The porch was about eight feet across. The steps were right in front of the entrance next to which was located an empty porcelain front porch light socket with a string hanging down which was attached to a small metal pull chain.

A loud crack of lightening and thunder jolted me and immediately an event occurred—a ball of electricity emerged very slowly from that socket. I can still best describe it as larger than a basketball and made up of a godzillion tiny sparks which individually resembled small lightening bolts. It paused for a second after attaining full size, descended slowly down the wall to the porch, then rolled past my very own body less than a foot away, down each of the steps getting smaller and smaller as it rolled down the sidewalk, and disappearing before it reached the street.

Well, people actually saw that tornado and no one wanted to believe me and they certainly weren't gon'na believe this either so I saved it until that night when I quizzed Miss Laura about plain old everyday lightning and thunder—or is it thunder and lightning—jeez. You know that old gal told me about how lightening developed and how the thunder occurred and what not to do if caught in a storm out of shelter, and you don't need to believe this either but she told me about ball lightning and that only a precious few special people had ever actually witnessed it and maybe it was the basis for the "ark of the covenant" and much more and I didn't know what to think. God I was excited. It was over a week before I actually got the nerve to tell her about my experience and she said that perhaps I was one of the chosen few and would always be under a shield of protection. She actually believed me and was glad that I had been alone since the experience would be mine with no need to share.

She then told me as much about her first husband, and my grandfather, Mr George Washington Slewter, as she ever related to anyone—ever. She told me how he came to Caddo Gap to teach at the academy when she was a senior and he was twenty-four and how they immediately fell in secret love. He never made a move until she had graduated and he came to call. He was the perfect gentleman and seemed to know everything there was to know—except how to cure tuberculosis—for he was infected but she didn't care. I have the original love letters old George wrote to "Miss Laura", asking for her indulgence at the dance Saturday night. These letters are as nice and gentle as you would expect from such a brilliant mind. She also told me that he had related a story about how he was sitting one day with his twin, Thomas Jefferson, in Shiloh when ball lightning rolled between the two of them.

Chapter 15

D URING MOST OF 1940 Clyde just ambled around the country spending time in Illinois, Ohio, New York, Colorado, Virginia, Texas and Washington, D.C.. No one really knew what he was doing or how he survived but he managed to work at odd little things, mostly door to door distributing samples of new soaps or cereals. I guess the main thing to emphasize is that he never had a pay check job but he always had enough spending money.

I believe the 1930's produced more social meddlers per capita than any other period in history. We probably had more "meddlers" than "meddlees." The communists ranted and raved, The "new this" and the "new that's" planned for the "couldn't be'es", the "technocrats" the you "name em's" were out there planning something for everyone, but, the worst of the bunch, then and now, were and are, the Fabian Socialists.

The seat of this organization was Oxford and was championed and founded by George Bernard Shaw, Annie Besant, Sidney Webb, Edith Nesbit, Hurbert Bland and H.G. Wells in the late 1880's. They believed in forming a revolution with publications and seminars and produced a series of "Fabian Essays" in 1889. These essays became the foundation of the labour party, in Great Britain, which advocated nationalization of private industry and utilities. They in essence believed, and still believe, in controlling the citizens of a country by exercising control over wealth, creating a committee of "responsible experts" to do this and long range "evolutionary" goals.

My definition of a Fabian Socialist is "someone with a constant incessant urge to give away something which belongs to someone else." God knows that the United States of America is up to its ass in these people.

Politically, I place my self some where to the right of Henry of Anjou—or Henry Plantagenet if you like.

My bias is that no one typified Fabian socialism any better than Franklin D. Roosevelt. The Kennedy group of folks, presently, qualify high up as did Nelson Aldrich Rockefeller's maternal granddad Senator Nelson Wilmarth Aldrich. He, old Wilmarth, is the guy you want to blame for the "Aldrich Plan" of 1911 which became the basis for the Federal Reserve Act in 1913" when a few folks got together on Jekyl Island, Georgia, and it just got better and better for fewer and fewer and it doesn't take a mental giant to figure it out from there.

And in the third year, F.D.R. created "The Social Security Act." That would have been 1935.

The S.S. Act Amendments of 1939 caused a form of mandatory contribution and gave a number to every American collecting a paycheck. It was supposed to be for anyone twenty one or over, and some employers even required kids to have one but I doubt that they, the employer, ever actually did anything more than keep the meager contribution for his own. My first one dates back to age thirteen.

Clyde never got a job that required this sort of thing and

even if he had he would have lied about his name and address so no one would have been able to trace him.

He would return to Kansas City periodically and take up with Beryl where he left off. Everyone they knew just naturally assumed they were married and neither ever dispelled this impression. I guess it's safe to say they didn't have any close friends anyway and no one knew much about their past.

Beryl continued at the T.B. Sanatorium in a pretty steady fashion, always working the midnight shift and apparently never complaining—but in those days I don't believe there was any differential in pay—she was a night person. She also continued drinking but as I said before, this was episodic.

The old story about a guy you didn't know drank at all until one day you saw him sober might correlate with Beryl. She was a terrible house keeper and kept trinkets and knick—knacks everywhere collecting dust and dander. Newspapers on the floors, dust pan and broom where it was touched last and a bathroom that looked like the men's room at the coliseum. Dishes, however, were always washed and rinsed clean and put away in an expeditious manner and her uniform for work was always spotless and you would never be able to find any physical evidence of booze. A real dichotomy.

And then after a short time together, the explosive, thrashing, spiteful, malicious, maniacal anger of the drunk too wretched and vile to pass out, striking out verbally and physically at another pathetic shell of humanity attempting to counter with like depravity. God,—I wonder what it must look from the inside?

Beryl was a very plain and mousy appearing woman with a tiny mouth and thin lips which appeared to be puckered most of the time. She wore bright red lipstick and heavy reddish rouge powder just on her cheeks. Her hair was henna and always seemed to stand on end, like she had just been electrocuted.

She could never select the right dress for any occasion and always wore dumpy looking club heeled shoes which looked like they were rejects from the second hand store. I guess unaware is the best description of Beryl's appearance in general—but remember, when it came to her uniform—two different people.

Beryl had some family living in Arkansas but never visited them. She never traveled with Clyde and except for infrequent trips to Kirksville Osteopathic Hospital, for manipulations, she never left Kansas City. One has to wonder why she went to Kirksville since they had a perfectly fine Osteopathic School in Kansas City. Content to stay in one of the one bedroom apartments listening, during her time away from the hospital, to which ever gospel preacher happened to be laying it on thick over the radio or sometimes going to one of the "public fits"—otherwise known as hallelujah- praise ye the lord—tent meetings, which became more and more frequent across the country.

Some mediocre misfit with a name like Brother Nick Nostril could come into Bug Struggle, U.S.A. with a truck full of folding chairs, a tent, a blond tart, who usually looked like she killed after mating, and six or seven characters right out of a Wallace Berry movie. In a three evening hustle Brother Nostril could purloin what few coins the locals had left over from the last such screwing they got and be over the state line before the neighborhood flock knew what hit them. Elmer Gantry was a true and anointed envoy of God compared to most of these pieces of waste but it seemed like the gullible "tongue talkers" could hardly wait for the next rotten bastard to show up. They just never ever got any smarter and even Miss Laura was guilty of attending these sideshows on occasion.

Well I guess Beryl suffered from that affliction known as periodic religious obnubilation, which is a condition suffered by more people than would like to admit.

As far as can be determined, Clyde never in his life set foot inside or amongst any religious setting although Beryl caused him many radio hours of listening to the hoots and eructations coming from some of these thunder ranting paragons of hypocrisy.

Clyde, of course, let these punctuations fly right by because he never ever attempted to pass an uninterrupted thought through his brain and even Nick Nostrils incantations required a thought.

Beryl would, as likely as not, fly into a rage when Clyde wouldn't, or couldn't, understand that the preacher was talking directly to him when stating "we're here to do good to others" and Clyde would ask "and what are the others here for", or some such answer which would immediately set the chain reaction into motion and end, likely as not, sometime the next day.

Clyde was, it is safe to say, the "stump" in Beryl's "river of discontent."

As for monetary gains, something must have been going right because, as 1940 came to a close, some more real estate entered the portfolio—a 21 acre piece of farm land with a small house close to Independence and another set of apartments. Paid for in cash, no questions asked.

IN 1940 MAGNIS and I seemed to have a split in our social affairs. That is to say Magnis didn't want me around when he was with his friends. I was eight and he was fourteen and God knows six years at that time of life is like night and day. Impossible to convince the eight year old that he can't run with the big guys. Magnis was in high school. A Little Rock High School Tiger! They had only one high school in those days and it was about four miles from where we were now living for the second time on Riverside Drive. Magnis would have to walk east on Pulaski—actually Cantrell but remember, we called it Pulaski Highway—past the Missouri Pacific Hospital south across the train viaduct to connect with Cross Street and then zigzag west down past the State Capital and then south again to 14th and Park which was where the high school was located.

This is the same high school now called Little Rock Central High of Orval Faubus infamy. Everyone remembers Old Orval—but how many remember that on the Sixteenth of September 1957, Elizabeth Eckford did exactly what Old Orval didn't want her to do?

As the crow would fly—I still don't know from where that saying comes—there was a much shorter route but unfortunately the Union Station and all of the train tracks in the world either started or ended there and ran parallel with Cantrell until they all converged to go under the viaduct and on to God only knows where.

On any given school day, Magnis and friends, living on Riverside, met on the corner and headed down the hill and straight through a lumber mill located between Cantrell and a very large drainage ditch slough. The slough ran parallel with the railroad yard. Everyone suspected that alligators lived in that slough.

They built a raft from boards they stole from the lumber yard and poled this across the slough, dodged moving trains, went under standing box cars or climbed over the connections, dodged the yard security cops, emerged at the depot building then south a few blocks through the capital grounds and further south along Battery Street to school on 14th and Park Street . They saved about two miles by doing this.

The only problem with this route is that it took them right through the "red light district" which was a tough section of town and which was about where the Children's Hospital and the 630 freeway is now located. When all the gang walked together it was okay but if only one or two made the pilgrimage trouble would more likely than not materialize in the form of two "trolls" demanding a duty before passage.

Magnis was fairly tough in a fair fight with someone his own age and size and when he had to be but was pretty slow afoot. In fact, he really didn't like to fight, and he was the slowest of all the friends.

I believe the British expression is "Oh shit."—You thought I was going to say "hard cheese."—Right?

These two thugs had the idea that Magnis and his

buddies were the rich kids—like I said, everything is relative.

I hadn't mentioned it before, but Magnis was also really smart in the head. That is to say when it came to math and physics and chemistry and dull stuff like that. Oh, and diplomacy. Come to think of it, he has never been very smart in any thing else except those things.

Well anyway, back to my story, after several months of this gauntlet run, Magnis started using his brain because as he calculated it—remember he was good at math and calculations—he wasn't gon'na last the semester, what with getting his "bell rung" several times.

All good diplomats have a way of keeping several lines of communication open at all times.

One day Magnis convinced the trolls—both of these guys were older than Magnis—that his daddy was the chief of detectives in the Little Rock Police Department and that he—Magnis—had access to a mold which his daddy had confiscated when raiding a counterfeit ring—and he could produce nickel slugs which could be used in telephones and the new Pepsi-Cola cooler machines which allowed you to slide a soda down a track after you deposited a nickel.

Well, Magnis actually did know how to make slugs out of lead and antimony and created a plaster mold that would have been the envy of any decent counterfeiter. One surface had a rough resemblance to a nickel and the other side was blank since the size and weight was all that was important—but the dummies didn't know that.

In addition to taking chemistry, math and other tough subjects, Magnis had an afternoon print shop class where they were learning to use a new Linotype machine, which as everyone knows melted Lead and Antimony to form print type, which eventually ended as the Friday afternoon high school newspaper. Magnis could melt and pour five of these slugs in a very short time and did so right in the print shop class where the Lead and Antimony waste was never missed.

He bought his passage whenever necessary with ten slugs worth half a buck to the trolls. This worked up to the time we moved again and he thought he wouldn't be exposed to the trolls again but they showed up after school one afternoon and made their demands.

What to do? Being the good diplomat he was, he made an anonymous phone call to the Little Rock Police Department, using a slug of course, and reported some pretty specific information on illegal activity going on with the use of slugs over in the "red light district." The ever diligent police department took care of the problem and diplomacy once again "seized the day."

Outside of using that slug to make the "anonymous" phone call, Magnis never used one of those slugs for his own gain. And that's the truth—or so he says.

I had started the fourth grade at Peabody Grammar School and had figured out that I didn't know who— whom—or what I really was.

I knew I didn't have a daddy and no one, including Miss Laura, ever told me what happened. When it came time to fill in some kind of form for the school records, I usually wrote "dead" or sometimes the name of Ada's latest "friend." When I did this, and she found out about it she would run amok.

I always knew how far I could take her on this when I started pressing her on the details of "my daddy" before she would go completely ballistic and tell me that I didn't have a "daddy" and that she had found me under a rock or one of her many other corrosive colloquial phrases.

If Miss Laura was around, she would more than not try to sooth things by saying something like "Well I swan Ada why don't you tell the boy all about it and be done with it."

Ada would then go after Miss Laura and rage all over her for the next ten or fifteen minutes during which time Miss Laura would motion for me to slip out of sight.

What really got me worried was the fact that Miss Laura also never volunteered to tell me even though I knew she knew and I believe she knew that I knew that she knew. Magnis often told me I was adopted.

I told lots of my friends that my dad was killed in the big war in France and this worked well on the ones who couldn't add or subtract or know that there hadn't been a war since 1918 and I would need to be at least twenty-two.

I fell in love again that year with an auburn haired girl with a heart shaped face and green stuff between her teeth. It was a short and sweet romance and not really rewarding because Billy Tiger—his name probably was Tagert, but he was the meanest kid in the school so, I thought it was Tiger since everyone knew how mean tigers were—decided that he was gon'na be in love with her instead and just beat the crap out of me before I even knew what hit me and right in front of the girl and everyone else.

I wasn't really that much in love with her anyway since I couldn't figure out what made her teeth green and it worried me a lot.

Throughout history, man has proclaimed things like "in the good old days" such and such happened and how "they just don't make 'em like they used too."

I have a quarrel with this because most things are better than they used to be.

If you told a man he could drive forty-thousand miles on a set of auto tires, in 1940, he would consider you a lunatic. You were lucky to get eight-thousand—and this with more holes than you would care to remember. A car battery lasting sixty months—good God man!

And socks! ! !

Well have you ever really considered socks?

You damn bet'cha. I considered socks when I was eight years old in 1940 in Little Rock, Arkansas.

About twice a year—I have no idea from where the money came—I went with Ada to J.C. Penney and got fitted with a pair of brown oxfords which had a simulated wing tip design across the toe and the salesman had these magic eyes which allowed him to say "looks like a perfect fit to me Ma'am." Jesus, they hardly ever fit and on top of that Ada always said "Better give him another half size so he can grow into them" and the sales guy always agreed. No one ever asked me how they felt and as far as I knew J.C. Penney was the only place on earth where shoes were sold.

From the shoe department to the sock department. You thought I would forget about the sock thing right ? Never—Socks were and are the enemy.

Both man and child have a right to socks that work right. Ada would go through the stack of whatever size socks went with what ever size shoe I was now in possession of and make believe that I was picking out my very own expensive colorful stripped socks.

I believe three pair was the number in mind. However, things would change at the last minute and Ada would manage to remember something else she would need and if we bought the stripped expensive socks she couldn't get whatever it was that she had remembered that she needed to get, and besides that, the three pair of brown socks, which didn't cost as much, would actually allow more wear since

81

if a hole wore in the heel of one you could match it with another and "mate up."

"Wonderful idea! Right Laurel?" "What do you think?"

Well I don't ever remember getting to answer.

"We'll take these three Madam—Won't we Laurel?" followed by "And don't you argue with me Laurel Hardy"—both names used always indicated that it was a good idea not to open my mouth.

In this sort of tight situation I could usually divert things by either pulling something from my nose or would reach around to give the seat of my britches a tug, a vigorous ass scratch and a dig—I think I had worms quite often because I sure needed to scratch a lot.

This would call for another one of Ada's famous unconstrained colloquial sayings which would make me aware that she was gon'na knock me into the middle of next week—but she never did—in fact Ada never struck me with anything except a switch until that day I already told you about when she smacked me in the kisser and again when I was sixteen when she gave me a right cross to the chin which I greatly deserved and maybe I'll tell you about if I have time.

The verbal torment would last all the way from the sock counter to the street and then drift off to some other universal collection of facts totally out of cognition to an eight year old and I always thanked God there were no hedges or trees downtown Little Rock.

I have to say that Ada never carried a grudge or even looked back. Justice was swift. Once punishment was meted out, the incident never came up again.

Okay, what about socks?

It wasn't actually the socks—it was the God Damned rubber elastic that the silly bastards put in the socks.

Didn't these rotten, irrelevant, fictitious, affected, misbegotten excuses for "sock engineers" even think about or have any consideration for us poor obsessive compulsives in need of socks which would not slide down from our skinny little legs and be swallowed by our shoes?

I like socks with strength of their own which will stay up on my legs where I put them. No sock should be allowed to be manufactured or sold which doesn't reach to the knee. Now that just seems intelligent to me. European men and golfers still wear socks which barely reach the malleoli and I really get anxious when I see such things happening to people. I have this incessant urge to remind these poor devils that their shoe has eaten their sock. Occasionally I feel the urge to actually pull them up for others.

In 1940, after three washings—or less—the rubber—elastic would fail and the sock would become this rather substantial size tube which forever fell into a heap awaiting its inevitable fate. That is to be eaten by the shoe.

This condition was absolutely intolerable to me and I was totally occupied with devising a method for overcoming this horrible punishment positioned on me by the "Sock God."

I'm not exactly sure just when I first understood this dreadful discomfort which came from this "sock condition" but I do remember having to stop and bend about every fourth or fifth step to pull my socks up to the proper position. This maneuver impeded progress and required setting aside any books or parcels each time.

The solution to my problem finally came to me during one of my many unsanctioned walks downtown after school. Unknown at the time of inception, the solution did come with a price.

The method I devised was, I thought, a clever way of taking about five steps and abruptly halting my steps, balancing on my left leg then curling my right foot behind the back of my left ankle just at the Achilles area and hoisting the wayward sock up to its proper location. I could then take five more steps and perform a like maneuver with my left foot. I perfected this to the point that only slight hesitation was required and could make, what seemed to me, almost normal progress.

However, others had now discovered my "little problem."

I believe the first suggestion, of something gone wrong, came with my being removed from my seat in the second row of the classroom and nudged toward the back of the room in a coaxing fashion—much as one would a Labrador Pup when newspaper training. First thoughts through my mind were that she—she being the teacher—had probably detected me playing with myself—later high school terminology tagged this as "pocket pool"—and boy was I gon'na get hell from Ada if they could track her down to our present address. Ada had chided me about this practice of late but the reprimand went unheeded.

I probably needed to "sock attend" at least once during the trip to the last seat in the row and was then asked if there was anything she—she being the teacher—could get for me.

Well, when she said that, I figured she hadn't seen me playing with myself after all and maybe she just thought I didn't feel well. I felt fine. In fact, I was already beginning to enjoy myself because I was real close to a window and could probably do anything I wanted to do clear in the back. Remember, I could already blow a bubble from my eye, multiple spit bubbles from my puckered lips and had almost perfected the first three bars of "Stars and Stripes Forever" passing gas.

Only a few minutes passed before "Billy Goat Gruff"—this was our name for the school principal—came into the classroom.

He had a whispered conference with the teacher during which time many glances projected toward me with the appropriate and timely head bob gestures required for a high current discussion such as this one.

I got'ta tell you, by now, I just didn't know what could be going on so I raised my hand number one, cause I was about to pee in my pants and Jesus, how the hell would I explain that, since I couldn't explain anything else because I didn't know anything else and scared just isn't—I wanted to say ain't but Ada never allowed me to say that word—the proper word. I believe sheer panic would be very appropriate.

My mind raced over the past week of illicit actions trying to reconstruct all of the things I had been involved in and I knew I was screwed up like "Ned in the Third Reader."

Finally the two of them approached me with very kind smiles on their faces and seemed to want to comfort me. Well I told them that the main thing I needed right then was to "go make a tinkle" which was Ada's polite way of telling someone you had to urinate—we, Magnis and I, also weren't allowed to use the "common" term "piss"—and that if not allowed very soon, was "sure as bears can't fly" gon'na tinkle all over the floor.

They thought that that would be fine and why didn't I do it right away which is exactly what I did.

When I came out of the restroom—we didn't call it a bath room because you certainly didn't take a bath in one of those rooms—well, you certainly couldn't rest in one either—"Billy Goat Gruff" asked me how long I thought I had been having this "little problem" and since I didn't know I was having any "little problems" I said I didn't really know which certainly couldn't qualify as a lie.

Well, had I seen a doctor and what did he think? You got'ta remember, I wasn't even sure we were living in the right place to be going to this school so I told them what I thought they wanted to hear which was "Yes I'm seeing him all the time and taking the right medicine and everything."

They seemed relieved about this time and assured me that they would do all they could to help me through this thing and were certainly glad that I had a Mother and family who cared so much and were seeing to my needs.

Well I thanked them for caring and at the same time wondered if Ada was even gon'na let me live after she found out what ever it was that I had—or did—or got into this time.

During recess I became a pariah but I managed to "overhear the under talk" and gathered that everyone thought I had something really bad and maybe I wouldn't even live through the day.

I certainly didn't know what the hell seizures were but I did recognize what fits were because one of Miss Laura's friends from church used to have them and foamed at the mouth and peed in his pants and I certainly qualified with having peed in my pants but I never ever foamed at the mouth except when I blew my spit bubbles. "Oh Jump'in Jesus"—that was one of Uncle Louie's favorite expressions—what am I gon'na do.

After Ada kills me Miss Laura will probably do it again and she never ever even laid a hand on me except to hug

86

me.

When we returned from recess the teacher let me know that if I ever felt a real bad one coming on that I should be sure and let her know so she could make sure I didn't swallow my tongue. I told her that I would be grateful for that and spent the rest of the morning in the back of the classroom playing with myself, blowing spit bubbles and trying to swallow my tongue.

At lunch time I think I managed to get clear of the classroom and down the hall before the "sock God" spoke to me and I had to extricate my socks. I was fully aware of all the eyes in the world watching my every move. What I wasn't even partially aware of was why they were watching me at all. I really couldn't remember doing anything different today than I always did and I certainly never had a fit or anything like that.

I had stopped in the cloak room for my lunch and went out to the playground and over to the corner beyond the swinging bars where I looked at the folded newspaper Ada always used to wrap my sandwich. We never got sacks— they were too expensive. I got a lot of long looks and even more "walk by's" and besides that—God! ! !—Ada used to make things for lunch like a jelly and gravy sandwich because that was what was easy to do—and today she had fixed boiled mashed sweet potato with catsup.

While sitting on an old block of concrete enjoying this epicurean delight I totally lost my breath when I looked up and saw Alice standing in front of me and I will never forget those green eyes and that little smile which was saying "I care". She was the most beautiful and smartest girl in the school and I didn't even know she could ever care about me but she apparently did. She didn't say a word. She just looked at me and spoke to me with her eyes.

I asked her if she would like to share my sandwich but after seeing what it was she declined and asked if she could eat her lunch with me. I was so overwhelmed I didn't know how to act but did manage to shake my head yes.

You won't believe this but she reached into her sack and pulled out the greatest looking peanut butter and banana sandwich I had ever seen. Peanut butter and sliced banana was, and is, my very favorite sandwich combination in all this world.

I declined her offer to share and I knew I was in love. She asked me if it hurt a lot and I told her truthfully "not much." And then I asked her "what is it I have?" And she told me I had something called "pretty maw seizures." She wasn't sure what that meant and certainly, if the smartest girl in the school didn't know, I couldn't be expected to know.

I asked her how everyone knew I was having these "pretty maw seizures" since I didn't even know I was having them. And she said she didn't know either, it was just what the kids had overheard "Billy Goat Gruff" say.

Well you got'ta know that by this time I was feeling the best I ever felt in my whole life so far and just couldn't wait to marry Alice and when she told me that she knew that we both lived in the same direction I just about swallowed my tongue accidentally—something I had spent half the morning trying to do on purpose—and became so rattled that she thought I was going to have a "pretty maw" and reached over and touched my forehead and boy, I just lost it. I didn't even care if Ada knew—cause I thought "I'm gon'na get in Love."

I didn't tell Alice though.

By the time lunch break was over we knew a lot about each other and had agreed that since we lived in the same direction we should walk home together.

Holy smokes, all of this happening in just one day.

I can't remember how I made it through the afternoon, but I did and there she was outside in the hall waiting for me.

We started west on 4th Street and of course Alice observed and tried not to let on each time the "sock God" problem touched me and I was in such love that I didn't care whether school ever kept or not and especially didn't care about "pretty maw" or anything else.

By the time we reached Cross Street, which was about five blocks, we were holding hands.

We turned right on Cross Street, North one bock and she said "This is where I live." Right on the corner of 3rd and Cross! I knew right then that someone ought to write a song about being on a street where someone lived and feeling good about it.

There was a short chain link fence around a grassy backyard which bordered Cross Street and where a very pleasant looking man in brown pants and shirt was busy with a pull knife shaping this marvelous looking long bow. I had never seen anything like it. He had bows in all stages toward completion.

Alice greeted him with "Hi Daddy—come meet my new friend Laurel." He did just that.

He explained how he made his living making these bows and talked to me just like I was a grown somebody. He even took a finished bow from a stand and shot an arrow into a makeshift target. Boy was I impressed.

He told me Alice was almost an expert archer and that maybe someday I could go with them to Fair Park where they had targets. I wondered what it must be like to have a great dad like Alice had and thought about asking him if he knew what "pretty maw" was but thought better of it.

About that time Alice's Mom came out the back door with some coffee for her man and a glass of Kool-Aid for Alice and me. I never had it so good.

They asked me about my family—not in a snooping fashion—but rather in a friendly caring way. I of course lied and told them that I lived with Ada and Miss Laura cause my dad had been killed in the war and they looked at each other with a knowing nod and I imagine some kind comment.

Well, I figured I had used up my welcome and excused myself, as I had always been taught to do with grownups, gulped the last of my Kool-Aid and said good by to Alice and asked if I could walk to school with her the next day.

She agreed that I could.

I got home and asked Miss Laura what "pretty maw" fits were all about. She asked me why I wanted to know about something like that and I told her about this poor kid at school who was having them and she just shook her head and said "Poor little thing."

Chapter 17

THINGS JUST GOT better and better as the days went by. I had now been in real love for about six weeks and whistled day and night.

"Lord only knows what's happening to that boy!" Miss Laura proclaimed often. I had shared my feelings with Magnis and he told me that it probably wouldn't last because these things seldom did.

When I asked him why, he said that everyone knew why, and as soon as I got to be his age, so would I.

I guess I thought that was as good an explanation as any and went off to whistle "When You Wish Upon A Star", which was the closest thing to a love song I knew.

Smitten is the best term I know to describe how I felt.

Alice and I had been meeting daily in front of her house for our stroll to school and one day she said: "Laurel, does it hurt when it happens?"

I confessed that I didn't know because I didn't know what it was that was happening and asked if she knew what it was supposed to feel like.

We had stopped to have this exchange and I told Alice that the very next time she saw me having a "pretty maw" she should tell me immediately no matter where we were or what we were doing. Five or six steps east on 4th Street and

Alice blurted it out.

"Laurel, what did that just feel like?"

For the first time I realized what it was all about.

We sat on the curb and I opened my soul to the one I knew I wanted to spend the rest of my life with.

She understood the "Sock God" concept and skinny legs and sock eating shoes and spit bubbles and apparently everything else I brought up and then confessed that she had also considered being with me for the rest of her life and decided that we wouldn't tell anyone else about the fact that I wasn't having "pretty maws" after all. We would let it be our secret. "What they don't know won't hurt them" was how she put it.

God!! What wisdom.

Alice also let me know that the next day she would solve my problem, which she did with two wide rubber band like pieces from her fathers long bow work bench and which she lovingly slid over the brown J.C. Penney fake wing tips and up to the top of the cheap brown socks covering my skinny little legs and carefully folded a short inverted cuff over the rubber so as to be unseen by those without a reason to know.

"Jump'in Jesus"—I said to myself and quivered all over just thinking about having my "problem" solved.

We held hands and turned for school and I made it almost all the way before my socks needed slight assistance.

A LICE, IT SEEMED, was the only   one in the world, besides Miss Laura, who recognized that I wasn't dumb.

My world was that of an observer taking it all in and stacking it away in my memory banks.

Since no one in the family—except Miss Laura—ever really asked me to express anything, I wasn't sure I was allowed or required to express anything except yes and no and I dun'no.

I guess I took exams in class and must have passed them because I was never held back in school—remember, I was advanced from the first grade to second grade after only two weeks when I started—but, most things the teachers would talk about left me with the idea that I seemed to already know about what ever it was. It never seemed important to me that the Pilgrims landed on Plymouth Rock in 1620—only that it was some time in the early part of the 16th rectangle since Jesus got himself killed.

My memory bank looks like a whole bunch of these rectangular things stacked one on top of the other, each divided from left to right into four parts. I file things into these stacks and quarters even though in the early parts of my life I didn't understand what I was doing, only that I was doing. And I guess carrying on a conversation with Miss Laura was the only exercise my brain ever got until I met Alice. Magnis was so smart he didn't even need to study to get excellent grades and I was considered untrainable so I only got to listen to Magnis, not converse.

Alice seemed to be on my wave length and brought out the best in me.

I even stopped playing with myself but didn't give up spit bubbles or practicing "Stars and Stripes Forever".

My "pretty maws" seemed to be under control according to all of the busy body observers and the other kids seemed to warm up to me just a bit—although I suspected it was because Alice was so popular and she spent most of her free time with me.

On most days after school we spent some time in front of a beautiful house on 4th Street which had a park like setting for a front yard with shade trees and lawn and a great looking rock retaining wall just the right height for sitting.

Alice understood me and seemed to be able to anticipate what I was going to say which is exactly how I responded to her.

I think Alice had said something to her mother because she now brought an extra sandwich and most days an extra apple or another piece of fruit for me to share.

Her mother probably realized that I hardly ever got enough to eat although I never remember going to bed without having something to eat for dinner, though it might have only been cornbread crumbled into a glass of buttermilk and eaten with a spoon.

This whole episode—even though lasting slightly over four months—had a profound life long impact on me.

Only eight years old and I learned how fragile life really is when one morning I waited for Alice—which never had happened before since she was always waiting for me.

I went on to school and was already on the "late report" and had to explain to the teacher that I had had a "pretty maw" and Ada had to take me to the hospital but I was alright now and whatever else I thought she might like to hear.

The teacher was real sorry that I had some "little problems."

I guess she was well ahead of her time since she never referred to seizures and never ever asked about my self esteem. I'm not even sure today what the term self esteem really means. God, I already knew by age three that all you got for not crapping in your drawers was not having to go clean yourself up—you certainly didn't get a self esteem button.

I worried all day about Alice and headed for her house first thing after school.

I was pretty anxious when I knocked because I knew it wasn't any of my business why Alice wasn't in school. I waited a few minutes and knocked again and still no answer.

I went on home and sat under the China Berry Tree until Miss Laura came to find me and asked what was wrong.

You know? At age eight, one time can become always.

All that night I wondered why Alice hadn't said something about not meeting me and actually, my first reaction was not for Alice but rather the horrible thought of rejection.

I made it through the night and headed down the hill

from Riverside and past the Missouri Pacific Hospital in pretty good spirits—at the viaduct, I got anxious and by the time I reached the little coffee shop with the pear tree I was a mess and I had to pee very badly which I did behind the sign.

When I neared 3rd Street I could see that Alice wasn't there.

I approached the door and before I could knock, Alice's mother opened the door and greeted me.

Before I could ask about why Alice was mad at me Mrs Smith said "Alice is very sick Laurel." "She's in the hospital with sleeping sickness and we're very worried about her."

I was devastated and began to cry. I managed to tell Mrs Smith how sorry I was and how could I help and probably all of the other meaningless things an eight year old could conjure up.

Mrs Smith simply reminded me about how much Alice cared for me and that friends just kept good thoughts and said some prayers.

I didn't know how to pray since no one had actually taught me how but I was reasonably sure that God didn't require all of the ranting and raving which took place at Miss Laura's sideshows and also reasonably certain even God couldn't understand the mumbling which I had witnessed the times Ada dragged me to the Catholic Church.

I ran all the way back home all the while wondering where God hung out most of the time and figured it couldn't be anyplace close to our house since China Berries stink and the house wasn't much.

There was an old Civil War rampart with a circular gun emplacement which commanded a promontory overlooking the river which was about a quarter of a mile from our house. I headed for this sanctuary and the shade of the big trees sheltering this little bit of history.

I was sure God knew about this place and I had my first conversation with the "Big Guy"—one way of course cause if it's a two way conversation they lock you up—which lasted a long time and which was interrupted with spasmodic crying at least on my part.

No one from home knew I was missing and the Truant Officer didn't show up that day for some reason and I wasn't missed.

I headed back to Alice's house and stopped along the way to swipe a flower from the planter at the Missouri Pacific Hospital.

When I reached her house I knocked and knew something bad had happened because when her father answered the door I could hear sobbing from inside.

I handed the flower to Mr Smith and asked if he could get it to Alice to help her feel better.

He answered "I'm sure I can Laurel—at least I'll try— Alice died a little while ago Laurel but I will try—thanks for being such a good friend Laurel—I'm sure she loved you a lot."

He said goodbye and I walked home with my head high and without a tear.

I was very angry with God.

CLYDE AND BERYL continued to live in Kansas City but Clyde still made frequent trips to other states and always came back with large amounts of cash.

October 1940 found most of the world in a turmoil and found Clyde likewise.

On September 23rd 1940, President Roosevelt had signed the conscription bill the congress had passed the week before. This bill laid down the rules which in essence allowed the government to register 16 million men ages 21 to 36 and subject them to be drafted into the army for one year.

October 16th was the date chosen and registration was to take place at the appropriate voting district office. The army was to choose 800,000 from this draft registration each year and after completion of this one year training the conscripts were to be kept on an enlisted reserve status for ten years or until age 45.

The only wholly exempt person was the Vice President of the United States. The President was not exempt because he was in fact the Commander in Chief of the Army. Members of congress, governors, legislators, judges and federal employees were not exempt unless the President found their work essential.

The law stated that: *"After registration, but before actual induction into the service, conscripts remain subject to civil laws."* The Department of Justice was ordered to: *"nab and prosecute men who evade registration or falsify statements at this stage [civil penalty: imprisonment up to five years, a fine up to $10,000, or both]." After induction: "they are of course subject to martial law."*

Therefore: *"If they fail to report on the day and hour specified for induction, they will be classed as deserters and be tried by court martial."*

Five days after filling out the questionnaire at the local voting precinct a serial number would be assigned. Since there were several thousand voting precincts across the country, thousands received the same number. Don't ask why they didn't use birthdays as they did in a later draft—they did it this way.

When your number came up, you were required to fill out a detailed questionnaire which probed into all aspects of your life.

Local draft boards studied the returned questionnaires and divided them into four classes : *[1] eligible for immediate service; [2] deferred because of necessary civilian job; [3] deferred because of dependents; [4] ineligible because of physical or mental incompetence.*

Ordained ministers and theology students were required to register but were not to be drafted. College students likewise needed to register but were not subject until they finished their semester.

Objectors: *"by reason of religious training and belief"* were to be classified for non-combatant duty and might be assigned to *"other work of national importance."*

Those landing in class [1] were then subject to a

99

physical exam which few failed since you qualified even if: *"blind in one eye, partially deaf, minus one big toe or two little ones."*

Clyde, wasn't missing any toes and he certainly was no theology student or for that matter even Vice-President and should October the 16th become a reality, he would just happen to be thirty six years, eight months and nine days old—leaving him one hundred and fourteen days too young.

When the evening of October 15th arrived, Clyde was just beside himself. He had his face in a bottle and he ranted and raved and jumped up and down like Rumplestielsken and blamed Beryl, God, Franklin D. Roosevelt, Herbert Hoover, someone named "sum-bitch" numerous times and evoked epitaphs from the depths.

Beryl finally couldn't stand it any longer and left the apartment. His yelling got worse and most of the tenants in the apartments yelled back at him to shut up which just poured fuel on the fire.

It suddenly flashed through Clyde's mind—well that's not exactly true—since nothing ever "flashed" through Clyde's mind—that maybe there was a way out of this "horrible mass of pain what's been heaped on my shoulders" and which had apparently singled him out from all other mankind.

Clyde now began to formulate—mainly to the walls and his bottle—why he didn't even need to register since he had never worked at a job where he received a pay stub and he was as close to the unknown man as anyone could be and actually he wasn't even Clyde C. Dodge.

Clyde ran through the bottle he had been sucking on and marched down to the local gin mill pretty puffed up with his brilliant problem solving shrewdness and joined some of his drinking cronies. He didn't tell anyone about his situation, he just decided to listen and learn which was a first for him. Most of the locals thought Clyde was older than he really was and no one asked about his status.

Several at the bar were pretty excited about getting drafted since it would at least mean a steady pay check and some amount of security. Others, like Clyde, were trying to think of ways to get around it.

Beryl joined him some time later and was surprised at his change in comport. He seemed more sober although he had been through about twice as much booze as was normal for this time of the evening and proudly told her about his decision not to register and how he had come to this conclusion and, expecting congratulations for his wise deductive reasoning, received instead a simple shake of Beryl's head and "Clyde, sometimes you act like you ain't got the brains God gave a green worm."

"Your memory is shorter than your belly button, Clyde, where were you in 1938?"

Chapter 20 It Always Works Sometimes

THE FINAL MONTHS of the year passed and 1941 kind of slithered into being as I remember it. We were still living in the little house on Riverside—probably lived there longer than any place I could remember.

I was really having a hard time dealing with what had happened to my friend. I had never been able to form a relationship or friendship with neighborhood kids because we were so often in the transient mode. Except for superficial playground banter I never really got to know any of my schoolmates. In those very few months, Alice had become the object of my life.

Miss Laura listened but for the first time, didn't seem to understand my feelings. Apparently even this exceptional lady's mind was unable to separate the desperate singular feelings of an eight year old boy from the rigidity of God, as ascribed to by the followers of The Good Man Christ, and adulterated and bastardized by the hoax on man known as religion. Spewed forth with sanctimonious proclivities by Papal edicts, Calvinistic guile and self anointed and self appointed clerics and preachers, the bible, as interpreted by the particular reader, gave answer to each problem, and yet failed altogether to understand the crushed heart of a child.

I tried talking to Magnis but after several tries, which got me nowhere, I gave up and internalized my feelings and in a cognitive manner withdrew into my self and shut out mankind.

I developed several tics which this time were real and certainly would never be solved using a rubber band. The major one seemed to develop with my thoughts about how cold it must be in a grave and manifested in the form of an internal shiver sensation which originated in my anterior neck above the level of what would later become my Adams apple and descend in a wave fashion down to the lower part of my rib cage. This tic was imperceptible to any but the most astute observer.

The second tic involved my lower right lip and seemed to fire off ad lib. It was a slight but obvious contortion downward and I have no idea even to this day what psychogenic protrusion triggered it.

Magnis picked up on the facial tic right away and figured that I must have been overdosing on "loping my mule" and did counsel me on the subject of self abuse but I assured him that was not the case. I don't think he believed me but I also didn't care because it was the truth.

I guess the only thing that saved me from myself during the first months of 1941 was that for the first time in my entire life—except for those daily meetings with Alice—I now had something to really look forward to.

We were going to California in the spring as soon as school was out.

Trixie and Uncle Louie were making all of the arrangements for us to join them in Los Angeles and one day in late May a tough looking man wearing an expensive tailored suit showed up and delivered an almost new 1939 Chevy four door sedan and instructions from Uncle Louie that the man said were to be followed to the letter.

It was almost Damon Runyan like. He gave Ada the ownership—registration papers which he said would "stay in da name of da boss" and gave her exact instructions about which routes to take to Los Angeles and several papers with names, phone numbers and addresses instructing her who she should contact in almost every town along the way should she need any sort of help or have any sort of trouble. Further instructions entailed an envelope which she was to open only when reaching Las Vegas and that a special package was to be picked up in Hot Springs.

The nice man spoke to Ada like he was sure she wouldn't get it the first time through and would be coming back to review the hard part later. "Car wise or anywise Ma'am" "Tha folks'll take care ya Ma'am—don't you worry none." While making sure Ada got all of the instructions which had been placed in his trust he held a large envelope in his left hand and when he was sure Ada understood everything that he had been instructed to relate, he turned to Miss Laura and handed the envelope to her.

"Miss Laura?"

"I hope its okay to call ya Miss Laura" "Is it Ma'am?"

"Da boss says for me ta give dis package only to you and no one else." "He says you're to open it in front of me."

Miss Laura took the envelope from the man and opened it and I've got'ta tell you, my heart went right up through my throat. There was a stack of money an inch thick mostly twenty dollar bills. I didn't know there was that much money in the world.

He instructed Miss Laura about never flashing it or letting anyone know she had it and then turned back to Ada with more instructions about the fact that this money would get us to our first "refill" destination where there would be more when Miss Laura phoned a certain number.

He further instructed Miss Laura that Ada was not to have anything to do with any of the money except that there was an allowance in the stack of bills for a shopping spree for new clothes and travel things for the four of us which she—Ada—was expected to see to and also money for having some of our things shipped. We could ship Miss Laura's Singer foot treadle sewing machine and personal things and her feather bedding and all of the quilts she had made over the years and Ada could ship all of her books and kitchen utensils and her personal things.

Magnis and I didn't even have any "impersonal" things to ship much less "personal" things except for the old bicycle, with only one pedal, which had given good service when Magnis delivered his newspapers and a fairly beat up red, rusted "Radio Flyer" wagon which he tied behind the bike to haul the newspapers he and I delivered each day. My only possessions, except for the few clothes I had and the shoes I was wearing, were a yellow Tonka type toy dump truck in almost perfect condition and a slightly damaged genuine hand made 20 pound pull long bow and one slightly used target arrow.

Mr Nice Guy took Miss Laura aside and told her that he would drive her to the nearest pay phone so that she could make a collect call to Trixie in California as soon as he was sure that everyone understood the plan.

It turned out that after talking to Trixie, Miss Laura was walking on cloud nine and she returned whistling "Onward Christian Soldiers" and told us about a house that was to be ours, completely furnished and waiting in Los Angeles.

Even I knew why the money had been placed in trust

with Miss Laura. Ada still walked the wild side more often than one would care to remember so she had been placed second in command and separated from the opportunity to be separated from the money.

Mr Nice Man—we didn't actually learn his name—was extremely satisfied with his presentation and prepared for his departure with the deportment of the perfect gentleman.

Miss Laura and I walked to the small corner grocery store and for the first time in my life I got to pick out what I would like to have for dinner that evening.

I chose hot dogs with real Wonder Bakery hot dog buns, with baked beans and for desert asked Miss Laura to make a bowl of banana pudding with vanilla wafers and Royal Brand vanilla pudding.

Actual fresh milk came to our table very seldom. We mostly got canned evaporated milk diluted with water when we got milk at all. Miss Laura picked two glass quart bottles from the cooler and on top of that went to the metal lined water cooled soda tub and told me I could pick any flavor I wanted and one for Magnis.

I chose Grape-ete and can still taste that wonderful flavor today.

Talk about flying high. I walked back to the house beside Miss Laura like I owned the world singing and whistling "Three Little Fishies"—"and they swam and they swam all over the dam"—and knowing that Magnis and I would have a great time trying to eat every bite of his "most favorite desert in all this world."

We got home and Ada had already gone off in the new Chevy to impress her friends.

Miss Laura, Magnis and me—what a feast. Miss Laura had secreted a second bottle of Grape-ete for me and a Hires Root Beer for Magnis and we drank these later that evening while listening to the Red Skelton Radio Show.

SPRING OF 1941 and no one had heard anything from or about Clyde or Charlie except maybe Ada and she wasn't telling.

It seems that Clyde had escaped the draft simply by listening to Beryl and not complying with the law. She rightfully figured that if anyone came looking for Clyde C. Dodge he could deny that such a person existed since he had never legalized the use of this name. Beryl further decided that since he had never applied for a social security number, filed any tax returns or been officially identified in any fashion he could be just about anyone he chose to be. Clyde helped a little by remembering that he had an older brother who had died at age 4 and was buried in an unmarked grave at the Black Springs cemetery.

Beryl proved to be a master at the planning and had a better idea. She sent Clyde on an immediate run to Reno, Nevada, where he set in motion a legal "six week resident seeking a divorce" status. After several weeks he made a false police report claiming he had been robbed of all his worldly possessions. Clyde was still pretty nervous making a police report.

It was duck soup getting a new ID in the form of a Nevada drivers license. The hotel where he was staying confirmed to the authorities that he was who he said he was and had registered as Mr. C.C. Dodge, and that was about all there was to it.

His name, if subjected to questioning, would be. Clyde C. Dodge, born July 10, 1903.

The only hitch in this scheme was that of the property which had thus far been acquired and grew again when Clyde returned from Reno.

Clyde now did something he had never done before. He consulted a lawyer. This really aggravated him since it cost money but even more so because he didn't trust lawyers.

He got the name of a rather shady attorney from someone at a gin mill, made an appointment and at the proper time got dressed up in his standard grey Dickie Brand work shirt with matching pants, white socks and Sears—Roebuck blucher style rubber soled work shoes and the ever present sweat stained brimmed felt hat.

The office—if you could call it that—was a walk up on Vine Street above a bar right in the heart of the red light district. In 1959 Jerry Leiber would write a song about Kansas City at 12th Street and Vine and finding some crazy little women there. I doubt that this area has changed much in these many years.

Clyde picked his way around the debris on the stairway and found himself in a hallway with only two doors. One on either side. The sign on the door to the left of the hall said "Private", the one opposite said "Efrom E. Lebowitz, Esq."

Clyde knocked on the "Lebowitz" door and almost immediately the door behind him marked "Private" jerked open and scared Clyde half out of his skin. He let out a shriek, did a spin and came chest to face with Efrom E. Lebowitz, Esq.

Clyde jumped back and gawked down at a face which could only be attached to a lawyer of the caliber one would expect to find on Vine Street.

Efrom E. Lebowitz was no more than five foot five and resembled a version of the comedian Buddy Hackett with a Groucho Marx mustache and large horn rim glasses. He was even more disheveled than Clyde—which really took some disheveling—and you guessed it, had this large cigar clinched between his teeth.

He ordered Clyde to turn around and face the wall and Clyde complied without giving it a second thought. The sleazy little bastard frisked Clyde and seemed to enjoy the process.

Satisfied that Clyde was clean, he reached around and opened the "Efrom E. Lebowitz" door and motioned Clyde inside the room which resembled a boars nest which any male college sophomore would have been ashamed to step foot in.

Lebowitz told Clyde that it would be alright if he called him Mr Lebowitz and asked what he thought Clyde would like to be called.

Clyde told Lebowitz that his name was Clyde C. Dodge but that Lebowitz could address him as Mr Dodge.

To which Lebowitz replied "Ok Clyde seems fair enough to me." "Wha'da ya want" and "How'ya gon'na pay fer it."

Lebowitz seemed to perspire and excrete fat from all of his pores as he puffed the cigar and when Clyde reached into his shirt pocket for one of his ready rolled cigarettes Lebowitz was quick to point out that he didn't allow smoking in his office.

When Clyde pulled out a roll of cash Lebowitz became very attentive and told him that maybe it would be okay if he smoked—to which Clyde retorted "Ah sure as hell wish't y'all could make up yor gol'dang mind cause I'm git'in mighty nervous be'in in here with y'all anyway." "Y'all jus make me awful scared an I don't even like yor high-fa-lutin ways no how."

Clyde managed to convey to Lebowitz what it was he needed done by the legal profession which was to some how or other make Clyde a business and transfer all of his property into this business.

Lebowitz, during the course of discovery, asked Clyde how he got all of this wealth and Clyde told him "It ain't non'na yor matter." Clyde had by this time regained some of his guileless crust and realized that he, not Lebowitz, was calling the shots. Lebowitz was a thick skinned piece of sludge who would perpetrate any transgression for a fee. However, of all the many things Efrom E. Lebowitz, Esq., was, dumb he wasn't.

The height and breadth of the transgression depended solely on the amount of money which crossed his pudgy sweat dripping palm.

I have to believe now—although I doubt that Clyde believed or for that matter even thought about it—that Lebowitz saw this cash cow and suggested that Clyde ought to form a Massachusetts Business Trust Organization to which Clyde replied "That's persactly what I had on my mind Mr Lebowitz."

The old insert is that you never want to milk a cash cow dry.

Lebowitz realized that Clyde was pretty dumb but after having come to this conclusion rather early on also realized that Clyde was at least smart enough to have pulled off what ever it was that he was pulling off and this put Clyde way out in front of anything he himself had been able to do

111

thus far.

The basic truth was that Lebowitz was jealous of Clyde's success. This mediocre misfit—he wasn't even a first class misfit—had acquired all of this real estate and all he—Lebowitz—had to show for his years of labor through college and law school was a shady two bit law practice and a monthly rent on a real shabby two room office. Yea, he got some extra curricular compensation from the girls downstairs when he sprung them from the pokey in quick time but this simpleton smelled like a long term relationship and true to his hunch, Lebowitz and Clyde did lots of business over the next few years.

God! How Efrom E. Lebowitz, Esq., loved an all cash deal.

A Massachusetts Business Trust Organization was also know as A Pure Business Trust Organization and was a very legal "hybrid" which was neither Corporation nor Partnership. It has been suggested that this was how all "old big money" was buried in those days.

The important thing to Lebowitz was that he had a feeling about where Clyde had obtained this wealth and also had a gut feeling about what harmful feats Clyde might be capable of if cornered or pressed. He had heard many stories of this "Clyde Barrows" type from the Ozarks' and after all, this guy was also named Clyde and his "lady friend" was named Beryl. Beryl and Clyde ? It got this fat guys attention.

It wasn't long before Clyde possessed a set of papers showing "The Bearer of This Instrument" to be the Sole Trustee of "Ozark C.C.D. -A Business Trust Organization" which in turn was named as Trustee of among many other things "Black Springs Land Company—A Business Trust Organization" and naming Efrom E. Lebowitz, Esq., as legal correspondent.

Black Springs Land Company was now the owner of record of all of Clyde's real estate holdings totaling over $150,000.

Efrom E. Lebowitz, Esq., didn't know from where the money came nor, at this time, did he wish to know. He only knew that as legal counsel he now had a management agreement and took a percentage of the monthly rent. Things looked good and life was sweet.

On the other hand, Clyde and Beryl still lived in the one bedroom apartment and actually nothing had changed. "Living well is the best revenge" apparently didn't apply here.

E.E. CUMMINGS wrote a poem titled LIV [Roman Number 54] in his book of poetry which he called 1 X 1 [One Times One]. He didn't publish this until 1944 but I believe he must have known about me in the spring of 1941. He closed the third stanza with "forever was never till now." He ended the poem and the book with "we're wonderful one times one."

Think about the anxieties an eight and a half year old boy can kindle during a month and a half wait for something which can only be imagined to begin with. The wait is impossible and each night the Technicolor dreams grow more profound and more creative. The actual day will never come because six weeks is a lifetime. It truly is 1 X 1 and maybe even 1 X 1 squared. "forever was never till now."

I hadn't even been taken to J.C. Penney to get the new things I was supposed to get for our trip. In fact no one told me much of anything except Magnis and he didn't know much himself and he was fifteen and knew everything. Ada always kept everything a secret and Miss Laura knew that the only thing she controlled was the money sack. She also knew she couldn't let it out of her sight. I knew only anxieties and my tics got worse and I got a rash on my fanny from scratching so much and Miss Laura took some of the money from the sack and went to Walgreen's Drug Store and bought some calamine lotion and some horrible tasting medicine to worm me. It didn't help.

Enough of that. The fact is that my world collapsed again one day less than two weeks after the departure of "Mr Nice Man."

Ada took "our new car" out one night and didn't return for two and a half days. No one knew where she was until she was discharged from the hospital and came home in a cab. That beautiful wonderful smelling shiny black, as close to new as I thought I would ever see, 1939 Chevy sedan was still submerged in water at the bottom of a gravel and sand pit out on Arch Pike.

Ada was a mass of pain, lumps, bruises, cuts and scrapes. That she was alive was a miracle. The police reported that she was going south on Arch Pike which would indicate that she was not heading toward home. Perhaps back to the Venetian Inn which later proved to be where she did most of her tanking up. At any rate, she skidded off the road hit a piling and into one of the many gravel pits which at this time of the year were mini lakes. She was so crocked that she didn't even remember what happened.

It was around one a. m. and some Good Samaritan, whom she had passed—"go'in bout as fast as that car could go and gol'dang out'ta control at that—about a mile afore the accident happened."—saved her life. He jumped into the water, pulled her from the wreck and drove her to General Hospital and told the medical staff what had happened. She was unconscious for about six hours and listed as a Jane Doe. The Good Samaritan left the hospital without identifying himself and didn't get further involved.

The police found the car the next afternoon but never did find Ada's' purse and since the car was registered out of state it took time to track it down. Ada didn't make any attempt to have us notified, she just stayed in the hospital and licked her wounds. If the whole world should try to enter her cave, or challenge her in any fashion, she would flick them off with all the hate and venom she had stored up over these years. No one told Ada Laura Slewter Lubeck what to do or how to do it.

Miss Laura just shook her head and said "Well I swan Ada if you don't beat all." "I hope you got it all out of your system girl because the Good Lord just gave you the lesson of your life"—"I'm not sure I'm gon'na be around this old world long enough to raise those boys to manhood and you better get your self straightened out and all together and I mean now." "How do you spect we can get this family to California now?"

Uncle Louie heard about the problem from his friends almost as soon as did we and needless to say, really blew his top.

Miss Laura got through collect on the phone, to Trixie, shortly after Uncle Louie had received his information call, and told her everything that she knew and begged guidance and forgiveness. Trixie of course had first concern for Magnis, Miss Laura and me. I guess she realized that things could only get worse if we were not where she could watch over us—at least financially. She told Miss Laura to sit tight and wait for a new plan.

Ada was by this time even more obstreperous than anyone had ever before seen her.

Imagine a tiny wooden framed house less than fifteen feet from its neighbor with a bare floor living room no more than 12 x 12, a 10 x 10 bedroom attached on one side, a tiny bathroom extending from the other side, and a closet which had been made into a hallway through which one entered a kitchen where Magnis and I slept. I got'ta tell you that just keeping out of the way was a full time job even in normal times but when Ada was really wound up and had her fuse lit it was prelude to a catastrophe.

No one was spared. The entire world had joined forces and contrived against her and a more paranoid cacophony never dismantled mankind with such rapier like righteous indignation before or since. It was the most amazing and yet terrifying experience of my life and she was stone cold sober. The amazing part was that she never broke anything or did anything except pace back and forth and rave.

She detested humanity in general, abhorred people in particular, desecrated and profaned all religious endeavors, marked certain individuals for future disdain and traduced and verbally desecrated that staid boulder of kindness—the person who in 1907 had incubated the particular egg chosen, through random selection, to be fertilized during hallowed love emanating from a premier union and which through the miracle of DNA replication, amalgamated into the living organism, which—she must have finally understood—was what she hated most.

Ada now had undergone complete and total catharsis and was, following her next heartbeat, ready to move on to whatever lay ahead and gave no further cognizant thought to what had transpired in the past.

I had witnessed this sudden intuitive realization—an epiphany—from my hiding place in the closet hallway peeking through the curtain which substituted for a door.

34 year old Ada Laura Slewter Lubeck pursed her lips and took a deep breath through her nose, walked over to Miss Laura, chucked her under the chin, leaned over the

chair where Magnis had been transfixed and tousled his hair then walked straight through the curtain where I sat, dumbfounded and thinking that nobody knew I was there, lifted me to my feet and hugged my head to her waist. Ada had never ever hugged me before. She then walked out to the porch, sat on the steps and sang a song I had never heard. In fact I don't think anyone had ever heard her sing a song before. Her voice was female kin to Louis Armstrong as she pronounced each word very distinctly—"There's a somebody I'm longing to meet, oh how I need someone to watch over me." I don't believe Ada ever took another serious drink of alcohol for the remainder of her life.

B Y THE TIME Trixie and Uncle Louie had put things back together it was June of 1941 and Hitler's Germany had overrun most of Europe, the Italians had occupied Albania forcing King Zog into exile, nylon had already been invented, Latvia, Lithuania and Estonia were "annexed" by Russia, Winston Churchill was Prime Minister of England which somehow caused Rudolph Hess to jump out of a plane over that very same country, and for what purpose we will never know. Orson Welles produced Citizen Kane, "Have You Met Miss Jones" and "My Funny Valentine", both by Rogers and Hart, were heard daily and Artie Shaw and Glenn Miller did Hoagy Carmichaels "Star Dust" and—we—headed toward California in a 1940 four door Pontiac sedan, mole hair seats, whitewall tires and a six cylinder engine.

I don't have a clue about how everything for our trip was put together, I just remember the last day of school and everyone running up and down the halls yelling and shouting and singing "The teachers sure been full of it—but now she's as loose as a goose—she needs to sit on a toilet—but she can't cause she's big as a moose."

When I got outside on the playground I saw Billy Tiger ready to cross the street and about as far away as he could

119

be from me and still be on the same block. Since I knew I wouldn't ever return and he probably couldn't run me down from that distance, I called him a fart face and a piss ant and ran like hell in the other direction toward home.

I stopped running after about three blocks and found myself in front of the beautiful old house with the rock wall where Alice and I had spent our few moments together. I forgot about the miscreant activity which I had undertaken a few moments before and sat on the wall just thinking about her and asked her how she was doing and had a pretty good talk. I told her where I was going and wished she could come along and that I was sorry I never brought any flowers for her cause I didn't know where they took her but I would someday when I found out.

There wasn't anyone else I needed to say goodbye to except Mernon and he wasn't around cause he was helping his daddy gather in the catfish trot lines down by the slough and he wasn't much of a friend anyway. So, the next day I climbed in the back seat between Magnis and Miss Laura with nothing of my own except the clothes on my body and a clean brown and white striped polo shirt, a pair of short pants, two pair of brown tubes, two pair of under shorts which were three sizes to large and hand me downs from Magnis and a black wool overcoat all of which were stuffed inside a pillow cover and hugged in my lap.

Ada's friend Helen had decided to go along with us as far as Las Vegas and would share the driving.

We arrived in Hot Springs after only a couple of hours and suddenly all of us were abruptly told by Ada to get out of the car and wait at the park where the main hot spring flowed out of the hill.

She told Miss Laura and Helen that she had a special job to do and would be gone only a little while.

After she drove off Helen and Miss Laura talked about Hot Springs being a haven for the gangsters and was considered a neutral territory—meaning, as I interpreted it, that they checked their guns at the door—I didn't know which door—and waved white flags when they went out.

I was certain that Ada was never gon'na return and immediately let Miss Laura know my feelings and proceeded into my tic routine.

True to her word, Ada was gone about 35 minutes. We climbed aboard and off we went.

We hadn't gone more than a block before I blurted out—"Did ya see any gangsters who didn't check their guns at the door?"

"Oh God Laurel don't even think that kind of thing" Ada said, with the most serious intonation I had ever heard her use.

We were headed toward Oklahoma City after we veered north and passed through Fort Smith Arkansas so we could pick up route 66 which was somehow or other eventually gon'na get us in the vicinity of Las Vegas.

I don't remember much about this early passage except that we drove for hours before stopping for the first night somewhere in Oklahoma where we pulled into an auto court and rented a room for the evening. For the first time I slept on a full sized bed with fresh starched sheets and a pillow which smelled like "Listerine." I fell asleep after counting the flashing blue neon sign go on and off more than two hundred times. At the crack of dawn I was wide awake and wondering what this place looked like in the day light and how the sign had known to stop blinking and was disappointed to find that we were in the middle of no-where with nothing but more rolling nothing surrounding us. I'm not sure what it was that I expected but whatever it was, this wasn't it.

I had never been in a shower before, except a run through at the boys club, and had my very first shower with my own little miniature bar of soap. God! And a clean towel all for me.

When everyone was ready and the Pontiac had been repacked, we drove a short distance and pulled into a truck stop cafe and an experience at "eating out." I could order anything I wanted as long as I ate it all.

I ordered fried eggs, pancakes with maple syrup and butter, fried potatoes and biscuits with honey and a big glass of milk. I ate all of mine and Magnis ate even more. We headed west again and after about 60 miles I suddenly thought I was gon'na die. I hadn't told nor had anyone asked about the last time I had "made a big job" and right there, somewhere between where ever we had been and Oklahoma City, I needed out of that Pontiac and I mean like right now.

Ada pulled the car over and Miss Laura, already having figured out the problem, opened the door and directed me toward a bush. Having never experienced anything like a camp out or a trip to the woods, I literally didn't know what to do so I dodged behind the bush and well! It was an awful experience.

The next stop was a filling station where Miss Laura did a pretty good job of cleaning me up out behind the building with a bucket of cold water and what was left of the little bar of soap. I was rather rank and ripe by the time we stopped for the night.

Magnis has never, even after all these years, let me forget the day I "ruined all of Oklahoma" and I still get tense when I smell maple syrup.

Miss Laura didn't know how to drive so Ada and Helen

traded off and the miles ticked off in slow motion time. On the fifth morning we reached Kingman, Arizona, which is where we headed North West to get to Las Vegas. We had stopped late each night when we found an auto court that looked fairly respectable. Miles thus traveled were premeditated, deliberate and calculated by the boredom gods to nurture vexation in a nine year old mind which further made way for a geometric transference progression to the adult figures present and thus directly proportionate to the square of the distance. Or something such as that. I learned early on that "are we there yet" was not gon'na go over well with Ada although Helen and Miss Laura seemed to understand and Magnis gave endless nudges in my ribs, middle knuckle—dead leg punches—to my thigh and egged me on unmercifully. I got blamed for every "dead rat smell pants ripper" Magnis created and my own as well.

I counted telephone poles, numbers of knobs on top of the poles, tested to see how far down my upper lip I could coax a nose snail without loosing it to gravity and played with myself until Miss Laura caught me and told Ada "I swan Ada if that boy don't stop, his whizzer is gon'na shrivel up and drop off ." "Laurel! Why can't you be like a normal boy and just say a prayer when that urge gets you." "Jesus talked about things like that in the bible but I guess you never got to that part did you"—and out came the ever present bible opened to some scripture pointing out how some one drank some poor little lambs blood instead of playing with himself and since I couldn't think of anything as disgusting as someone drinking lambs blood I looked up at her and did one of my tics which caused her to rub her upper lip between her thumb and index finger like she always did when she was perplexed and didn't know what else to say to me.

Magnis let everyone know that he read in the Boy Scout Manual about how unhealthy it was to do this and that he had been telling me to stop—but, just when he thought he was going to score some real good points I managed to rip off a rather substantial "pants ripper" which I blamed on him.

I knew I was gon'na get blasted and it didn't help my situation any when I blurted out "I'll bet Jesus farted a lot and blamed it on —" I never even saw it coming. I don't know how Ada managed to keep the Pontiac on the road and still get off that backhanded hay maker swing which missed me completely and smacked Magnis right in the jaw. She didn't realize she had missed me so I let out a scream anyway just in case she was thinking about swinging again.

Helen, who had been dozing in the front passengers seat, came awake thinking my scream was associated with the end of the world and let out her own scream which resulted in her losing her lower dental plate which was an episode I'd never seen before and was one of those things which struck me so funny that I started laughing and boy that too was the wrong thing to do.

Ada had managed to pull the Pontiac off the road and was on her way out of the door saying "I'm gon'na strangle that boy right here and now and leave him beside this road and nothing can stop me."

Well, I had enough sense to know that she probably was really gon'na do it so I wedged as deep as I could get beside Miss Laura and as Ada yanked Magnis out of the back door and bent over reaching for me she too succumbed to mother nature and blasted a musical note. This absolutely fractured my funny box and doubled me up into uncontrolled fits of hysterical laughter.

With that she began to laugh and cry at the same time while telling me through hands covering her face "Laurel Hardy Lubeck—I do believe you are the most exasperating kid I've ever known and I keep wondering where I ever found you and why I don't put you in a home somewhere with the rest of the cracked brains I'll never know—but I guess we're stuck with you."

"Now I guess I better get us to Las Vegas."

We got to Las Vegas just as the sun went down and after we found where Helens friends lived and said our hellos and goodbyes we took more time looking for a phone booth where Ada made a quick call and then a second stop which was on the same street as the train station.

I wondered why Uncle Louie hadn't just put us on a train in Little Rock and headed us west.

It was already dark when we pulled up to the curb and I thought we would be staying here for the night but instead, Ada instructed me to stay in the car and not even look around and she would be only a minute or so.

Ada went to the trunk of the Pontiac and lifted out a valise who's zipper was secured with a small padlock, and which had escaped even my eagle eye, then closed the trunk.

When walking across the rather wide street she seemed to have difficulty managing the weight of the valise and shifted hands twice before entering a building which was across the street and half a block down from the train depot. She climbed the stairs just inside the glass entry door and disappeared from my sight.

Miss Laura, now riding in the passenger seat, had closed her eyes and nodded off as soon as the car stopped. Magnis had been sleeping since we left Helens friends place.

In no time at all I needed to pee rather badly so I climbed out of the car and headed for the same door Ada had entered.

I climbed the stairs. At the top there was only one door and I walked through it without knocking and immediately blurted out "Where is your rest room?"

Well, this was the wrong thing to do because inside this smoke filled but otherwise almost empty room three rather malevolent looking characters whipped snub nosed revolvers from someplace and aimed them at me.

The one to my right had been the recipient of the valise and he let it fall to the floor as he reached for his gun. It made a substantial thud but the contents remained a secret.

Ada screamed and I wizzed down my leg and reeled off half a dozen tics before I realized I probably should have done what Ada told me to do—which was to stay in the car.

"Oh God Laurel look what you did to the floor." "Don't hurt him—he's not wrapped real tight and sometimes he acts like he has a couple of loose gears an he don't remember anything for more than a minute or two anyway isn't that right Laurel?"

I stuck my finger up my nose and blew a bubble from my eye which needless to say just about cinched that story.

Ada then stepped behind me, put her hands on my shoulders and as she began to back toward the door pulling me along the toughs each blew a sigh of relief and holstered their guns.

I was doing really great and had already forgotten the wet pants, sock and shoe but Ada had a terrible time getting down those stairs. At the bottom landing I turned around and stuck my finger up like a pistol and said "bang—bang" which was another wrong thing to do or say.

Perhaps Ada was right—maybe I wasn't wrapped too tight.

Ada grabbed me in an under arm "step-over-nose-hold"—which is the best description I can remember, having never before or since been grabbed like that—and dragged me all the way across the street at a gallop.

When she reached the Pontiac she opened the drivers door and hurled me past the steering wheel and up against Miss Laura, climbed into the seat and in the same motion hit the starter button, put that machine in gear and we were off.

I could never remember having that much fun and fancied Ada as a "gun Moll" driving the get-away car after a bank heist. I straightened myself upright and immediately was on my knees in the middle of the seat looking backyards for the pursuing police car and telling Magnis and Miss Laura—both of whom had been startled awake—that "Ada just got robbed by three bad guys or maybe we robbed them—I'm not sure"—and—"Well, anyway we're making our get-away and the cops are gon'na get us if this moll don't put her foot in it." "They were gon'na rub me out with their gats cause I pee'd on their floor " —but I was cut off with—"No question about it Laura he's gon'na be the cause of my demise."

There was also no question about the fact that Ada had reached the end of her stretch factor. Her heart was racing, her apocrine glands were profuse and the three catecholamines her adrenals were capable of producing were expended and without further potential.

She wanted to maim me for sure but by now was only physically capable of pulling into a coffee shop parking area where she got out of the car, gently closed the door and went off mumbling to herself without Miss Laura getting out even one "Well I swan."

I have always wondered what "I swan" meant and have sometimes wondered what might have been packed in that valise. It could have been anything of value except narcotics. "Junk" as I was to learn only several years later was absolutely and without question a forbidden transaction.

JUST ABOUT THE time we were in Las Vegas Clyde took another one of his excursions across the country only this time he headed East. Beryl stayed behind as usual and attended to her job still content with the night shift. The two of them continued to live in one of the one bedroom apartments in Kansas City. Apparently Beryl was still a victim of what she was told by Clyde or perhaps she knew much more than she let on. No one will ever know. I already indicated that she was much brighter than Clyde when it came to thought process and reasoning but she didn't have great resources when relating to deft things. Don't misunderstand, she could lie like a champion when cornered. She just didn't have the raw survival meanness of a Clyde.

Clyde never actually told her when or where he was going when he hit the road but she was bright enough to generally get him to reveal the direction and during his absence she would go daily to a well supplied news stand, not far from the TB Hospital, and scour the out of town papers for other things she suspected Clyde might be involved with. Robberies and bank holdups were always first things that came to mind although he always assured her that he wasn't involved in anything more than what she already knew he was involved in which was basically nothing.

Clyde's defection each time left Beryl with terrible mixed feelings. She had never really loved anyone in an honest affectionate way and very likely was one of the pitiable individuals here on earth truly incapable of honest caring love. She thought she might have liked Clyde at one time but now had grave doubts about even that. She mostly feared him physically but also feared that if something happened to him things would telescope back to her. She was also greatly troubled about how she would manage to protect herself from any authority since she didn't really understand the amount or from where the money came. She had some comfort knowing that she had an ace-in-the-hole in the form of a lie she had fostered off on Clyde sometime back.

She informed Clyde that she had written a "confessional letter" telling all and had placed it in the hands of an attorney with instructions to be opened only if not contacted by her personally at least every six months.

They were actually tied together by a rope from the past. Each held the loose end of the others noose and neither could afford to let go while life continued. The ultimate shackle and stalemate.

Clyde seemed to have some future plan in mind concerning the investments but never shared it with anyone. It is possible that he fancied himself as a real wheeler and dealer although he never demonstrated any form of grandiosity or moved in any fashion toward lofty living. He was driving a 1936 Ford coupe with a 60 horsepower engine which certainly didn't get anyone anyplace very fast or give one the feeling of power. It was however a very reliable car.

Clyde had been gone almost three weeks and was pretty frazzled looking and really odiferous that evening when he drove up to the apartment house. For the first time he wondered if he should have phoned instead of just showing up in order to give anyone visiting Beryl a chance to vacate the premises since he wasn't sure what he would feel even if he should break in on a tryst.

Beryl probably did most of her "messing around" the first few days Clyde was gone but we will never know for sure. Only—according to Clyde later in life—that she did.

He had been drinking since he left Chicago and had picked up three pints of Gin—just enough to tide him over—in the little town of Trenton which is about one-hundred miles north-east of Kansas City. Dusk had just turned to night when the county sheriff, who had been following him since he left the state store, pulled him over about five miles west of town. Panic struck hard—Clyde had five twenty dollar bills in his pocket and almost thirty thousand dollars in a paper bag stuffed under the seat. He also had a snub-nosed 32 revolver in the same sack.

The last thing Clyde needed had just happened. Before the sheriff could get out of his patrol car Clyde reached into his pocket and pulled out a twenty and instantly rolled down the window about two inches, slipped the bill out through the crack and rolled up the window, leaving most of it hang outside like a flag.

The sheriff got to the window just as Clyde realized this might not have been such a great plan. The sheriff grabbed the twenty which he stuck in his pocket and instantly yanked the door open and pulled a sweating, terror stricken Clyde out of the seat, threw him to the ground then lifted him with both hands by the grey Dickie Brand shirt, tearing it in the process, and threw him onto the hood of the Ford face down.

Clyde was certain he was gon'na die, either from fright, a heart attack, a stroke or the sheriff's gun which was now pressed right into the back of his head. He tried to speak but instead, he shivered from head to toe and evacuated his bowels and bladder. Yep! Crapped right in his pants which most assuredly saved his life because the sheriff was so surprised by this repugnant act that he forgot his plan— which was to clean out Clyde's pockets make him run for it and then shoot him. Instead, this "Scattergood Baines" character just told Clyde to turn his pockets inside out and when the other four twenties fell to the ground he picked them up and walked back to his patrol car and drove away.

Clyde took off his shoes and socks, stripped off his now brown and grey colored Dickies Brand trousers and his underwear and cleaned him self up using two of the pints of gin and a rag he kept for checking the oil. He had a substantial mental struggle over whether to discard the Dickies in the ditch or toss them in the trunk of the car— after all, they were almost new. With vexation and anguish, the ditch won out. But only after a car full of teenagers came slowly by whistling and shouting and Clyde realized he was standing beside the road wearing only a torn Grey Dickies Brand shirt.

He had two more identical sets of "Dickies", which were several weeks dirty, in a cheap Montgomery Ward brand cardboard suitcase in the car trunk and quickly got dressed.

When Clyde walked into the small apartment it was a toss up as to whether his mood or his stench was the most foul.

The apartment was a mess and several empty glasses and gin bottles were lying about. Some uneaten food, obviously for two, remained on the table and Beryl's dress was in a pile in the middle of the living room. In the bedroom Beryl was lying across the bed in her under slip and nothing else, dead drunk and didn't even know he was there much less how he smelled.

He went into the small bathroom, took a fast bath, then went back to the bed where he pushed Beryl onto the floor in a heap and climbed under the sheet then finished —in one long gulp—the remainder of the gin left in the bottle on the night stand which Beryl had failed to draw down before she passed out.

Sleep came quickly but the nightmares worked their way slowly and frighteningly across the rest of the night.

Beryl came out of her "coma" about 7:00 am and realized that things weren't exactly right. The first thing of which she was aware was that she was very cold and terribly uncomfortable. Her head was splitting and she was unable to move her right arm which was totally numb from pressure brought on from lying on the floor with the arm stuck under her chest which was the position she had assumed when pushed from the bed.

She managed, with much difficulty, to stand up before addressing the "lump" she saw under the sheets—"Hey! whatever yor name is—y'all better get out'ta here before Clyde gets back if you know what's good fer ya."

These words fell on a snoring Clyde with no effect and Beryl stumbled around to the other side of the bed and shook the "lump" before she realized she had made a pretty serious mistake.

She made her way to the bathroom then silently dressed, and slipped out the door.

Phil Harris used to tell Jack Benny: "I feel sorry for folks who don't drink cause when they wake up in the morning that's as good as they're gon'na feel all day."

When Clyde managed to become functional it was almost 3:00 pm and he felt as miserable as a still living human being could feel.

He made his way to the paper sack which he had stuffed behind the sofa cushion and counted the money and when satisfied that it was all there he put the snub nose into the secret hole he had managed to create behind one of the kitchen drawers.

He then found what he assumed were clean under shorts and a wrinkled set of grey Dickies.

He hadn't shaved for 2 days and failed to look at himself in a mirror—not that it would have changed anything—picked up the sack of money and headed for the Ford Coupe.

When he arrived at Efrom's office he trudged up the stairs and found a note tacked to the door informing the world that he could be found down stairs in the gin mill.

Efrom was in the back booth with one of his "girls" attempting to play kissie lips as a prelude to an episode of hide the weeny, probably right in the back booth, and he actually imagined this to be a romantic seductive interlude.

He wasn't happy about the interruption but when Clyde scooted into the booth he told Goldie to get lost, shook his head and said "Jesus Christ Clyde you look like something the cat drug in and the kittens wouldn't eat"—"How about a drink?"—"Buffo bring Clyde one of them new things I been drink'in"—"One of them manhattans"—"Jesus Clyde you got some funny smells com'in from you." "What you been into anyway?"

"Jus shut yur big trap an lissen ya grease bag bastard"—"an don't y'all ever tell me about smelling funny."—"Ya'll must'a been kissin tha south end of that

Goldie while she was headed north an yur smellin yur upper lip."—"I'm aim'in ta buy that big farm over at Independence an that there other apartment place an y'all better get yur dead ass up ta that office an make them papers right."

"You got enuf cash fer this Clyde?" "It's gon'na take maybe thirty thousand to close."

"I got most now and tha rest real soon."

THE NEVER CHANGING detritus which is located between Las Vegas and San Bernardino, California, is another of God's gigantic mistakes. An average of about 40 miles per hour was all that could be expected on most roads in those days. Air conditioning in an automobile was almost unheard of and open windows were out of the question for Miss Laura because she said "I can't hear, what with all that wind rushing past my ears an blowing my hair an what if some bee was to fly in and sting Laurel—you know how you swell up Laurel—remember last year when that bee flew up your nose?"

"Why your whole head swelled up like a mush melon—remember that Ada?" "Laurel? You remember that?" "We stuck chewin tobacco soaked in turpentine up your nostril and wrapped your head in warm sassafras an china berry mash cataplasms an that didn't even do much good."

Good God—how could anyone ever forget something like that? I mean—a bee flying up your nose—and how many people have had chewing tobacco soaked in turpentine shoved up their nose—much less a big hot wet rag soaked in sassafras tea, smeared with a big wad of mashed up china berries and wrapped around your whole head? Have you ever smelled ripe china berries? As close to absolute putrid as you can get. I wonder why all the carrion eaters in the world don't flock to the southern United States in the summer just to be close to that smell.

"I'm kind'a glad I wasn't home that day", Ada said. "It probably saved his life alright—but where did you ever get the idea of using china berries as a cataplasm?" "How did it feel Laurel?" "I mean how did the bee feel up inside your nose?" "Did it tickle a lot when his wings buzzed?" "Boy! I bet that old bee was surprised when he found out he couldn't turn around in there." "Poor thing was prob'ly scared half to death." "How'd you ever get him out'ta there anyway Laurel?" "I wonder if he left his stinger when you got him out?" "You know the poor things die after loosing their stinger." "Did you know that Laurel?" "Did you know that Magnis?"

"Magnis—you didn't have anything to do with that bee goin up Laurels nose did you?" "It just dawned on me that you got stung a bunch of times a couple of years back an some how or other blamed it on Laurel an you knew damn well Laurel didn't have a thing to do with it!—Didn't you?"

It was amazing how Ada could extrapolate and associate thought patterns so quickly.

Magnis was giving me rib jabs and whispering that he was gon'na tell and I was trying to figure out how to get out of it if he did. But, I didn't really believe him.

The truth was that I caught all those bees in a fruit jar and decided to transfer them to a paper sack to experiment with how bees might make a "humming" sound against the paper sack much like a comb and tissue kazoo.

The problem came when I didn't hear any noise and opened the sack because I thought they had all died. Well, once more I learned how and why not to do something. That bee flew up my nose so fast I thought I'd been shot with a rubber gun. Magnis about died laughing and I thought I would die from the pain. I blew and blew but the damn thing had stuck his stinger in my middle turbinate and I couldn't reach him with my fingers to pull him out.

Magnis was helpless from laughter and besides, he always vomited when faced with anything physiologic anyway. So, I ran half a block back to our bathroom and found a pair of tweezers from the cigar box where Miss Laura kept her special things and then pulled that "hummer" out of my left nostril. Well! I had now disproved the idea that when bees sting you they can't inject their venom without loosing their stinger cause when I released the tweezers grip he flew away—stinger intact—and I began to swell up just like Miss Laura said I did.

What a question—did I remember when the bee flew up my nose!

We went through the wide spot in the road called Baker and finally reached the agriculture check station just east of Barstow and the excitement of almost being wherever it was we were supposed to be was overwhelming. And then came Barstow which was only slightly more depressing then than it is now as I tell this story.

We made it to Victorville and Ada found a place to stay this final night. It was grubby and only a little less scary than a certain movie motel of later fame.

Early the next morning we began the final leg of our journey to our new home and headed down winding Cajon Pass to San Bernardino and west on Highland Avenue also know as Route 66.

Somewhere along this road not too far from San Bernardino we passed a memorable sight which has forever remained in my mind. An honest to God tepee village. It turned out to be a motel with stucco rooms shaped like tepees and I raised a fuss—for about fifteen miles—because we didn't spend the night in one of the tee-pees instead of that awful place where we had spent the night. I said I was positive I saw a real Indian and lied and whined about it and Magnis egged me on until Ada bopped me a light onc on top of my head.

We found Pomona and went past the Kellogg Arabian Horse Ranch and damned if Miss Laura didn't know all about how Mr Kellogg—from 'Corn Flake fame'—owned this beautiful place and about his life history and expressed the fact that if I studied real hard maybe I could "Buy something like that someday."

When we reached Rosemead Boulevard we turned South to Slauson Avenue and then headed West to our new home.

The excitement was almost too much and even Ada was anxious and started singing "You are my sunshine—my only sunshine."

"You know Ada!" Miss Laura said—"Mr Jimmie Davis made that song real popular last year when he was running for Governor of Louisiana—you know that man could really sing a song and I do believe he got real rich from writing it."—"Why—He even rode his horse up those capital steps"—"Ya know, my sister Penny—your aunt Penny—Ada—your great aunt Magnis"—"Now pay attention you boys because your Aunt Penny once met Mr Jimmie Davis and said he was a right nice man"—"An isolationist but never the less a real nice man." "Now that sure is interesting isn't it Laurel?" "He sure is the governor alright."

I forgot to tell you that Magnis was the splitting image

of Carl Switzer with freckles on his freckles and one of his front teeth slightly overlapping the other in what I always thought of as just the right way a real guy ought to look. He was real skinny and all his friends in Little Rock had called him shadow—a nickname he was eager to shed—and he had this perpetual grin which pulled his upper lip down and slightly to the right. I always figured this was because he was trying to cover up that crooked front tooth but he swears it was just the way he was. Oh, and by the way, Carl Switzer was Alfalfa from the "Our Gang" series.

Well, anyway, Magnis had his famous "shit eating grin" going full surge and began to snicker with excitement and I got excited even more because I thought it was great that some man rode his horse up the capital steps—hell, I'd never even seen a real horse except in the Tex Ritter movies we watched at the boys club—and then I realized Magnis wasn't even paying any attention to Miss Laura but was all "snickered up" cause we had just passed the sign 'Welcome to Stanford Park' and he was first to see it.

I had never actually believed it would really happen and now it had and I was trying to think of a good song that I could sing but that search was superseded by my need to pee and I told Ada about it and she just kept right on singing "You are My Sunshine"—and Miss Laura just kept right on talking about Aunt Penny and the governor and Magnis just kept giggling and I didn't need to pee very much after all and wondered if Alice knew where I was.

CLYDE VENTURED OUT shortly after his meeting with Efrom—heading east once again and when he returned he had more than enough cash to complete the two transactions and had Efrom do the paper work which, when completed, made one of Clyde's trusts owner of a one hundred twenty acre farm outside of Independence.

A rather substantial creek bordered the property and almost all of the one hundred twenty acres were prime black agriculture land.

A very well kept two story farm house overlooked the entire property from a small hill. It was well fenced and came equipped with a tractor, a disk, a planting drill plus all of the other implements needed for farming and a well maintained flat-bed Dodge truck.

Just below the farm house a beautiful old wooden barn touched off the perfect picture of rural "Americana."

Clyde figured he could just climb on the tractor and start plowing and planting and harvesting. Not a single thought about the fact that he had never before been closer to farming than the manure from the pony ride in Kansas City.

He hadn't even bothered to tell Beryl that he had been

looking for something like this to buy so when the transaction was complete he gathered up his meager belongings, drove out to the farm and moved in without even telling her.

She, of course, didn't question Clyde's absence since their relationship hadn't made much of a recovery since the episode late in June and by the time she realized Clyde wasn't spending any time in the relationship it was September of 1941.

She did manage to track him down in a gin-mill one evening and remind him that their alliance wouldn't be all that easy to terminate

In the past months Clyde had taken up with an alcoholic nymphomaniac named Panama who had drifted in from Cincinnati after meeting him there during his last foray.

She was such a mess she made Beryl look beautiful by contrast but Clyde, as usual, was having a terrible time extricating himself from this predicament and welcomed all the help he thought Beryl would give him.

Well, Beryl wasn't into giving help right at the time but she did come up with a plan for letting Clyde swing in the breeze for an indefinite period. She told Clyde that the Public Health Department had been nosing around the apartment asking questions about him and a woman he had been involved with in Cincinnati who had recently been diagnosed with syphilis and very likely was tubercular.

This got Clyde's attention and he immediately bought Panama a one way train ticket to Chicago, put her on the Santa Fe Chief and gave her enough money to establish herself in the first bar she found when she arrived. She was so drunk when this took place that she didn't even know where she was until she had spent a week in Chicago.

Clyde didn't tell Beryl when he made his way to the

public health clinic and claimed he didn't have money to see a private doctor and lied to the clinic by giving a false name.

His chest x-ray was read as negative and after forty eight hours the TB skin test was negative but the medical laboratory took more than a week to get the results of the negative Wasserman and Clyde, don't you know, was even more of a mess psychologically when this part of his life had become history.

For a long time after this experience Clyde took up celibacy, in both the allusion and actual meaning of the word. He thought periodically about asking Beryl to come out to the farm and take up with him but she really wasn't interested since it would be such a long way to travel each night to the TB hospital —or something like that—and she wasn't a good driver to begin with. She continued to live in the little apartment and had occasional liaisons with dolts and dimwits from here and there. Mostly she drank gin from a water glass, listened to the radio gospels and waned into bouts of depression but always managed to be on time for her shift.

September of 1941 wasn't a good year for the rest of the world either. The war was not going well for England and Churchill had failed to convince FDR that the USA needed to join in the carnage. A little bit of mundane tongue in cheek citizen comfort materialized when rumor had it that John Gutzon Borglum had completed his Teddy Roosevelt thing in the Black Hills of South Dakota. The Redstone Arsenal in Huntsville Alabama had been secretly commissioned and opened three months earlier and was up and running full blast making incendiaries, explosive weapons and even some form of special war gas. The local citizenry had managed to dispense with their racial bias and local Negro and Caucasian managed to work very well side by side until the plant got so large they needed to import outsiders to fill jobs and these outsiders couldn't handle sharing a restroom—well, you know what happened—and the "The Ink Spots" popularized the song "I don't Want To Set The World On Fire."

The farm had been fallow for two years and Clyde decided that the next spring he would plant pop-corn as a cash crop since so many people were going to the movies and all of them seemed to eat pop-corn. He thought that all he had to do was disc the land and plant the kernels. He gave no thought to how he would be able to harvest, shuck, sort, grade and sack the finished product much less how he would market one hundred acres of this specialty produce. We already know many of Clyde's shortcomings but Clyde didn't seem to know any of Clyde's shortcomings. However, he had acquired considerable wealth in a very short period of time and certainly without any manifest vehicle or channel so one could not assume that growing pop-corn wasn't the right thing to do.

When asked by some of his sloshed cronies down at the gin mill about how he managed to own a farm he told them his grand daddy left it to him and when questioned about how he would suddenly become a farmer, and know what to do, he gave them one of his favorite arcane sayings which was "Ah think ah'll jest study on it" . When Clyde uttered one of these sage responses the cronies stood in awe which attests to the probability that the average IQ present during any particular gathering was close to that of a green worm.

The 1940 draft law was now about a year old and at least that far back in Clyde's thoughts which is to say, he didn't remember it at all. He never listened to any news on the radio and wouldn't understand what was going on any place else in the world anyway so with that tacit approval Germany went right ahead with their invasion of Yugoslavia and Greece and the Japanese captured Hong Kong and most of Indochina and Erwin Rommel got himself promoted to Field Marshall after raising all kinds of hell in North Africa. All of this just goes to show you how ignorance distributes itself throughout the world because by Sunday afternoon, Kansas City time, on December 7th, Clyde was right belly up to the bar telling the silly bastards next to him "I prodicted x'actly all about this here thang clear last summer but y'all wudn't lissen." He had done nothing of the sort but some of those around could even remember him telling "how those Japs was ah gon'na a-tack Ha-wa-u", but no one seemed to remember just when that little bit of information had surfaced. It didn't make any difference to Clyde that he in fact had no idea where Hawaii was located, much less why anything like this would or could happen.

Panic suddenly struck Clyde's innards when several of the bimmies, drawn up in his circle, began to blare about going down to join up in the army just as soon as the place opened on Monday.

Shades of his dishonesty started to ooze through his mind as it came back to him what he had done the year before. Something about being jailed for a long time and maybe even facing a firing squad.

Clyde needed out of that gin mill right now and lunged toward the door, violently pushing several of the poor whisky brave souls aside, spilling their drinks and causing talk that lasted the evening.

Even as his hyperventilation accelerated, he was sure that what he needed was more air and less patriotism. By the time he reached his Ford he had managed to light one of his cigarettes and had begun to sweat rivulets. By instinct he started the car and headed for the TB Hospital where he hoped to get counsel from Beryl. She had to help him, she was in as deep as he was by his reckoning but he didn't have a clue as to how she might help.

Beryl was busy on her shift when he arrived and refused to talk to him until she got off work at 11:00 pm. She told him that he could pick her up when she finished and that was that.

When 11:00 o'clock came, Clyde had been without a drink for almost six hours and was about as organized as a circular firing squad. Beryl barely had time to close the car door before he bombarded her with questions from "what'im I gon'na do?" to "wher'm I gon'na go?" "How'd I get in'na this here messacrap?" and "How'm I gon'na git out'ta this here messacrap?" "An don'ya jus gim'me no crapabout ever thin's gon'na work out okay cause I never wud'da done it if it warn't fer you—an y'alls in jest tha same messacrap as is I an don't never fergit it."

"Goldamn it Beryl I ought'ta slap hell out'ta y'all, stick ya in'na sack an bury ya somwheres." Wow! Well, you must remember, Clyde was really good at endearing himself to others with his finesse, love and his compassionate thought process.

Beryl was petrified and started to jump from the car when Clyde gunned the engine and squealed the tires pulling away from the curb. He was going much too fast to risk jumping so she bunched up as close to the door as she could get when Clyde said "Oh hell Beryl—I ain't mad at y'all I'm madder-in hell at me an I ain't a know'in whut ta do." "I wus hope'in y'all might have some answer but ah guess ya ain't."

146

"Goddamm it ya stupid sum-bitch ya ain't got ah lick ah brains sometimes." "I told ya ah. . . . ah bunch ah times I got ah certificate an it's legal an you jest like ah goose—ya wake up in ah new world ever stinkin mornin—an lord a pissin Clyde I out'ta jest let em cum an take ya away but ah won't so shut yor stupid sum-bittchin mouth long enuf fer me to say it."

"Yer name is Clyde C. Dodge an I never knowed whut tha C. stood fer an ah don't know how ta find out—I never knowed him that much anyways." "I never even knowed whur he cum from." "Maybe C. don't stand fer nuthin." "We can go ta Little Rock an find out maybe." "Maybe no one cares." "That bunch he run with wus no good no how an then went an got killed."

"We got'ta stick together Clyde—we cain't never split up." "Lets go out yonder ta tha farm an act like farmers till this here war thang blows over."

SUNDAY MORNING, DECEMBER 7, 1941, is indeed permanently stored in my memory bank. When the news came over the radio, which had only one green eye, I was lying on my bed reading the Sunday comics.

Miss Laura was very excited and ran through the house in a dither. Ada had been dating a Marine Lieutenant stationed in Long Beach and had been out with him the evening before, getting back home very late, and was sleeping in. A gathering of the four of us took place and Ada made a phone call to Trixie and just about everyone else she knew in Southern California. Of course, none of those called knew as much as Miss Laura about how, where and why.

She, as I recall, knew the history of how the Japanese Emperor Hirohito had inherited the Imperial Throne from his father The Taisho Emperor, Yoshihito, that he was about 40 years old and probably didn't really know much about what was going on relative to his war lord leaders. She even knew he was a marine biologist. She told us about the Japanese attacks on China and their aggression in Southeast Asia, and thought Chiang Kai-shek was a really bad guy but at least he was "fighting those dad-gum communists" who were even worse than he was. She got sidetracked telling about Han Chao-shun better known as Charlie Soong who was a young Chinese man who ended up in Boston and educated by friendly Methodists at Trinity (Duke University) College, sent back to China as a missionary and fathered one of the richest dynasties in modern history.

His female offspring included Ai-ling who married into one of China's richest families, Ching-ling, who married Sun Yat-sen, and later became Mao Tse-tungs Vice Chairman of the Peoples Republic of China and last, but certainly not least, May-ling, better known as Madame Chiang Kai-shek. The sons, three in number, amassed individually, three of the greatest fortunes in the world. I asked and she told us much about Pearl Harbor and the Pacific Fleet and a pretty good summation of why the fleet had been caught without warning and preparation. We found out from her that many islands in the Pacific had been given a Japanese Mandate and had been occupied by them since shortly after the First World War and I tried to imagine how far away these places were from Stanford Park—about seven thousand miles.

When we had arrived at Stanford Park six months earlier it seemed that most of my dreams had come true. Trixie and Uncle Louie had prepared for us a small but clean vine covered house in a very good middle class neighborhood. It had a living room, two small bedrooms, a small dining room and a fairly large kitchen which had a breakfast area and an alcove partitioned off which was just the right size for the bunk beds and a dresser which had been set up for Magnis and me. We still tell people we slept in a closet when we were kids but that's not really true. Believe me, we had never had it so great.

There was a lawn in the front and a small back yard with a vegetable garden. I don't know what happened to the Pontiac but Uncle Louie furnished Ada with a 1938 Dodge 2 door sedan that he had won in a poker game. It didn't belong to us but no one else knew that and we even had a garage where it was kept most of the time since Ada took the streetcar to work every morning.

Ada had gotten work almost immediately at one of the factories in the Vernon area and could easily commute on the great transportation system then in place and if there was a depression in Southern California I don't know where it was located. Ada brought home more money in a week than she did in a month in Little Rock and coupled with the fact that we lived rent free and only paid the utilities, we were in great shape.

Uncle Louie owned a sports arena where he promoted amateur boxing on Wednesdays and professional wrestling on Fridays. He had been doing this since leaving Las Vegas and not many of the 3000 seats were ever vacant.

Magnis was given a job hustling soda to the fans. He bought a twenty four bottle case from the "house" for a dime a bottle and poured it into eight ounce wax cups to the fans for a dime. It was against the "State Gaming Commission Rules" for fans to have the bottles and it doesn't take a genius to figure that every two bottles gave him an additional eight ounces since soda came in twelve ounce bottles. This was called "the stretch" and "the stretch" produced, as if by magic, twelve extra cups per case—or—the dollar equivalent of thirty six bottles per case—or—in real money—three bucks sixty. The "hustler" got to keep the difference. If it was a particularly busy night, Magnis could "hustle" forty cases and make forty-eight bucks. Not bad for a 16 year old—he averaged about

80 bucks working 3 hours 2 nights a week.

You had to be twenty-one years old to hustle beer and Magnis could hardly wait for the next five years to pass because the beer "hustle" was even better. Uncle Louie knew all the tricks.

The Alcohol Beverage Commission better known as the "ABC" kept pretty close tabs on all alcohol sold in the state. The two biggest breweries in Los Angeles seemed to be "The Eastside Brewery" and "Lucky Lager Brewing Company. They had both twelve ounce and quart bottles available. Well, no self respecting "beer hustler" wanted to work with 12 ounce'rs because you used ten ounce cups. Any good "hustler" could fill four or five wax cups from a one quart bottle.

Foam was the friend. One silver quarter per cup. The "hustler" bought the quart for six bits—nine dollars per case—and if he didn't get back twelve or thirteen bucks per case something was wrong with his pouring.

Sometimes it seemed as if every one of the three thousand fans drank at least four cups of beer twice a week. God! What a lot of beer flowed through that place. In addition to the two "beer hustlers" a rather substantial bar existed in a side "refreshment" area where you could get the best—and I really mean this—hot dog or hamburger in Los Angeles. Maybe I'll tell you more about this later—on second thought—maybe I won't.

When Uncle Louie placed his order on Monday for a beer delivery Wednesday morning, he would calculate what had been "laid off" the past week and cut it in half. He had to pay 24 cents a quart wholesale—$2.88 a case. Well, the ABC wanted to collect a substantial, even for those days, 10 percent tax on the collected retail sale and the breweries were responsible for reporting exactly how many cases

151

were delivered. Uncle Louie just hated taxes of any kind. I don't know why he didn't order kegs of beer which seemed to me would have been easier to "stretch" but he must have had his reasons. Each fiscal quarter, from the reported number of cases, the ABC could extrapolate their due.

Monday afternoons found Uncle Louie and me out among the Italian owned delicatessens and liquor stores scattered throughout the area. Six cases here—six cases there and pretty soon forty—fifty cases through the back door and all bought on discount. No tax on food and all sales through the deli's were written as food. He would pick me up after school and I learned at the side of the "master of hustle. Sixteen hundred to two thousand dollars two times a week on beer alone.

Uncle Louie had something for everyone. He found some type of canned lemon concentrate which probably sold for a dime and mixed two cans with a pound of sugar, water and ice in three ten gallon ceramic crocks which had spigots. Total cost about thirty five cents and retailed for $38.00. No trick left to chance. Thirty-eight bucks paid for the ushers and the janitors.

No pop-corn was allowed since Uncle Louie believed that pop-corn would swell up in your stomach and make you feel bloated and therefore you wouldn't want to drink as much beer and coke. Peanuts, which were slightly salted, were absolutely different.

One of my jobs was to sack the peanuts.

On Tuesdays "The Mellos Peanut" guy delivered several 100 pound sacks of old fashioned goobers and I spent Tuesday evenings putting 15 of these slightly salted—triple jointed delicacies into red and white striped sacks. I got so good at it that I could estimate 15 by the handful, load them into a sack, grab the corners, give the sack a spin and create closure in a matter of seconds. The sacks were then counted, potential revenue estimated and stacked with loving care cause I already knew that when I got to be thirteen years old the "peanut concession" belonged to me.

These days we all know what it means to "launder money" but Uncle Louie was some sort of an original and I was perhaps the original "money ironer.

Imagine the "hustlers" and the bar tenders and the concession stand folks literally stuffing wads of wet bills into money aprons tied around their waist.

On Saturday morning, I became the "main Ironer. In fact I became the only ironer.

Uncle Louie or Trixie would mysteriously appear with several overflowing cardboard boxes of soggy crumpled money in addition to that which had come from the ticket booth.

I guess we hadn't been in California but a few weeks when Trixie began to notice that I never seemed to forget much of what was said and had a real ability with numbers and subtly started finding out about me by asking questions and apparently setting me up to check my prowess.

She had some talks with Miss Laura and Miss Laura told her—"the boy has the gift' Trixie—he knows more than I know most of the time—and it just seems like your daddy's extraordinary mind got transferred right there into that brain of his—sometimes he does startle me but he isn't strange like many of his kind are—I think Ada knows but she won't let on or talk about it—I think it scares her—you know about how your daddy and his twin brother were— don't you Trixie?—your daddy died when you were so little—you don't even remember him—never got to know him—but you do know—don't you?

Well! It wasn't long before my job was to sit at an old-fashioned hot iron mangle and make crisp, dry bills from those soggy crumpled ones.

As the bills exited from this roller, I made neat stacks of each denomination, counting them into the appropriate dollar value and wrapping them with a rubber band and a small slip of paper which told the exact amount in each stack.

After the first several weeks these totals were never questioned nor rechecked. The whole process was over in about two hours and recorded as such.

I didn't get paid in a particular way, or a particular sum, I just sort of never wanted for anything. I was being a part of a family and feeling like I finally belonged.

I also didn't have a clue that I was any different than my new found friends in my new found neighborhood. Wally—Andy—Ernie—Kip—June—and Brenda. We still keep in touch after all these years—except Ernie and Kip both of whom died and went to heaven—and Wally, who changed his name to something I can pronounce but can't spell, shaved his head and joined a sub-cult of Epistemologists who limit their study to the nature of the study of epistemology—or something like that—well, anyway, you can see him but you can't talk to him—that is to say that you can see him studying and you can talk to him but he won't talk to you.

People have asked me about pocketing a buck or two here and there. The need to "steal from myself" never occurred to me and I can't remember from the day we arrived in Stanford Park ever feeling poor again. If I needed a dime for a comic book I wouldn't get just a dime. I would get half a buck from Uncle Louie or Trixie. All I had to do was tell why I needed the dime and as long as the purpose—not the price—was reasonable, so be it. I spent hours trying to master the words "aluminum" and "indubitably" and never did until long after.

Magnis started his sophomore year at Stanford Park High and took mostly science and math courses. Magnis, I found out much later, had a little bit of "the gift" but it was limited to mathematical things. How strange—my least gift was mathematics.

By the middle of the afternoon of December 7th I had borrowed binoculars from Uncle Louie to look for Japanese planes flying in from the west. Andy, Wally, Ernie, Kip and I then hurried to a vacant lot behind the sports arena and expanded a trench and a deep tunnel which was leading under the fence of a neighbors back yard and which had been in progress since the summer in case of Indian attack. We were certain that this was the place to be when the air attack—which we expected at any time—came. We were diligent—indubitably so.

All of us were enrolled at Central Street Grade School and Andy could chin-up thirty-five times on the play yard bar. I could do three. Ernie could run the fifty yard dash in about six seconds. I could run the same distance without stumbling or falling. Wally could swim across the Pacific Ocean in the community pool. I could stand at the shallow end. Kip weighed one hundred fifty seven pounds. I weighed eighty one. June and Brenda both stood five foot four. I was five foot three. Perceive however that none of them ever mastered an eye bubble and my "Stars and Stripes Forever" remained nonpareil and I, in some manner, and unknown reason, embarked on a life long fondness for Jimmy Durante.

THE TRIANON BALLROOM in the little L.A. suburb of South Gate was a great place to spend a Friday or Saturday evening—that is if you didn't want to see a wrestling match—and liked to dance to the big bands. Ada was still seeing this Marine Lieutenant I told you about—remember? She had met him at Uncle Louie's arena sometime late summer 1941. He was from Texas and had graduated from the Naval Academy at Annapolis and then chose the Marines instead of staying with the navy. Promotions were slow in the depression days and he had considered leaving the military and using the engineering degree he had earned—and— even talked to Ada about family things. However Ada, at the time, Ada being Ada, couldn't give this much serious consideration. After all, she was still married in the eyes of the law. Within days after the bombing produced World War II, he had been promoted to Captain and believed it would be only a matter of weeks before he would be promoted to Major. Physically he was a very big and powerful man, was within days of being Ada's age, that is he was 36 years old and within months of being only a memory.

Magnis thought the sun rose and set somewhere right

dead center of Billy John Boscum and spent every minute he dared—picking his brain about Annapolis. How to apply, what to study at Stanford Park High, what it was like being a plebe and almost drove Ada crazy because even though she couldn't—or wouldn't—admit it she was becoming attached to this big lovable hulk and just a little bit jealous of time since she knew his Second Division Marine Armored Unit would be the first to get shipped out to the Pacific.

It was now March of 1942 and Singapore had fallen to the Japanese the month before, William Saroyan was still relishing the fact that he had refused the Pulitzer Prize for his 1939 play "Time of Your Life" and was in the process of writing "The Human Comedy" and was himself trying, and without help, to polish off most of the spirits in California and showed up one Friday evening to watch the wrestling matches and renew an old friendship with Uncle Louie and told him he was just wandering around researching material for another story he was writing. I have no idea how they met, or where, but I do know where and when I first met Chancey.

Chancey Sekimora. I had never before seen such beauty. Her parents enrolled her in the Fourth Grade at our Central School in September 1941 and I knew I was in love again.

She lived on the east side of the Central School District and we lived on the west so I never got to see her walking to and from school.

Her father was Nisei and a U.C. Berkely graduate. He had a PhD. in biochemistry and had been in the research lab at Gilmore Oil Company but recently accepted a teaching position at Cal Tech and had just gotten his family moved in to Stanford Park. His father, who had a PhD in math from USC had died in 1938 and was Issei, born in Los Angeles in 1889 . His grandfather had migrated, with a brother, to this country in 1885, married a Nisei and received his citizenship in 1888. This made Chancey a Sansei which meant that she was actually third generation American born and had a longer American heritage than Saroyan or Durante—each of whom would qualify only as Issei.

One beautiful part of living where we lived was that you could walk from home to the movies or the Eastern Columbia Department store in fifteen minutes and from there the library was only one block and I even had my very own library card. The librarians would get quite annoyed with me because they claimed that I took too many books from the shelves and of course they had to return them to their proper place since no one except a certified librarian could possibly understand the complex "Dewey Decimal System" and I got constant lectures about how to read and study a book and how I should take my time and complete Jack London's "The Call of The Wild" before starting another and all the time I thought I was doing it right. I didn't even know it wasn't normal to read a whole page just by looking at it briefly.

I spent countless hours perusing words and staring at Chancey who also loved to read and spent a lot of time in the library. She also stared back and our eyes would meet and I would always blink first and blush. On three occasions we talked at recess about the Sunday "funny papers"—we both loved "Lil Abner"—and another time about a funny song we had both heard called "The Old Apple Tree" which was in a corny comedy movie called "Swing Your Lady" and featured some guy named Humphry Bogart. Then one day in March while I was staring at her across three library tables she completely floored me from afar with a wink and a puckering of her lips into a kiss and I turned a fever red and needed air and headed for the door. I was totally incapacitated and prostrated my self against the cool of the large granite stones which allowed the library such dignity while also holding up the roof and hoped the second law of thermodynamics would hold up in this court—that is to say heat flows from hot to cold.

I hadn't been under this jurisdiction more than thirty seconds, with my eyes closed and my face pointing toward the heavens like Moses on the mountain, when Chancey found me and I was sure that some magic conveyance was going to plunge forth from above and afford us a trip to the stars or some such breakthrough. Her coy voice broke my delusion: "Here Laurel you forgot your coat . . ." She touched my cheek with the palm of her hand in a gentle loving fashion and gave me a gentle kiss on my cheek as she walked away then looked back and said: "Don't forget to put it on." We had never touched before.

I am fairly certain, but not positive, that Uncle Louie never met Admiral Isoroku Yamamoto who had been wrestling with a most ambitious plan to totally destroy the remainder of the U.S. Pacific Fleet. However, the Japanese naval mastermind sold Admiral Chester Nimitz short as a fighter and besides that, no one had bothered to tell Yamamoto that the U.S. had broken the Japanese "Purple Code" the year before and "Old Chester" knew pretty much where and when the attack would take place. Consequently, 1942 would prove to be a real bad year for Isoroku, especially at a little known place called Midway, a real good year for Saroyan in Fresno but on the miserable day of 28 March my heart was taken away for a second time.

Chancey Sekimora disappeared from my life as quickly as had Alice. I didn't understand then and I don't understand now how or why it happened. I figured she as likely didn't understand how or why it happened.

I had already activated a conviction which I would carry for the rest of my life: "Life is indeed a series of controlled surges of outrage."

I was nine and a half years old and half way through my fourth school year. All my buddies were half way through their fourth school year and were almost eleven years old. I think maybe Wally was twelve. He failed the first grade.

Ernie, Andy, Wally, Kip and I walked to Central Street School every day and you have no idea how I felt about having these buddies. They treated me like a regular guy and just sort of tolerated the fact that I hardly knew anything about anything—that is the real important "anythings" like how to catch, much less throw a football, how to swim, roller skate or throw dirt clods dangling from the end of a grass handle.

They also relied on me to absorb the important things in class and sum it all up for them before a test.

Brenda and June were just like big sisters and sometimes managed to intercede just in time when I decided that I was much too big for my britches and walking on thin ice. Wally had a tree house in a giant oak tree in his back yard and we spent countless wonderful hours talking big stuff and eating ice cream bars purchased from the Good Humor Man on his daily rounds of the neighborhood. Kip was sort of a good guy "putz" who never wore underwear and I can't remember the number of times we "pant'zd" him and sent him home nude.

I already knew all of the worlds cuss words in English, Italian, Spanish and a few in French since Uncle Louie spoke each of these fluently. Strangely enough, when the four of us were together we rarely used profanity and even then, something like "damn" or "oh hell" was the biggest talk and I was the one most likely to articulate this. I don't think I have ever heard Wally utter even a mild profanity even to this day.

Wally—who was the strongest—could also whip each of us individually so occasionally we would gang up on him just for meanness knowing even as we did so that we would each be brought to justice respectively at a later date one on one and usually out of the blue and when least expecting it. He never seemed to forget this "obligation." He was methodical and strong and had a favorite wrestling hold he had learned from watching Wild Red Berry and which Wally called "the extender"—that is to say he could grab you and try to pull your chest from your pelvis and would not stop until you would holler very loudly "please stop Uncle Wally." Somehow those words seemed to placate him. You need to understand that none of this was done with malice, it was just "Don't Tread On Me" pay back.

From the week we first met, these guys were my friends and Trixie and Uncle Louie adopted all of us.

We were fixtures at the Friday night matches and met all of the of the great and near great wrestlers of the day. Most of these wrestlers were superb athletes and real gentlemen outside the ring. Uncle Louie was the boss and many of them thought that I was his son and treated me as such. I can never forget Danny McShane, George Dusette, Pavo Katonen, Ray Steele, Antonio Leoni, Jimmy Londas,"The Greek God" and certainly not "Wild Red" Berry who was one of the meanest men in the ring and equally gentle outside of it.

161

I met the great boxing champion Jack Dempsey on several occasions when he showed up to referee the wrestling matches and Max Baer—another boxing champion—on another occasion.

I went also to the Wednesday night boxing but was never allowed to stay through the entire card since it was a school night.

People constantly asked Uncle Louie about wrestling being fake. He had a pretty good stock response—"These guys are professionals and they know how to work with each other."

I had full run of the arena including the dressing rooms and I can attest to the fact that the bloody cuts, broken bones and any loose teeth were always mistakes—but nevertheless real. No such thing as fake blood in those days. There were fake feuds which were put on for future attractions but the fact is that except for rare occasions they were good friends out of the ring who socialized and traveled together. The one thing common to all was that they were all superb physical specimens and most were intelligent business men who invested their money wisely. Another outstanding characteristic was that they were—each and every one—generous with their good fortune.

At least two times each year Uncle Louie staged a "Charity Night" and the "show" as it was called was all "Pro Bono Publica"—these guys wouldn't even think of asking for transportation or expenses—they just did their part and never asked for recognition.

So far it sounds like men had a wrap on professional wrestling—not so—"Now entering the arena—Miss Mildred Burke—World Champion Lady Wrestler" Uncle Louie's booming voice would announce over the loud speaker and down the aisle this very attractive muscular lady would bound. She was as feminine and sweet as a person as she was tough and powerful to her opponents.

Mildred just loved me and my big ears and I can still remember standing in the aisle one evening when she bent down, picked me up at arms length, drew me to her for a squeeze and a kiss on my cheek. She was great friends with Trixie and we all went to Sonya Heine's ice show one evening. What a terrific lady. I still have one picture of her with Max Baer and another of her with a playful headlock on the great singer Al Jolson.

It seemed that Uncle Louie and Trixie knew everyone. An endless stream of movie stars would show up and each would be greeted and seated personally by Uncle Louie or Trixie and with as much ceremony or privacy as was required or requested by the celebrity. I guess I thought that I was really something because I got to meet most of them including a gentleman with an unkempt ill fitting grey double breasted suit, sleepy eye lids overlooking three rows of puff bags beneath each eye, a trimmed mustache with a six o'clock beard shadow and a crumpled brown snap brim hat with brown shoes badly in need of polish. I certainly wasn't impressed since I had never seen him in a movie and didn't remember ever hearing the name Howard Hughes.

Billy John Boscum came from some place—where he was stationed was actually a secret—as often as he could to see Ada. Magnis and I knew that he was by now a commander of a marine tank unit getting ready to go some place and fight—which is exactly what he had been training for all his adult life.

One night when leaving the "Zamboanga Club—The Home of The Tailless Monkey" out on West Slauson where they had stopped off for a nightcap—Ada still didn't drink alcohol—they encountered three uglies who said something unkind about Ada followed by a demand for some money. Two of them had knives and the third one had only about three seconds of consciousness left from the onset because Billy John Boscum broke his left collar bone with the first move of his right hand which was a Judo cut and dislocated his jaw and shattered most of his teeth along with most of his maxilla when the immediate second stroke came—a short powerful upward stroke which landed the heel of his left hand directly underneath the jaw. The result of this was one hell of a backward whiplash followed by instant unconsciousness and one third of the overall battle was in the books.

With what seemed to Ada to be one continuous motion, Billy John whipped off the thick, wide leather tunic belt, worn by Marines in those days, held the leather tip in his right hand and wrapped two turns around his open hand then made a fist—and faster than a whip, he whacked the closest knife right out of the thugs hand and without losing any momentum swung the heavy brass Semper Fidelis buckle over his head and crashed it across a startled face almost ripping a terrorized eye from its orbit and continuing on a figure 8 trajectory, crashed the second knife from a helpless hand by slashing the punks knuckles followed by an enormous thud to the left temple and instant senselessness. A seizure producing and finishing wallop to the temple of the chap who's eye had been partially enucleated finished the job without even raising the heart rate of the safeguard.

Several witnesses were present from the onset and Billy John was urged by the growing crowd to disappear and not wait to be involved with the police. Someone said that they would inform the police that the three had attacked each other.

Billy John knew that any implication with a civilian, regardless of the circumstance, would demand enquiry and confinement to the base while an investigation took place and he couldn't bear the thought of not being able to spend some more time in Stanford Park.

Ada and Billy John Boscum found his 1939 Ford Tudor in the parking lot and headed east on Slauson Avenue.

That weekend would be the last time Ada would ever see Major Billy John Boscum, United States Marine Corps. He was sent to Hawaii within the week with his unit and was killed during the second day of battle on Guadalcanal, Solomon Islands in August 1942.

CLYDE AND BERYL spent the early part of 1942 getting organized out on thefarm and for the first time Clyde was beginning to realized just how much work it required to be an untutored and unorganized farmer much less a well trained organized one. He made one mistake after another with the tools.

The first big mistake was showing off for Beryl about how to drive the tractor. She told him she didn't want to learn since she could barely drive a car but Clyde kept badgering her until she tried. She took off down the field and attempted to shift gears on the run—something you just didn't do with that vintage tractor. That transmission just went "clunk" and stopped and it certainly wasn't something Clyde could fix. It took several weeks to find a shade tree farm mechanic to even come out to the place to look it over.

"You know Mister—what's-chur name again?— There's a war a goin on an I don't even know if I can get parts fer this here thing." "What er ya grow' in out here anywise—I got ta know ya know—if its a war crop y'all are a grow' in I can prob'ly get ah release fer parts but if it ain't it'll sure take ah long time doin."

Clyde had managed to drag the tractor up to the front of

the barn. He did one of his foot shuffling routines and circled around the dead tractor several times spitting and uttering profanities and kicked each tire as he went past. "Gol-dammit don't ya know it wud'da happen like this?" "That Gol-dammit Beryl dun this ah purpose—I told her not ta have dun it anywise." "I never knowed a woman what cud ride ah trac-tur anyhows an fur yur in-fur-ma-chun we been gett'in ready ta plant special popcorn fur tha army." "Ain't that right Beryl?" "Sides, thur's ah purty good re-ward in' nit fur y'all soon as its fixed."

The shade tree mechanic was going counter clockwise around the tractor as Clyde was going clockwise and every time Clyde spit a bunch of brown tobacco juice the shade tree mechanic did likewise and every time Clyde kicked a tire likewise.

"How much y'all sp-osc that thar bonus gon'na be wurth—what y'all say yer name wus agin?"

"Ah didn't say whut my god-damn name wus that ah re-co-lect an it an't non ah yer god-damn matter so jus tell me whut it's ah gon'na cost and fix tha god-damn thang an I an't gon'na lissen ta no more ah this here crap."

"Don't pay no attention mister—whut's yer name?" Beryl chimed in; "He's jest worked up cause tha gum-ment been ah lay-in on him ta get busy with tha plantin. An I bet'cha ah hunnert dollars reward wud jus be fine." "wha-chu think Clyde?"

"Yea, wha-chu think Clyde?" echoed the mechanic who was by this time kind of enjoying the intimidation he had been capable of generating. "An if ah get started right away I cud be thru by Thusday." "That's if tha parts release cum thru in time." "I bet another hunnert wud fix that ol' release tho." "Wha-chu think Clyde?" "Think another hunnert wud fix that ol' release?"

167

"Ah got me ah long mem'ry like ah el-le-fant an y'all better not fergit that. Jes get on bout yor business an get it done and no more back mouth-in." "Ah got me sum plantin ta do."

The mechanic drove his truck to the local junk yard and bought a discarded Ford tractor transmission for fifteen bucks painted it with grey enamel and had it installed by the next afternoon whereupon he demanded one-hundred seventy five dollars for the "new-re-bilt" transmission and "two-hunnert fur tha ree-ward y'all obliged me an ah hunnert fur tha war release pre-mit." But not before he had admonished Clyde about "An't that mary-wanna ah grow'in down yonder by tha crick side? Looks like y'all already dun sum plantin ta me."

Clyde really erupted with this exchange and with hands flailing in all directions and feet dancing like he had been tossed onto a bed of hot coals he spotted a short thick stick which he grabbed and started swinging back and forth in a menacing fashion as the mechanic backed slowly toward his truck in a defensive fashion and then quickly swung the door open. He pounced into the drivers seat and while attempting to roll up the window he saw Clyde reach into a bulging pocket. The mechanic was sure that he was reaching for a gun and as he screamed Clyde pulled a large roll of money from his pocket and peeled off five one "hunnert" dollar bills which he threw through the half raised window opening and in the high pitched ozark twang he attained when this angry said "Ya better be gone offen my property afore ya can make one more scream. An this better be tha last ah hear frum ya or it'll be tha last anyones gon'na hear frum ya."

Five hundred dollars was twenty dollars more than Ada had earned in ten months of hard work in Little Rock the year before.

Well, Clyde actually did manage to get his crop of pop-corn—it was anything but special—drilled in in time for the summer growing season. The rows looked like someone with a severe case of labyrinthitis or impending drunk-ness had careened back and forth and the whole field looked like it had a bad case of the mange since some areas were rather bare, followed by, or preceded by, substantial blotches of growth, depending on whether it was being observed coming or going. All of this was the aftermath of having bounteous piles of corn kernels spill on the ground when a drill feeder tube would break open, which had happened often, and usually without being noticed. Lurching, contrary to planting, comes to mind.

Clyde had not been able to come to grips with the "draft dodging" thing and in lieu of this, inducted a rather penetrating case of dyspepsia coupled with an embarkation of colitis. And about this same time—wouldn't you know it—the septic system, the workings of which Clyde never quite understood anyway, suddenly decided to become affluent and stop leaching. He re-activated the outhouse which had been de-activated when the house had been modernized by the previous owners. From John Crapper back to Chick Sales in a shudder. Sorry about the name dropping.

In any event, Clyde lived on pins and needles wondering just when they would come for him. They never did. He actually beat the draft and the closest he ever came to a tank was one very short period when he took a job working as a cleaner in a Kansas City company which produced aircraft auxiliary drop tanks.

Not long after the shade tree mechanic episode, Clyde had a visit from the local sheriff. The sheriff wanted to talk to him about "some stuff reported to be growing on yor property."

Clyde was ready for him. He had gone almost immediately after the mechanic left the farm and plowed under the marijuana which had been growing along the creek. He even ran the disc over the area three times to plow it under "Good an plenty." He took it as a slight but not a major set back since he knew where to find an abundance anytime he needed to "Lay some off." It was only a tiny part of his enterprise and he didn't wish to compromise any of the "big stuff." The truth is, that Clyde had not even planted this "cash crop." It had been present when he first looked at the farm and he made no mention of it to the previous owner nor gave a hint that he even knew what it was. He just figured he was buying a bonus.

Anyway, the sheriff had arrived without any announcement and made some subtle talk about things and such and then in his best and most investigatory vernacular, suddenly became aggressive and started lecturing Clyde about the evils of drugs. He let it be known that he did not condone this sort of thing and Clyde chimed right in with agreement.

Clyde let it be known that just a few days ago he had "discovered this filthy weed ah grow' in down by tha crick and drived my tractor here right over tha top ah that stuff." "I took ta plow'in it right up soon's ah recognized whut it was." "Y'all knows we jus bought this here place an tha folks here before us—ah thank his name wus Hackett—or sump in like that—wus jus no damn good ah grow'in somethin like that." "Jus cain't trust no one no more can ya sheriff?"

"Mister, I don't know nothin bout you but I do know bout Jess Sackett cause he happens ta be ah cousin ah mine an I don't take kindly ta say' in nuthin about ma kin." "Now, ya hear me?" "If there wus anything grow'in what was e-legal here Jess Sackett didn't have nuthin ta do with it." "I gon'na have me ah look around this place an if I find anythin I'll be back and you can count on it."

Well of course the last thing Clyde wanted or needed was a run in with the law and here he had put his foot in his mouth and hadn't really even tried and as the sheriff drove down toward the creek he muttered to himself about "How could ah have known Ole' Bracket or Hachett or Sachet had a gol-damn sheriff fur ah cuzzin what was a ride-en this here end ah tha county." "God dammit if not fer bad luck ah wud-den have none a 'tall."

The sheriff came back by the house about twenty minutes later and informed Clyde that he could see that the crop had been destroyed but admonished him that he would be "making regular rounds through this here place from now on."

It was then that the sheriff decided that he better get some information from Clyde and asked for a drivers license and a draft card.

Clyde had never been asked for a draft card before and his throat went dry and nothing came out except "Let me study on whur that might be."

Beryl had been observing the whole thing and stepped in just in time. "Sheriff. We jus moved frum Nevada an had most our things lost an all our importunt papers wuz lost an Clyde—show tha sheriff yor Nevada drivers license—ya still got that left."

Whereupon Clyde regained some of his composure and went inside and returned with the Nevada drivers license he had obtained several years before. It was outdated but it was all he had since he never bothered to take a license in

171

Missouri and he certainly didn't have a draft card or even a registration paper.

The sheriff was writing Clyde's name and rural box number in his little note book when Beryl once again came to the rescue. "Ya know sheriff—cud ah speak ta ya ta tha side fer a second?"

The sheriff drifted over toward the shade of a tree with Beryl at his side and she said "Sheriff, Clyde ain't quite right in tha head ya know. Had his skull broke ah few years back an tha gum-ment went an declared him 4-F fer tha draft." "Poor thing—we an't married ya know—but I'm ah nurse an ah do tha takin care ah him—but we live like we is married—y'all understan Sheriff? Why he don't know whuther he's ah foot or horseback most ah tha time much less whuther he's 1-A or 4-F in'na draft."

Clyde heard every word that was said and was doing another one of his slow boils and almost lost it when he realized that Beryl had completed the con and the sheriff came back to get into his car when he turned to Clyde and said "Poor devil"—got into his car and drove away.

Clyde immediately launched into Beryl about how bad she made him look and acted like the aggrieved party when she spun around and said" you still ah dumb sum-bitch Clyde I jus saved yer ass frum bout fifty years in'na prison an this here tha thanks ah get. Well let me tell ya Clyde y'all can go right ta hell with out look 'in back as fer as it concerns me an ah think I'm goin back to Kansas City an ah don't care whut y'all do."

She went in the house and started to pack some clothes and Clyde trailed in before long with that hang dog look he could develop when he realized he had been more of a jerk than usual and tried to apologize in the only way he could—that is to say he attempted to rationalize most of his actions.

Beryl listened with reserve and kept on throwing things into the suitcase. She finally told him that she just needed to do some things in the city and not to be concerned because she would probably get over this latest hurt and let him know pretty soon.

"How much ah that money y'all got left frum tha last trip Clyde?" "Ah need sum fer livin afor ah get back on at tha hospital."

Clyde drove Beryl back to the little apartment and just kind of dropped her off.

He headed immediately for Efrom's office but only made it as far as the gin mill. He was greeted by several of the "bimmys" and in a little over an hour was really sloshed. He woke up alone and in a strange bed which was located in a strange room. It was obvious that someone else had been with him at some time during the blackout period but he had no memory of it.

He really felt rotten and tried to make it through an open door into what appeared to be the bath room before he threw up. He didn't make it. He did have on some under shorts but no undershirt. A filthy rusted bath tub fitted with a pipe which extended from a single faucet handle coursed upwards along the wall and then bent in the direction of a rusted tin can with holes in the bottom. This acted as a shower and after a few minutes and without benefit of any soap he looked to no avail for a towel. He went back to the bed and ripped off what appeared to be the remnants of a sheet which he used as a towel.

A look around the room was totally unrewarding—one tiny window, a straight back chair, a ready to fall and dilapidated pedestal type bed side stand and the filthy bed with a wrought iron head and foot board and a torn blanket hanging from the side. Empty gin bottles were strewn about with no sign of any sort of drinking vessels but the worst revelation was that none of his clothes, not even his shoes, were to be found.

Clyde didn't know where, what or when so he peeled back a corner of the old newspaper which was acting as a window cover and attempted to reconnoiter—actually he was connoitering since he had not previously connoitered. The only thing he saw was a window which was identical to his and about three feet away. He also determined that it was daytime.

Next he opened the door a crack and was able to see that he was in what appeared to be a motor court. He waited to see if anyone was around before sticking his head out further. Nothing was stirring so he went back to the bathroom and wrapped the filthy wet sheet around toga style and ventured outside.

His first encounter with life was a mangy German Shepherd dog gnawing on what appeared to be the remains of a much smaller mangy German Shepherd dog and who apparently thought that Clyde had some design on his possession and growled and lunged at him with bared teeth and managed to tear a large piece of the sheet. Clyde screamed, jumped several feet and was heard nor seen by any one.

The dog returned to his feast and Clyde struggled to maintain any balance this binge and splitting headache had left him. He struggled toward what seemed to be the front of this enterprise which consisted of twelve clapboard sided cabins, six in a row facing each other. The front one was the designated office by the fact that a pink neon sign displayed "Cupids Cabins" in italicized script and blinked off and on.

When Clyde opened the door he saw what was little more than a modified version of his abode and occupied by one really ugly, really large, hairy version of a male person standing behind a makeshift counter holding a tiny hairless Chihuahua dog which had a pink ribbon collar from which a pink heart and an arrow sticking through it hung. Clyde had no sense of smell right then but had he, he would have been appalled.

"Well—morn'in" said Clyde.

"Sal-mos even 'in" said the person.

"Oh!" said Clyde

"Yea!" said the person.

"That Cupid?" said Clyde pointing to the Chihuahua.

"Nope" said the person. "I'm Cupid." "This here's Thor."

"Listen!" "I was wonder' in eff'en y'all cud tell me where ah am an how long ah been here?" "Sum one done run off with ma clothes an ever thin else as y'all can plainly see."

"Ah can tell ya where ya is an when ya got here." said Cupid.

"Well! Is ya gon'na tell me or not?" said Clyde after having waited what seemed much too long.

"Not till ya pay me fer tha rest ah this here day I an't. Supposed ta be gone by noon." said Cupid.

"Well ya can see plain as tha nose on ya face ah an't got nothin ta pay ya with. Ah jest got'ta sheet on ma back." said Clyde only now noticing what was left of a nose which looked as if it had been partially bitten off.

"An thet an't y'alls sheet, it's mine an it looks torn an thet's gon'na cost ya." "Ya cum in here three days ago an paid me fur three days. That woman left in ya car yestuday an ah an't know'in any more." "Sure sounded like y'all had

175

ah scufflin good time while it lasted tho."

"Whut happen ta ma clothes?" Clyde started to shout and even as the first nasal twang came out of his mouth he realized he was not in the cat bird seat and tried to apologize—"Lissen Mr Cupid—ah apologize fer that thar outbust—but ya got'ta know ah am a hurt' in an cain't thank straight." "Did ya recognize that woman Mr Cupid?"

"Yea I knowed her alrights. Cum in heah wunce in'na while an bring sum poge like you what don't know no betta. An she get out afor ya knows whut hit ya. How ya gon'na pay fer this anywise?"

"Jest whur am ah anywise?" "Ya got ah phone here bouts?"

"An't got no phone." "Sheriff usually cum long an chat bout three o'clock ever day. Ya'll can settle with him when he cum."

"Well, are ya gon'na tell me whur ah am or not?"

"This here's jest about six mile north ah Olathe on Kansas City Road. Jes whar'd ya think ya was?" said the person.

"Olathe!!! Well that's clear in Kansas." shouted Clyde.

"Well!!! Jes hold up ah minit mister standin with no clothes an ah sheet. Ah course Olathe's in Kansas. Ah'll be dam'ed ef y'all an't tha dumbest sum-bitch ah ever did talk ta."

"Well anywise here cum tha sheriff an y'all can tell ya sad tale ta him after he get thru laffen at whut he gon'na see."

"Hi sheriff. Got'ta little prob-lum here ta-day but ah spect ya can take good care it eff'en ya know whut ah mean. Seems Mr hot shot here done got hisself rolled an stripped by sum fast shuffle broad."

Clyde broke in: "Ya said ya knowed her ah little while

ago."

"Never seen her afore sheriff. This here feller cum in three day ago an ah thought they was mister an missus. Turns out was sum tramp what run out on him." fibbed Mr Cupid.

"Has he broke tha law besides run' in around haf nek-ked Cupid?" asked the sheriff as he turned to Clyde and asked "Whut's tha name an lem'me see some identification proven who ya are."

Clyde's Ozark twang burst out again—"How in hell fire can ah be hav'in any i-den-ti-fi-casun when I'm ah stand'in in ma drawers with ah sheet wrapped round me. Now y'all jest tell me that!"

"Don't go gett'in testy just gim'me ah name mister." rebuked the sheriff rather sternly.

Clyde was so ruffled by this time that he almost said Charlie Lubeck but caught it just in time and said "Ah don't rightly know whut ma name is. Tha las thang ah remember wus gett'in hit in'na head an ah thank ah got whut—cha—call—it amon -nessa." "Ah don't know whur ah am, or who ah am or how ah got whur ah am or whut day it is!"

With that, the sheriff handcuffed him and put him in the back seat of his patrol car and headed out.

By the time they arrived at the pokey, Clyde had confabulated what turned out to be a real plausible story and one that would very likely save his bacon. It actually was clever and served him well.

At the sheriff station he steadfastly denied knowing who, what or why. They brought a doctor in for an exam and he reported that Clyde certainly could have been hit in the head and sustained a concussion and that it was not uncommon for post concussion amnesia to manifest in cases such as this.

The sheriff finally concluded that Clyde had not really broken any laws and did not legally have any reason to hold him but didn't feel right about turning him out since he didn't have any clothes.

This called for a transfer to the jail ward at the Johnson County Hospital where Clyde was put to bed and finally got some aspirin for his four plus hangover headache.

The next day the local newspaper got wind of and headlined *"AMNESIA CASE Brought To Johnson County Hospital"* always a big story since an amnesia victim could be just about anybody including a rich and important person.

The staff photographer for the newspaper came in and asked permission to take Clyde's picture which was exactly what Clyde wanted them to do. He even suggested that they might place his picture on the front page asking "Do You Know This Man?." He further suggested that it might be a good idea to send it to the major newspapers such as the Kansas City Star since he seemed to have a thought running around in the back of his head that he might even be from Kansas City. This idea also caught on and so the next day Clyde's picture was front page news "Do You Know This Man"

Efrom was having his first coffee royale' drink of the morning at his desk looking at the race results which he always separated out from the other parts of the paper when he spotted Clyde's picture staring up from the floor where the front page had been dropped. Efrom perused the story quickly, polished off the remainder of his "pick me up" and headed for the door snatching his coat from the rack.

Efrom by this time owned a 1941 Packard sedan paid for mostly from commissions from dealing with Clyde and headed this splendid machine in the direction of Johnson County Kansas which is to say in a South-West direction.

When he arrived in Olathe he immediately asked directions to the police department and upon locating same, went to the desk to inquire about the man who's picture was on the front page.

The Olathe police Sergeant informed him that it had been a county sheriff case but that he knew for a fact that the man was presently being held only in protective custody and that no charges had been filed and directed Efrom to the county hospital.

After signing the appropriate papers he was issued a visitors pass and escorted by a male attendant, whom Efrom believed to be a trustee, to the room where Clyde was still sleeping.

He gently nudged Clyde who awoke with a start and flipped over and sat up all in one motion.

Clyde quickly recognized Efrom and put his index finger to his lips to caution him not to say anything. He then motioned Efrom to bend so a whisper was all that could be heard.

He told Efrom about his idea and Efrom was absolutely amazed at the soundness and viability of this fabrication.

Efrom wrote himself some notes and headed back to the desk and informed the attending nurse and guard that he indeed did know this man but the man did not apparently know him. He further explained that he was the man's attorney of record and would immediately go to the Sheriffs station to obtain a release—which is exactly what he did.

SEPTEMBER 1942 FOUND me again enrolled in Central Street School as were all of my buddies. I decided that being ten years old was at least one year better than being nine. I continued to think about the importance of getting to be thirteen because, according to the physiology books I had scanned at the library, this magic number brought puberty and puberty brought all sorts of great things. I talked this over with all of the guys but each of them professed to already have pubic hair which was not true in every case since we all used the same dressing room at the swimming pool and I knew better. I let them have their white lies and realized that I really knew more than they did about the subject—at least book wise.

I decided to share my curiosity with Brenda and approached her with a straight from the shoulder query about this thing. "How many pubic hairs do you have Brenda? Have you reached puberty yet?" I asked, putting on my most deductive facial expression but verbalizing it with all the finesse of a hand grenade. She just looked at me like I had gone stark mad and knocked me flat with a doubled up fist delivered as a solid right cross to the jaw.

I was in the process of figuring that I had miscalculated

something when she sat down beside me and started to effuse sorrow for what she had done, took my hand with onc of hers and began rubbing my jaw very gently with the other. "I just don't know what caused me to do that!" she exclaimed.

"I don't know either" I replied. "I was just gon'na ask you if girls worried about it as much as boys—cause—none of the guys, including Magnis ever tell me thc truth about stuff like that anyway and now I guess it's not as important as I thought or you wouldn't have slugged me like you did."

"Oh you poor little thing Laurel. I sure do wonder sometimes what the inside of your mind must look like." She declared as she hugged me like I was a teddy bear and kissed me right where she had slugged me and rocked me back and forth right in her front yard. "Laurel Hardy Lubeck—I bet you and I are gon'na be friends for the rest of our lives—ya know that Laurel?"

"I'll keep you posted about my progress but don't tell anyone else cause no one else is gon'na really understand anyway and the answers to your questions are none and no." Brenda and me are still buddies and no one ever grew up with a better friend. From that day forward we could talk about anything—and did.

Ada was still in a struggle with grief over the death of Billy John Boscum and threw her whole emotional being into extra hard work at the now converted "defense plant" where they made fuses for some type of bomb. She always volunteered to take any open double shift and worked most Saturdays and some Sundays.

Miss Laura looked after the household and functioned as the mother figure for Magnis and me. She had been trying, of course, to console Ada and direct her toward other things but she knew as sure as she tried that Ada would internalize this latest maneuver decreed on her by the infernal gods and wax malice in promotion of her wrath toward them and would make them deliberate for a long time before damaging her again. You could feel the intensity of this angry power which discharged from her and yet you knew it was not directed even at the Japanese who had fought in the battle and killed the gentle giant whom she had been unable to tell just how desperate her love for him had been, but rather at the directors of fate and how desperate for perverse amusement they must be to have foisted yet another swindle on her unadorned, ungarnished quest of life.

Uncle Louie, who was too old for any kind of military duty but a good patriot, made special ticket prices for servicemen, that is to say they all got in free in uniform and he donated thousands of dollars to various service related organizations. He helped sponsor the local USO which somehow was hooked up with the YMCA and had a sleeping dorm which was open and free for all men in uniform.

I remember going with Uncle Louie to get all of the blankets for these bunks.

At this point I need to tell you how things worked. The boxing and wrestling games were controlled from a higher level which translates into "This is how much it is gon'na cost to promote these events." Uncle Louie had purchased a "territory" from "The Boss"—or "Top Tradition"—for who knows how much and 10% of "the take" and believe me the 10% wasn't a guess, it was right to the dollar. The Boss ruled everything west of Denver and lived in the Hollywood Hills. His name was Hayman Nicholas and he too had a "Boss" but I don't know his name. I recall making the "quarterly settlement" with Uncle Louie on several occasions. This was accomplished by driving to Hollywood with a brown paper bag full of the right amount of money and paying respects to the boss and any "others", who would be setting around the kitchen table, having a few minutes of small talk, drinking a quick cup of coffee, renewing old memories and then departing, simply leaving the unopened bag on the kitchen table. It sure worked right for them and I was absolutely sure on one of these occasions that one of the "others" was the same man Ada had delivered that valise to that night in Las Vegas on our trip out west.

He—Uncle Louie—had heard about "some unpatriotic son-of-a-bitch black market bimmy" trying to hustle some wool blankets in L.A. and immediately went to Hollywood to have "a sit down" with the "boss" who already knew about the hundreds of boxes of blankets and other things that had been hi-jacked down by San Diego while being transported to the Naval Training Center and it frosted him and Uncle Louie that any "motherless asshole" could "do something like that to our boys."

Well, I accompanied him on a windy November afternoon. He picked me up after school. When he needed company during what I called his excursions he would initiate the invitation with "Hey Laurel let's take ah' little ride." When he was contemplating things he needed a sounding board and I just naturally turned out to be a good one. That is to say, I never talked back—only listened. He would really get into conversations with himself and go through step by step what he was thinking—what he thought someone else was—or would be saying—or thinking and then turn to me while zigging down what ever street we were presently terrorizing.

183

I forgot to tell you, Uncle Louie was perhaps the worst driver ever behind a wheel and never had a drivers license because he could never pass the test. Without fail, when he opened the drivers door of a car to get in, he would reach into his pants pocket and extract a large chunk of money, which he was never without, and which would approximate one inch thickness and be clamped with a one of a kind money clip made from a beautiful gold coin . From this slab he would pull a one hundred dollar bill, fold it lengthwise and wrap this around his left middle finger. He called it his "officers friend." He also kept two free six month passes to the wrestling matches stuck in his shirt pocket. I can't remember how many times that combination kept him on the streets of Southern California. He could talk and/or buy his way out of anything.

Well, back to the "Unpatriotic no good son-of-a-bitch."

We were down close to the corner of 7th and Mateo Street and I had to do the address reading for him—I always knew that he couldn't see very well and that was the reason for my riding what he called navigator. We found the right place—he parked after a fashion and I pulled out some reading material from my back pocket.

He started for a large metal door which looked like it had been someplace else for a long time before ending up bolted to some substantial rusting hinges. He stopped, turned around and walked back to my window and motioned for me to roll it down.

"Follow me Laurel—I want to show you how it's done." "I don't want you to ever have to do it but just in case—well you know what I mean."

We walked through the heavy door into a small warehouse and almost immediately encountered the man in charge. A beat up desk with some papers sat next to a dirty sink, which seemed to defy gravity, made up the clerical part of this enterprise. Hundreds of cardboard boxes could be seen stacked four high.

The man in charge was about forty-five years old and was smoking a really bad smelling cigar. He asked Uncle Louie if he came to inspect the merchandise to which Uncle Louie answered in the affirmative. About that time another man stepped into sight from some place in the rear and stood his distance. The man in charge tilted his head toward me notifying Uncle Louie that he thought I should evacuate the area. To which Uncle Louie replied "Oh that's my boy and he's here to learn some diplomacy."

Uncle Louie always dressed in these beautifully tailored tweeds with hand made shirts and silk solid color ties and most often his huge head was topped with a hand blocked three inch snap-brim fedora rolled up all the way around and on this day he looked his finest.

I anticipated that some heavy bargaining and bidding was about to take place and I was exactly right about two seconds later when the man said "What's your offer pal?"

Uncle Louie turned to me and handed me a business card and said "Laurel read this to yourself and then take it to the nice man so he can also read it" .

I did as told and handed the card over.

After reading the face of the card the man turned rather pale and began coughing rather violently, dropped the cigar and sat down on the edge of the desk.

Uncle Louie said: "When you can control your self read the other side out loud so your moth eaten piss-ant friends back there can hear you."

The man began to read in a mumbling fashion when Uncle Louie stopped him and said in a rather sedate but authoritative voice. "I said—read it loud and clear grease bag so all the bimmies in tha back can hear."

'Drop 5 boxes of blankets and cash to run the USO for a long time at the Stanford Park YMCA let cops find the rest at the main gate at Naval Training San Diego . Then get a job in a war plant. I'll check on all of you. My son's a Recruit and I don't like what you did. H.N.'

As we pulled away from the curb I asked if what had taken place was diplomacy and Uncle Louie answered: "No Laurel that was just an exercise—didn't need to use any diplomacy this time." as he waved an "everything's okay" to the four very tough looking occupants of a sedan parked across the street.

A FTER CLYDE WAS released from the county hospital Efrom drove him back to Kansas City and then out to the farm where they sat for most of the afternoon drinking beer and concocting further plans for covering Clyde's trail.

Efrom was still impressed with the story Clyde had given to the Sheriff and kept repeating that he wished that he had thought it up so he could have charged a fee for it. This of course set Clyde on edge because he knew that he could never trust Efrom because Efrom just didn't "always play by the book" and as far as he—Clyde—was concerned was "down right dishonest."

The two of them finally agreed that as soon as Efrom could make the arrangements he would take Clyde to a doctor at the University of Missouri Medical School who specialized in neurology and forensic psychiatry and had seen many amnesia cases during his career.

Efrom claimed that he needed to know the real truth about Clyde's past but Clyde was not about to release any information about Charlie Clyde Lubeck being his real name or any thing about his background. Only that his name was Clyde Dodge and gave his age as 39.

When they arrived for the medical appointment a clerk

at the reception room started asking Clyde questions from an information form. He told her that he knew nothing about where he was born, when he was born, where he lived and let her know that if not for Efrom he wouldn't even know that his name was Clyde Dodge.

The clerk told him not to worry because Doctor Wolf-Smyth had handled many such cases and would certainly be able to help.

Clyde was pacing back and forth and Efrom's words of comfort only irritated him more.

He didn't like it that there were three patients in the waiting room who had bandages wrapped around their heads and numerous others with various forms of mental retardation, infirmities and one man with late stage Huntington's Chorea who decided right off that he didn't like Clyde and let him know about it with arms flailing and facial contractions and contortions preceding the explosive verbal vexations.

This further unnerved Clyde and he needed a smoke badly but there were "no smoking" signs posted and it was a long walk and an elevator ride to the outside so by the time Clyde's name was called he was almost as agitated as the hapless soul with the incurable hereditary disorder.

Finally the receptionist asked Clyde to follow her into the doctors office.

Doctor Wolf-Smyth was a man about sixty years old and had long waxy grey hair combed straight back with no part and no side burns. In fact his hair didn't seem to start growing from his scalp until two full inches above his ears. It was like a reverse baldness pattern. His ears were huge, the nose showed early signs of rhinophyma and this only exaggerated the bushy red mustache which cascaded over his upper lip and which would appear to obstruct normal eating and drinking—or at least make it a messy procedure.

His gait was that of mid stage Parkinson's—that is to say he walked on the verge of falling—and his hands were in a constant pill rolling movement also typical of mid-stage disease and which was noticed by Clyde as the doctor came from behind his desk to greet him.

His movement to shake Clyde's hand however was, as per usual with this central nervous system disorder, very normal and did not return to the tremors until he had let go of Clyde's hand.

The whole mustache moved up and down when he spoke but the sound was muffled. However, he was gentle of speech and began almost immediately asking questions about the recently acquired medical problem.

Clyde was scared to death and taken aback by this attention, stuttering and wheezing as he attempted to lie his way through the numerous medical questions.

After taking a long and exact history, Dr Wolf-Smyth ordered Clyde to go into the exam room next door, disrobe and put on a gown.

A nurse entered and took his blood pressure, pulse rate and placed a thermometer in his mouth and then began to ask her own questions which Clyde attempted to answer but each time he started to say something she told him to keep his mouth closed until she was through taking his temperature. Remember, Clyde was not one who could conjugate successfully even when not revved up as he was by now and went through yet another episode of hyperventilation which seemed to be his answer to each blind alley he found himself in during his entire adult life.

Dr Wolf-Smyth came into the exam room during Clyde's hyperventilation routine and began to ask him more questions in a fairly staccato fashion.

"What day did you say you last remember Mr Dodge? Was your mother dark complexioned?" "Did your father call you Clyde?" "Who is Mr Lebowitz?" "Where is your home?" "When did your mother pass away?"

Clyde had assumed that Dr Wolf-Smyth was incapable of this rapid speech since he equated his Parkinson's handicap with slowness of speech which is how the doctor had conducted himself during the earlier history taking event and he also assumed that he wanted yes and no answers which he attempted to give and this led to total frustration which continued to the point of syncope.

When he recovered from this transient episode he was totally and absolutely spent, which was the exact condition Dr Wolf-Smyth had wished to achieve—albeit with less effort than had ever before been required with someone lacking the inherent character quality and temperament of Clyde.

Dr Wolf-Smyth proceeded to do his physical and neurological exam and dictated his findings to his nurse who wrote in short hand. He used acronyms and medical terms which were greatly mysterious, and the whole proceedings befuddled the bee-jeezus out of Clyde.

Next came the dexterity portion which required taking apart and reconstructing a simple wooden pyramid puzzle—perplexity level age eight, time limit four minutes. Clyde had never even mastered the complexities of changing a toilet paper roll much less something this engaging and was still "Try'n to put tha damn thang back like it was." when the doctor gently removed it from his hands and dumped the contents from another box which contained four shapes—triangles, circles, squares and rectangles of three colors each—red, white and blue .

The instructions were to place the objects in stacks each

of the same color one on top of the other and in alphabetical order top to bottom and then arrange the stacks in alphabetical order by color of the stack left to right— perplexity level age ten, time limit two minutes.

Clyde was finished in less than the allotted time and looking real pleased—three circles red, white and blue, three squares red white and blue and so on with the triangles and rectangles.

Doctor Wolf-Smyth gave a sigh, a wry smile and a chuckle and ordered the nurse to "Send Mr Dodge down to X-ray for a skull series including a Towne and a Waters view and then prepare him for his electro encephalogram."

The "normal limits" x-ray report was phoned almost immediately to Dr Wolf-Smyth's office and was relayed to him even as the electrodes were being placed in strategic spots on Clyde's already thinning scalp.

The electrodes were glued to the scalp with some type of shellac which was made from beetles and gave off a musty odor. The electroencephalograph was a very large and complicated piece of machinery just loaded with vacuum tubes, and electrical coils of all sizes and capacities, and which was designed to measure alpha and beta brain waves and record such on a continuous wide strip of graph paper and gave off an electrical fire ozone odor which competed well along the olfactory route with the shellac and tended to scare hell out of most folks while just warming up. Every thing had to warm up in those days.

The technician went through the recording process with Clyde staring stark eyed and petrified—afraid to move a muscle for fear of being electrocuted which he was positive would come any time.

The tracing was reviewed by Doctor Wolf-Smyth while the technician sponged alcohol into Clyde's previously described thinning scalp all the while pulling and tugging the electrodes which gave up their hold unwillingly, each one extracting a squeal more shrill than the last.

As doctor Wolf-Smyth left the room he asked Clyde to get dressed and join him in his office which he did a short while later.

The doctor asked Clyde if he minded Efrom being present during the final portion of his consultation and received what appeared to be an affirmative grunt.

"Well Doc. What'd ya think?" "We think we know what happened and we're gon'na sue the crap out'ta those folks out there in Kansas you bet we are—God what'ta case we gon'na make." "Some one can't go round given other folks amnesia now can they doc?" "Will he be like this forever? Never to remember where he came from or who his daddy was or even when he was born'd?" "God what'ta way to go through life—not to. . . ."

"Hold on and calm down Mr Lebowitz." Wolf-Smyth broke in.

"First off, Mr Dodge—if that is his name—has at the worst a simple case of psychogenic amnesia and I'm not really convinced it isn't a pure factitious amnesia so don't go off half cocked and jump through too many hoops. I will prepare my report and send you a copy but I wouldn't be a bit surprised if this memory deficit hasn't returned to absolute normal as soon as the precipitating crisis has vanished and will so state in my report." "Now if you will excuse me Mr Dodge and Mr Lebowitz I have some really sick patients to care for."

"How will you be taking care of the professional bill?" asked the receptionist as they came through the outer office. "I believe you were informed that a cash settlement would be expected." "Your statement will reflect the professional consultation, testing, including the x-rays, EEG and a certified type written report suitable for deposition sent to you by certified mail and your total comes to ninety-two dollars and we don't accept checks."

Efrom paid the bill and they headed down the hall and made it into the elevator before Clyde gushed out "Jesus—H—Christ that som-bitch knows everythin an ah got'ta have me ah cigarcttc aforc ah bcgin ta quiver."—only to be warned against it by a little old lady in a wheel chair at the back of the rather large elevator and who was wearing what Clyde took for a dead beady eyed fox wrapped around her neck and her hands and chin resting on a silver headed cane stuck between her knees which she immediately snapped upward striking Clyde on his leg. "Didn't your mother teach you any manners you crude, unfinished, incomplete excuse for a posthetomy? Can you not see the sign which forbids that nasty habit? I suppose you also dirty up your already filthy mouth with the likes of snuff or some other God awful chewing substance and probably expectorate in a can or on the floor." "Please see that I don't brush against him as we do our exit Sturdavan." The towering chauffeur attendant standing behind the wheel chair nodded his head.

The complete medical report was delivered to Efrom by certified mail three days later and indeed gave Clyde the benefit of the doubt—but this little edge was all he needed to wax his story about being who he pretended to be if ever challenged and could extricate him from harms way with the war.

"What does that word fack-tit ... —however ya say it—mean Efrom?"

"Oh, it kind 'a means ersatz Clyde."

"Oh! That's about what I thought it meant Efrom."

IT WAS LATE in 1942 and Mercer and Carmichael got a lot of people to sing "Skylark" and three sisters with a man's name didn't want someone else to sit under an apple tree for some reason and Wally and Andy and I went to the California Theater to see "Donald Duck in Nutzi Land" which had Donald singing "Der Fuerhrer's Faze" but we knew it was really Spike Jones doing the song and making the "rassssspberrieeees" right in Hitler's face.

I missed Chancey a whole lot but had no idea if she missed me or even remembered or for that matter even really knew who I was.

I asked Miss Laura about what happened to Chancey and she admitted that she didn't know where "Roosevelt might have taken that family" or why. "You know Laurel I'm only second generation American and from Germany at that." "Did you know that your uncle Louie was born in Italy?"

"Came here as a four year old with his mother after his father died" "She was a United States citizen and married your Uncle Louie's father in Italy while traveling with an opera company." "He was born in Salerno and died two years after they were married."

"It sure makes a person wonder what could have been in the minds of those horrible people in Washington making such decisions." "No rational or reasonable assembly of brain matter could have been so wrong— which leads me to reckon that the idea came from some very disturbed, disorganized little minds—and what will remain even worse is the fact that no one will ever be held accountable for this insult—beware of the civil servants or officials or social doctors who make plans for other peoples lives Laurel."

"Every man should be held responsible for his actions—politicians are a scurrilous bunch of spineless wonders with their own improbable plots or pretenses and they too are never held accountable for their actions . . . an idiotic idea coupled with some grandiose, noble yet unworkable plan designed by some mediocre misfit ends up tumbling around the chamber . . . emitting a foul smell and wrapped with mischief . . . which then suddenly becomes the law and the best that can ever be said of such an execration is that . . . *It Always Works Sometimes* . . . But please forgive me Laurel I seem to get kind of confused and mixed up somewhat lately and tend to ramble."

"I think that if it's meant to be—you and Chancey will meet again." "You know that song the nice English Lady— Vera Lynn—recorded it over the transatlantic telephone cable?" "We'll Meet Again." "Listen to the words Laurel."

"You know something else Laurel?" "Song writers are probably the most intuitive, sensitive, perceptive therapists in the world."

And I started a lifelong commitment to song listening when on that very day I first heard someone sing "I Remember You" which had been written earlier in the year by Johnny Mercer and Victor Schertzinger. And I also never forgot those words from Miss Laura—*It always works sometimes.*

Christmas that year was one of my most memorable because I got the first symptoms of mumps about three days before the big day. I got an Ouija board and Magnis was the one who taught me how to use it. He cheated but I didn't know it at the time.

Trixie was the best partner for this. Her imagination was great and we traveled the universe . . . one letter at a time.

Uncle Louie loved to play poker but it was illegal in California except for lo-ball and some other poker game. These games were legal in certain cities and club rooms which were advertised and anyone with money could go in and partake.

However, the real poker games went on all over California in any city you could name. The two major games in Stanford Park were never over. Only the players changed.

The cheaper game was in the back room of a gin mill called "The Corner" and you entered through a door located at the back of a mop closet in the men's toilet. I never was able to figure out why anyone believed this was a secret. Even I knew it.

At any given time you could find the Police Chief or the Mayor and any number of councilmen and top businessmen around the two tables with six chairs—all constantly filled.

Uncle Louie took me with him one day just to show me the ropes and nobody even grunted at my being there. We stayed just a few minutes while he transacted some business which I learned later was indeed his business.

Uncle Louie owned this whole outfit. Boy, was I proud.

196

Even Magnis didn't know about it. No one in the family knew except Uncle Louie, Trixie and me.

Uncle Louie never played poker at The Corner because he preached over and over: "You never shit where you eat Laurel. And don't never fergit it."

Uncle Louie played his poker at the big money game which was a twenty-four hour, seven day a week marathon with only one table. A losing player, when leaving, usually just shrugged off his losses or if a winner would more often just grunt. No emotions here.

This game was in the back room of "The Club" and nothing kept it from public sight except a heavy canvas curtain that separated it from the tonsorial front portion. That is to say, everyone in town knew that Jack The Barber only ran his barber shop and some one else from "out of state" ran the back end. No one asked and no one told.

Jack cut hair and shaved faces and took short nip's from a lotion bottle which he kept on his shelf along with a myriad of powders, shampoo, aftershave and scissors and razors which he kept in a glass jar filled with some vile colored green solution. I got a hair cut every third Thursday afternoon and hated, as I do today, to get little hairs down my shirt collar. It gives me the "willie jeebers."

Jack had a partner and it didn't take me long to figure out which of the two was the better barber. His partner, who's name escapes me, always looked like his head should be in one of the pictures which were framed and hung so the customer could choose which style he wanted this week. Jack, on the other hand, looked like something that was just ready for harvest. I figured out that they cut each other's hair and I usually tried to manipulate my turn so Jack would do me.

I always chose the style that looked most like Earl

Flynn or Cary Grant or the star in the latest movie I had seen. No matter, I still looked like me with my big ears looking even bigger and some foul smelling palmade sticking the forelock sideways to the edge where it became almost bald.

Anytime I was in the vicinity I would pop in to see if Uncle Louie was in the game. No one bothered to stop me or even look up. Most knew me and didn't care.

The whole room would be warned of a stranger by a flashing blue light set off by Barkley the shoe shine "boy." Mr Barkley—as I was allowed to call him—knew everyone in town even though he wasn't allowed to live in town—was the Negro shoeshine "boy"—called that even though he must have been sixty years old.

Well any way, he had his stand set up right at the doorway and he pushed a button when a stranger appeared. Benny the Duck ran the card game and he would quickly waddle to a sliding eye level peep slot in the wall to see who might be coming.

If Uncle Louie was in the game I would watch for a while and knew that when I had observed two or three hands he would slip me a buck and with a motion of his head shoo me off.

Well, back to my story—one morning after an all night game at the club Uncle Louie came driving up in a car that was too neat to be true. For some reason he didn't want to take it to his place so he parked it in our tiny garage. He told me he won it on just one hand of lo-ball stud—"Some wheels for a 'little wheel' huh Laurel?"

This was the most gorgeous baby blue two seat white topped Cadillac convertible that I have ever seen. Everything that was not baby blue was chrome. The wheels were spoke and the whitewall tires must have been three feet in diameter. It had two flexible chrome plated super-charger pipes exiting from the side of the engine compartment that disappeared into the front fenders. Inside, everything was a light brown leather and the dash was some type of elegant gnarled wood which was polished so it would reflect your face. The gauges were all of chrome as were all of the fixtures which were designed to open the convertible roof and needless to say, the door handles were large, engraved, heavy chrome. The window knobs were accentuated with another touch of class—large polished knobs made from the same wood as the dash.

I just could not believe that an automobile could be this beautiful—but—I saved the best for last—This two seater became a four seater when you turned the chrome handle sticking out from where the trunk should have been—yea, a fantastic rumble seat with the same fine leather covering everything which could be visualized and the best quality moleskin covering everything else including the floor.

Uncle Louie said: "Don't tell your aunt Trixie Laurel this is a birthday present."

I had a hard time figuring that one out cause Aunt Trixie never in her life learned to drive a car. I kept my word and didn't tell and sure enough Uncle Louie came over on her birthday and drove off and had it washed and polished and I had my first ride in that car and it was cold and I sat in the rumble seat so everyone in Stanford Park could see me—big ears and all. When I saw someone I knew I gave "the right thumb"—we didn't yet know about the middle digit—later to be know as "giving the bird"—well, we pulled into Uncle Louie's driveway and he blew this horn which sounded like a fine tuned French Horn and Trixie came out to see what was going on.

Uncle Louie got out, handed her the key and said:

"Trixie—this is yours as soon as you learn to drive but until then I guess I'll sport you around in it." "Happy birthday kid."

I was sitting in the rumble seat beaming from ear to ear. Trixie was sure happy and I thought everyone in the country probably knew about this gift.

Uncle Louie said: "Laurel did you find something under your feet back there ?"

I then remembered a rather sturdy gift box I had been using for a foot rest.

"Hand that down here Laurel." "This can be your gift to Aunt Trixie."

We were still in the driveway when Trixie opened the box and found a full length mink coat which I think she liked better than the car.

I believe it must have been a 1937 or 1938 and it had white porcelain heads on the engine and it looked like it was going ninety even when parked at the curb. God I loved that car and the rides through town in that rumble seat. That Cadillac had no logo on it indicating what model or year it was and I never found out cause Uncle Louie totaled it in a wreck about nine months later and that brought us to the end of 1944.

THE DECEPTION, CREATED by Clyde, was working well. At the insistence of Efrom, as a part of his cover up, he applied for work In October of 1944. A Kansas City sheet metal company, which had a large contract to fabricate fuel drop tanks for a fighter plane called the P-51, had advertised for unskilled labor.

Clyde worked outside of the main building under a canopy with open sides where a rather slow conveyor setup brought aluminum pieces which had already been cut to shape and formed so that two of them could be welded along a middle seam to form one of these fuel pods. It was his job to clean these large parts with carbon-tetra-chloride.

This carbon—tet was supposed to remove any grease or other contaminants from what would become the inside of the fuel tank and further assure that the aluminum welding would be perfect. This task was accomplished by pulling these large parts from the conveyor into a very large tank of this carbon—tet and sinking them after which he would pull them back onto the conveyor so that they might drain on the return trip inside the building.

Well Clyde had been doing this task for about two months and had given up drinking during the day. He had made temporary peace with Beryl and the two of them were living in a duplex Clyde owned and which wasn't far from the factory.

One day two very large men in dark single breasted suits, with vests and snap brim hats suddenly appeared in his working area.

"You Clyde C. Dodge?" asked the bigger of the two as they flashed I.D's flipped from leather holders.

"I'm Hollister P. Dentworthy and my partner here is Slocum NMN—that stands for no middle name—Hood."

"We are investigators with the FBI -that stands for the Federal Bureau of Investigation-and would like to ask you some questions Mr Dodge."

"You are Mr Clyde C. Dodge aren't you?"

Well of course this was the last thing in the world Clyde had ever expected would happen and his first impulse was to leap between the two of them and make a run for it but for some reason he hesitated and then fainted right there on the spot.

When he regained what little prior sense he had he exhibited his—thus far main contribution to society—that is to say he began to drool down the front of his work smock.

Hollister P. Dentworthy and Slocum NMN Hood reached down and hoisted him to his feet with little effort and leaned him against the wall and he immediately slid down to a sitting position. At this moment he felt like something that had been passed through a dog.

Dentworthy squatted down right in front of him and said, "Mr Dodge we ain't here to cause you no harm only to clear up a discrepancy which was found on your application for work."

Doubting that Clyde knew what a discrepancy was he

said, "You do know what I'm saying don't you ?"

"Well if it has somethin to do with that there amanesia I been gett'in better at remembur'in thangs." "You just ask tha boss—I do a real good job with this here tetra stuff."

"We already asked your boss about your work habits and he told us you been doing a real good job." "Ain't that right Slocum?"

To which Hood uttered his only verse of the day, "Yea."

Dentworthy said, "Can I call you Clyde ? Well of course I can." "Clyde—it looks like on your job application you ain't done a bit of work for quiet sometime and we were wonder' in if you could fill us in a little about where you been and how you been makin your livin an things like that." "Do you know that this project you're work'in on is a pretty secret thing ?"

"Well I don't mean to say that your particular part is anything secret but—well—you know what I mean don'cha Clyde?"

"We are required to run a background search on all folks working on projects such as the one you been doing and we just now got around to you."

"Just where you been living Clyde?"

"I mean for tha last three or four years?"

"We just can't find nothin about you."

"Are ya married or divorced or maybe you're a faggot—what'ta ya say Clyde?"

"You know somethin Slocum? We never even asked Clyde if he has some kinda identification now—did we"

"Clyde you got some I.D.? Maybe a draft card or drivers license or somethin like that?"

Clyde had regained some of his thought pattern and managed to wipe his chin which by now had become totally dependent on gravity.

He realized that he somehow needed to get to Efrom but couldn't figure out exactly how. He then remembered a patient having a seizure in Doctor Wolf-Smyth's office and a question the neurologist had asked him about ever having urinated in his pants when unconscious or had he ever had a seizure.

Right then and there Clyde put on a seizure that would have made Amy Semple McPherson and her hysterical group real proud and topped it off with micutrating a puddle.

By the time he thought that he had them convinced, he indeed had.

"Mind turn'in him over Slucum so I can find if he has a wallet or not?"

Slocum NMN Hood bent down and with deliberate indifference rolled him face down and Dentworthy pulled his smock up over his hips and extracted a leather wallet which was totally soaked with urine.

With a disgusted look on his face he held the wallet out at arms length and said "Oh shit Slocum no one this dumb could be a spy and even if he is a draft dodger we'll be do'in our side a great big service just keep'in him here out'ta tha way. Anyway, I been told that that carbon tet crap will kill you almost as fast as a hand grenade. Poor bastard don't even know what's what an I doubt he could feed himself if not for the wages he gets here."

"Let's get ta hell out'ta here and write him up as cleared . Okay?"

Slocum NMN Hood shook his head okay and Dentworthy tossed the wallet back beside Clyde without even looking inside where he would have found the "Age Deferred Status" draft card with birth date Feb. 7, 1904—a legitimate drivers license from the state of Missouri with the farm listed as the residence address and the date of birth 2-7-04—all the handy work of Efrom Lebowitz, Esq.—and, tucked inside the fold down secret compartment found featured in all Woolworth's Five & Dime wallets—forty three—one hundred dollar bills.

The foreman had been watching the whole thing from a distance and after the investigators left he came to Clyde— stood over him—shook his head from side to side and said "We can take you to the doctor and make a further case out of this or you can tuck your tail and head on out. I think you got two days wages coming and we'll make sure your money gets sent to the address you gave us. Don't ever use us as a reference cause we never ever heard of you before. Get it ?"

Thanksgiving came and went and Christmas was just one big blur for both Clyde and Beryl with booze floating the "Yule Tide Log" and neither remembered a thing about the arrival of 1945 .

1945 TURNED OUT to be one of the happiest and one of the saddest of my life—almost.

Commander Abner Plummer Pinkney, M.D., U.S. Naval Medical Corp had been born in Merced, California, in 1907 and grew up the son of a prosperous grape grower. He attended College of The Pacific in Stockton for his undergraduate work, studied medicine at Stanford, interned at Los Angeles County General, did a four year general surgery residency at Queen of Angels Hospital in Los Angeles and had been in private practice back in Merced. He volunteered and was commissioned in the service of the U.S. Naval Medical Corp the first week in January 1942 and was given a three week course in military protocol and etiquette before being assigned to temporary duty as a surgeon at Pearl Harbor awaiting transfer for duty aboard the U.S.S. Lexington.

Some of you will recall that the Lexington was an aircraft carrier and "She" went down in the Battle of The Coral Sea in early May 1942 in what was later called the "first naval battle in history in which rival fleets never saw each other"—that is to say it was fought in the air and at a distance.

It was never determined exactly what happened except that a mysterious monstrous explosion occurred in the boiler room and this noble flattop went down along with this noble surgeon . . . only Abner Pinkney somehow floated back to the surface and it was exactly four months to the day since he had become "An Officer and a Gentleman." He noticed that he had a rather nasty wound involving his right hip but little pain except when he tried to move the leg. He was rescued from the water in a short while and never chose to talk much about it.

He was a big man—six foot two, two hundred ten pounds and solid. Very large—size nine surgeons glove hands—number 12 brogans for shoes and to me he always looked like a large version of Gene Kelly and before his injury he had really loved to dance and boasted that he was pretty good. He could still do the slow dancing stuff but the quick two-step had to be done in four or more.

Abner had never married and both his parents had died within six months of each other in early 1940 leaving him the sole heir to more than 1000 acres of wine grapes. As I said, he had been an only child and was very much a gentle, kind, loving and compassionate man and when he met Ada in the fall of 1943 he fell immediately and completely in love for the first time.

He was stationed at the Long Beach Naval Hospital after having recovered from the wound which left him with a permanent semi rigid hip with the resultant slightly shorter right leg and a limp.

Ada told him that she was still married and gave him the whole honest story about her past with Charlie Clyde Lubeck and the two boys she had been raising.

Abner let her know right away that what was important was not the past but what the future held. She was so taken in by this sincere and gentle man that she even told him about her time spent with Billy John Boscum and how she had grieved those many months and how the anger which she had harbored for so many years had beaten her down.

He also let her know that all of this didn't "Amount to hills or beans" to him. He never managed during his entire life to get his malapropisms, or "out of placers" as he called them, straight.

Another one was "You never want to put all your cats in one sack." That one served a whole host of situations as far as he was concerned. He liked to say that he was too shallow to understand the past and too naive to anticipate the future.

Abners call schedule at the hospital was heavy and consisted mostly of reconstructive surgery and a lot of burn care but he squeezed as much time as possible into Ada's life and getting to know Magnis and me. And that is exactly what he managed to do during 1944.

He had played some football in high school and at C.O.P. was a tail back in a single wing offense which was the rough, mighty and mean system they used before the arrival in 1932 of the most famous Amos Alonzo Stagg who changed everything to that sissy T-formation and on several occasions took Magnis and me to see USC or UCLA play at the Los Angeles Coliseum. I think you could say he really loved the game.

I guess his biggest thrill came one Saturday evening when we all—Abner, Ada, Magnis and me—got into his 1940 four door Chevy and drove over to Hollywood's Gilmore Field and watched Occidental College play College of the Pacific. After the game I found out that Abner actually knew this most famous C.O.P. coach and we got to meet him outside the locker room.

It was during one of those great afternoons that I decided once and for all that what I really absolutely wanted to be for the rest of my life was a football coach and that particular night "bolted the mast to the keel" as Abner put it.

By the fall of 1943 Magnis had decided that he wanted to go to The United States Naval Academy at Annapolis. He was a senior at Stanford Park High School and had very high grades but didn't really know what or how to go about getting accepted at the academy but Commander Abner Plummer Pinkney did and did.

Magnis got a call from the local office of our congressman only a few days before his graduation in the Spring of 1944 and started filling out papers like crazy. Somehow I just couldn't imagine Magnis wearing a sailor suit since to me he still looked like Alfalfa and was still real skinny and at six foot one and size twelve shoes walked like he had one foot nailed to a trash can lid. But boy was he good at math, chemistry and physics.

It was too late for him to be admitted to the United States Naval Academy Class of "48" so somehow in the summer of 1944 it was arranged for him to be enrolled at UCLA for one year in some special ROTC program and he would be transferred to Annapolis in 1945.

Amazing how sometimes things work when you know how things always work isn't it?

Even though so many splendid listings were booked on this stage of life known as the year 1945 the backdrop scenery got caught in the dark wet heaviness of gloom and the bright shining paper moon fell from its apogee over the pinnacle to the stage below to glow no more . I had just turned thirteen and Miss Laura, who in 1944 had been diagnosed with Lou Geherig's disease—amyotrophic lateral sclerosis—died and friends and family gathered silently at her graveside then read aloud, in unison, four words from a printed brief—"We shall miss you." Each laid a single flower on the simple oak casket and retired to his own thoughts.

The simple single flower service had, to everyone's surprise, been spelled out in a letter written by Miss Laura. As declared, Ada would be allowed to add her own simple inscription or lore as long as no reference to any religious persuasions were made.

This maxim struck Ada with such admiration and overdue respect that she scheduled those four clear, intelligible and meaningful words and I knew that her metamorphoses had been completed.

I refused to cry and later that day had another one of those talks with "The big guy" and admonished him for having now in my young life already taken two of my favorite people permanently away from me and I charged him greatly with the responsibility of returning Chancy to my path in life.

I didn't know if Chancy knew but I knew.

I spent the next week spinning "Summertime" from "Porgy and Bess" round and round and round in my mind and whistling the tune. It was the only song I ever heard Miss Laura sing or hum—except for those religious songs. Maybe she just understood the meaning of these gentle words.

THE FIFTH DAY of August 1945 arrived with Uncle Louie, Trixie, Wally and me driving over the "Grape Vine", which was a colloquial name for highway 99, winding its way over the mountains from Los Angeles to all points north.

We were headed toward Yosemite Valley National Park to see what Uncle Louie referred to as "paradise." or "a place Jesus wud'da kept for himself if he'da found it first."

We were pulling a small camping trailer behind his newest magnificent machine which was a 1941 Buick four door sedan with all the accouterments available.

I can attest to the fact that this machine would travel at 60 miles per hour in second gear because he had forgotten to shift and that is how fast we were going when Trixie looked up from her cross-word puzzle in time to see Uncle Louie nod off at the wheel and veer toward the soft shoulder of the highway. I lunged over his thick shoulders and grabbed the steering wheel easing the car back on the road but certainly not under control. Wally anchored my legs and gave me some "Left—No—Right—No Left" advice which was better than Trixie was doing which is to say wailing like a Cantor in a synagogue.

He awoke with the expected start and some here-to-fore

explosive expletive in Italian and slammed on the brakes which threw the Buick into a skid which turned the camping trailer into a magnificent centrifugal configuration reminding me of a carnival tilt-a-whirl and off we went straight as an Argentine bola whirling right down the middle of old North 99 when just as sudden as it had started, the camping trailer decided to become a centripetal force which for what-ever reason straightened us out and we continued north just as big as you please as if nothing had happened and Uncle Louie acted just like he knew what he was doing, stuck in the clutch and dropped the column shift lever into high gear.

We were not destined to make it to Yosemite Valley without at least one more major problem. The problem was the inevitable blown tire when traveling faster than fifty miles per hour for more than 60 miles—or so it seemed. Therefore, somewhere between Tulare and Fresno, the right rear tire went pheeewuu—romp-lugg-lugg—romp—romp—romp and this Wally and I changed while Uncle Louie kibitzed and cussed and damned the lousy tire companies and especially Mussolini who was—it seemed—the cause of everything that could or did go wrong for as long as I could remember—"Holy jumped up Jesus Christ Laurel it's too damned bad they didn't twist one of these lousy tires into a figure of eight like you would do a with a step-over-nose-hold and stretch his rotten neck off his shoulders instead of wasting a good rope. They hung him up by his ankles for a couple of days you know and most of those Ginzos thought his ass was his head and his whizzer was his nose till someone pointed out that his nose wasn't that small. If you ever act as dumb as that son of a bitch Laurel don't ever come around me cause. . . ." as he trailed off walking away with some other inaudible thought probably about Hitler which was not uncommon and since he also had no earthly use for communists it is not unlikely that he uttered something about "that foul putrid little bastard Stalin."

By the time he had gone behind a bush to pee again we were ready to travel and Trixie said "Louie it's a really good thing God only made one of you cause the world just couldn't handle two." "Laurel, you know that if bull shit was music your uncle would be a big brass band but he certainly would play some patriotic tunes."

Uncle Louie just laughed and put that Buick in gear and Wally and I looked at each other and burst into a terrible fit of laughing till our sides hurt and that made us hungry and Trixie gave us each a Bit-O-Honey and an apple. I assured Trixie that I just filed all of his expletives and sage sayings in one of my throwaway boxes and that Wally didn't ever say much about anything that was comprehensive anyway and this convinced her that none of his mannerisms would rub off or go forth. All of them did. I still sprinkle my conversations with his crusty sapient utterances, Wally still doesn't talk much to anyone and indeed, "The Big Guy" did make only one of Uncle Louie.

We got to this incredibly beautiful valley just before sunset and by the time Trixie, Wally and I got the camp site set up—Uncle Louie was totally inept at this sort of thing but was good at what he called schmucking—I have no idea what that means—at Camp Curry right alongside the river. It was dark and I got to build not only the first camp fire I had ever built but the first one I had ever seen.

From somewhere a far away voice yelled "heath cliff" and the echo reverberated across the valley dying as it bounced from the floor of the valley to the gigantic walls only to be quoted from another direction. . . . to be quoted

from another direction. . . . be quoted. . . . direction . . . .
rock formation to. . . . formation. . . . to. . . .

Wally found this manner of communication to his
liking because he was not addressing anyone—just an echo
and I imagine that he uses this as an allegory in his
teachings at his Epistemology coterie even as I write this
tome.

We cooked hot dogs over the fire and drank cold cokes
from those little light green bottles we had placed in the ice
cold Merced River which flowed august no more than ten
feet away and each molecule tripped over another in an
attempt to evade the tiny smooth pebbles obstructing the
pathway to the freedom of the ocean many miles away—
indifferent, apathetic, inattentive to the electrons swarming
around in a frenzied trek to anywhere except where they
were—changing energy levels—not infatuated—not
beholding and like some fickle trifle—without loyalty and
without disclosing or notifying the ephemeral and
temporary nuclear mate of their imminent random dash to
cohabitate with too many new infrastructures to understand
and in a never ending dash to somewhere else—any new
territory—and with the ability to be in a new frenzy with a
new core—or maybe it's all just a spirit—the following day
perhaps as far away as a narrow tributary emptying into the
Japanese Inland Sea after having mated with more masses
in just a few hours than everyone could in every lifetime
count.

We watched the traditional spectacular "fire falls" and
all of us wondered why this custom didn't set the whole
valley on fire since it was such a massive sphere of burning
wood and brush.

It was certainly the largest ball of fire I had ever seen.

While Wally toasted marshmallows for the four of us

Trixie wondered aloud if we, as the only know human race, would ever be able to know how many stars are actually in the milky way and just how long it would take for all of them to burn out.

She said that her gypsy fortune teller friend Mrs Saragova had read in the tea leaves that the world would end in the year 2012 after a rather large and momentous cataclysmic fire—or something similar.

Wally thought something might happen in maybe 50 or 60 years and Uncle Louie said that he didn't believe Mrs Saragova would know "a momentous cataclysmic fire if it jumped up and hit her on the ass with a big bass fiddle." "Make that two bass fiddles cause one wouldn't cover her ass." "An why the need to scare these boys like that Trixie—Hell you almost scared me cause you know I don't sleep well when I got important things like that on my mind."

I told them that I had been reading some really interesting things about atoms and molecules in a physics book and had listened to some scientists on a radio broadcast one night talking about them and we just might indeed be able to blow up the whole world someday but added quickly that maybe by that time we could travel to another world.

Uncle Louie said that he thought "physics" were something you drank when you got constipated . . . and with that Trixie hit him on the forehead with a sticky toasted marshmallow which stuck for a moment and then dropped to the tip of his bulbous nose only to be retrieved by his tongue flicking upward like a frog catching a fly.

We made it into our sleeping bags about 10:00 o'clock and Wally and I talked softly about what the future held for us with Trixie listening intently and Uncle Louie provided

215

his usual cacophonic snores interspersed with spurts of ptew. . . . ptew which seemed to calm the oral pharynx for the moment and prepare for the next earth shaking rattle.

As I posted my knowledge about things and such to Wally I was remembering the words—but not the meanings—of that radio broadcast I had heard one night not long before which originated from Princeton University and was a lecture by a Professor Einstein and the most fascinating thing was his explanation of our then known universe being curved—and—if you would point the most powerful telescope you could imagine in any direction you could see the back of your own head and that had reminded me of the 1931 e.e. cummings poem which starts off "Space being (don't forget to remember) Curved"—and when I recited the whole poem to Wally we had a great laugh and Trixie revealed her pretended sleep by laughing as hysterically as did we.

With such serene bucolic surroundings, who could remember hearing the last echo of "heath cliff" before submitting to blissful sleep.

And who could know that as we rousted ourselves from our sleeping bags with dawns first light that Hiroshima Japan no longer existed and that maybe some of the electrons which had been in this very valley yesterday in their frenzy down the river were involved in this shock wave of history.

I don't remember how we first heard of this news but I guess someone had a radio at the camp headquarters and the word quickly spread around the valley.

Everyone we talked to agreed that this atom bomb only weighed 5 pounds and was the size of a baseball and an absolute perfect sphere which was so highly polished that nothing could stick to it except a thin layer of gold and

Wally was sure that an atom wasn't that big and he was right but couldn't prove it and another kid camped not far away had come over to tell us that if we thought that was a big explosion we should see what would happen if you got an anvil as cold as you could possibly make it and hit it with a hammer which was as hot as you could possibly make it plus making it travel as fast as you could possibly make it go that. . . .

While I was telling him at the same time that if he thought that was something smart "What about being able to destroy a freight train with a bumble bee if you could get that buzzer flying fast enough" but my brilliant statement fell on deaf ears cause the kid was off telling someone else that this Wally guy said that it would have to be a pretty big atom to do as much damage as it did in Japan and it was mainly the gold that blew up but no one knew why gold would explode and when she heard this bit of information Trixie wanted Uncle Louie to put all of her gold jewelry in a box inside the Buick because she certainly didn't want to take a chance that it to would blow up. . . .

And so on throughout the morning everyone had a fabrication and we all knew nothing but we all knew something because. . . . and the "Enola Gay" is still recalled as the plane flown by Colonel Paul Tibbets over Hiroshima but few remember Major Charles Sweeney and Don Albury and Kermit Beahan and John Kuharek and the very noble Captain James Van Pelt of "Bocks's Car" which flew both missions and dropped "The Fat Man", which weighed 10,300 pounds and was over 1,000 pounds heavier than "Little Boy", on Nagasaki and all any of these excellent men really wanted to do was to be in Yosemite Valley skipping small flat rocks over the surface of the Merced River and awaiting sundown when "heath cliff" would again echo throughout the valley and the molecules— having learned a lesson- would now be less anxious to flow so quickly past the pebbles and even the electrons would somewhat moderate their frenzy on the Eighth day of August 1945 and on the Fifteenth day of August the four of us would return to Stanford Park and WWII would be over.

CLYDE HAD BEEN living mostly on nerves for the past year or so seeing FBI and other folks out to get him from behind every tree and wall so it was with great approval when President Truman made his announcement that the conflict had ended and all of our men could soon return to their homes and to private life.

His "trips out of town" had diminished and the net worth of his trusts (not including cash accounts spread about here and there) now exceeded half a million dollars, which included a 1940 Chevrolet 2 door sedan and eight sets of "Dickies" with enough white socks for two weeks wear if he changed every day, a brimmed felt fedora and black shoes. He had splurged and bought a rather handsome fur lined canvas long coat for the coming winter and moved back into one of the several nicer apartment houses which Efrom had advised him to buy in Kansas City.

He looked drawn and had aged considerably—loosing his hair rapidly and lots of his teeth. He claimed he never had a sick day but It's also likely he just couldn't remember all of the hundreds of hangovers. He was suffering greatly with his new found paranoia and would even make some pretense to monitor the adjacent area outside the men's room, hanging around until he was sure that the last donor to enter had indeed exited prior to his entering.

Beryl was still an off and on thing but she didn't seem to mind and they kind of did their thing together apart yet still tied forever by that intangible elusive bond neither talked about.

They mostly continued to fear each other. Beryl occasionally asked him where he got his cash but still didn't really want to know. She continued to scour the newspapers for bank heists and other scurrilous and indecent news wondering if Clyde was involved. Now and again she would intentionally get him sloshed beyond his usual but was never able to extract what she thought was her due. She knew, after all these years, that she could get any material thing she wanted from him. However, her wants and demands never amounted to more than penny ante and she never knew the amount of wealth he had hidden away nor any idea of the extent or worth of the property and trusts. She had some idea about the price he had paid for the farm but probably believed that was the big saucer and continued to work at the TB Hospital doing the best job she could do. She also began to occasionally slug down a patients dose of camphorated tincture of opium commonly known as paregoric which was used as a treatment for diarrhea. Most of the patients were so sick that they didn't know if they were getting paregoric or paradoxical. She didn't even know why she did this and became both contrite and constipated whenever it happened.

Clyde's life—even now—had simply never advanced.

A joint called The Verity had become his favorite haunt. It was located downtown just a couple of blocks from the Muhlbach Hotel and at one time had been pretty fancy dating back to prohibition days. It still had a peep hole in a thick wooden front door which entered into a four by four alcove with a second door made of metal which at one time opened only when a patron had been screened in the alcove. Several side rooms which had been used for gambling in the old days still housed active crap tables.

Knez Tesla—who claimed to be the first cousin of the genius Nikola Tesla—was about 60 years old, owned this establishment and was more than proud of his Serbian heritage. He seemed to always be behind the bar pouring drinks and bellowing profanities in his native language and in general ran things like he ran his life which was the equivalent of a guerrilla attack on an Albanian village.

Knez liked Clyde but the reason why must forever remain a secret since in 1948 a deranged female Turk came into The Verity and after listening to Knez rant the lesson learned at Kossovo Polje—the Field of Black Birds—stabbed him dead with a large stout hat pin through his temple. But that's not really a part of this story.

It is doubtful that Knez even knew Nikola, who had died in 1943, but he knew about his genius and had obviously read of his accomplishments and they were both Serbs and that was enough.

He liked to extol and eulogize Nikola and Clyde was the perfect "review'ie" because—he didn't know much and it's not that he couldn't remember, it was just the fact that there wasn't anything to remember and just agreed and drank.

One day Knez had been knoodling Clyde about how that pig headed Croat-Tito—had screwed up everything sacred and Clyde kept shaking his head like he knew what the hell Knez was talking about when two unsympathetic severe looking substantial size men wearing well fitted

221

suits and the proverbial felt hat came through the doors and took seats—one on each side of Clyde.

"I'm Punch and this here is Judy." said the larger of the two sitting on Clyde's right.

"You're Clyde—right?" "Think about this Clyde—We ain't got no ax ta grind but there are some folks out west who asked us to make a call on you and find out if you could see your way clear to take care of some private business in Los Angeles and since they would do the same thing for us in what you would call reciprocity—we saved them a trip since we're right here anyway an—"

"Hey you—you listen'in to what I'm say' in ?"

"Judy—speak some nice words to this bimmy I don't think he heard a word I said."

Judy grabbed Clyde by the back of his belt and started to gather things up with his fingers and kind of wadded up the seat of his Dickies in his huge right hand while lifting him straight up from the bar stool and it was pretty tight between his shorts and his testicles right away—like a one handed bums rush that didn't go anywhere but upwards. Then he bounced him a couple of times and it was all Clyde could do to get his breath.

Knez had come over and acted like he was going to say something when Punch made a "shuss" like noise from his puckered lips and said "This is Ginzo stuff little Serbo man—don't push your luck." and Knez understood all too well and found some glasses to wipe with the bar rag.

Judy was straightening out Clyde's back side with his hand like he was dusting him off when Punch said "Clyde—or what the hell ever your name is now— anyway—you got an invitation to a party from someone who might be named Louie—capish ? The party is gon'na be in Los Angeles one week from today and don't be late or we might have to come back here and talk big time—call this number the minute you get there—understand ?" and he handed Clyde a piece of paper with a phone number as the two of them got up and walked out like nothing had happened.

"Clyde" Knez said "Here it is 1946—a beautiful February day with the fruit trees getting ready to pop their leaves—fishing down in the Ozarks the best in the world—you got no reason to go to California that I can think of and besides that you don't seem to listen to a thing I say to you—Hell Clyde sometimes I think you don't have no brains at all—you could qualify as a Croat or worse yet an Albanian or even more worse yet a Turk."

"How come you never got married Clyde?" "You're not married to that Beryl lady who comes in here sometimes are you?" "She never seems to come around unless you'r here and don't say much of anything even then." "You know her a longtime Clyde?
Seems like it to me that you always fight—that right ?" "Is that what that was all about?"

"Knev—y'all know what bigamy means?"

"Sure I know what bigamy means—you think I'm stupid?"

"Well, what's it mean—I mean what's it amount to ?" "Efrom explained it ta me but I didn't understand cept I told him I did an then he asked me why I needed to know an then I figert he was gett'in to nosy so I clammed up."

"Well if you have never been married how in hell can you be a bigamist Clyde?"

"Well I have but I havn't I guess." "Oh crap, maybe it ain't bigamy, maybe it's somethin else I don't rightly know what it is—it's just too complicated I guess so I better get my ass out ta California."

He actually went out and bought a cheap double breasted grey wool suit, four white shirts and a neck tie which had palm trees printed on it, a cheap suitcase, gathered up some of his personal papers and left on the AT&SF two days later.

It was a 44 hour trip on the Santa Fe Chief from Kansas City to Los Angeles and typical of Clyde he went coach. God, he was indubitably (that's one of the words I spent months learning to pronounce when I was ten) without class. I bet he passed that same crossing outside of some tiny burg in Arizona that Magnus and I saw on our trip out west. The sign said: "It takes the Santa Fe Chief about 12 seconds to pass this crossing—whether you are on the tracks or not"

When he arrived at Los Angeles Union Station and found a hotel room he called the number on the paper and found it to be an attorney's office—a Mr Mario Montana in Hollywood.

After a short wait a friendly male voice introduced himself and indicated that he was expecting his call. He told Clyde that the matter at hand was being solicited by Mr Louie Benuto and was relative to an unattended, longstanding and abandoned matter only he, Clyde, could conclude.

"I will inform Mr Benuto that you have arrived in Los Angeles and have been in contact with me. That will satisfy the very first part of my clients desires, or demands as you please."

"You know Mr Dodge—it would have been much easier had you responded to the four letters we sent you over the past several months—if so perhaps these next few days could have been avoided. But indeed, that's how I make my living."

224

"Oh by the way, do you have legal representation here in California?" "Mr Efrom E. Lebowitz, Esq., cannot represent you here you know—he is not licensed before the bar in this state."

"And one more thing Clyde don't try to leave this state without checking with me, or you will be detained and I do not mean by the police. Do you understand?" "The food at the Main Street Hotel where you checked in will probably be just great for you." "Sit tight until you hear from me tomorrow morning."

He hung up and Clyde was still holding the phone as he wondered how the hell this stranger knew where he was staying—about Efrom Lebowitz—and what kind of food he might enjoy.

The next morning at 8:00 sharp the phone rang and Clyde recognized Mario Montana's voice. "Good morning Clyde—trust you slept well and have finished breakfast—got a pencil?"

"Write down these instructions." "I will go very slowly so as not to tax your synapses."

"My what?" said Clyde

"Never mind—be here at 11:00 o'clock this morning—take a cab to my office—northwest corner of Hollywood and Vine—second floor—Montana and Meyer Law Offices—should take you about 30 minutes and if you have hired a lawyer you better bring him with you. "Do you understand Clyde?"

"Well, you just hold on a second, let me ask you some questions there Mr Montana—what makes you think I'm gon'na stand fer treatment like this?" "You got no cause ta order me around like this—I reckon I got rights ya know—just mess with me an I'll call tha police—y'all better be careful—that Louie don't mean much to me anyways—I can take care of that big shit like nothin you ever seen."

But before he could go on Mr Montana cut him off saying: "For starters, draft dodgers have very few rights Clyde—or should I call you Mr Lubeck?" "See you in a couple of hours." and the line went dead.

At 10:15 Clyde pushed open the door of the hotel, stepped outside into the wind and cursed himself for forgetting to bring the new coat with him.

5th and Main downtown Los Angeles was one of the most sordid crossroads in America that February 1946 and something we would later label a jet stream was pulling cold air out of the Arctic ice masses and passing it through Southern California. The smudge pots out in the orange belt were polluting away and the cold air stung the skin.

He had to go back inside the shabby lobby to phone for a cab. There was no queue of cabs since folks staying at The Main Street Hotel didn't often need them and cabbies even when called asked to see the color of the money before hauling anyone anyplace.

The cabbie pulled away from the curb, headed over to Broadway and turned north until he came to what should have still been Brooklyn Avenue but which had already died, in name only, for some unknown reason—and had become Macy Street—turned left—and after passing under Hill Street through a tunnel Macy Street is reincarnated as Sunset Boulevard—God, Los Angeles was complex and Clyde was as confused as usual. It was, however, a pleasant drive along the south-eastern part of this getting to be so famous boulevard and in less than 30 minutes—just as Mr Montana had said—the driver turned right on Vine Street to the already famous Hollywood Boulevard and came to a stop.

The cabbie charged Clyde twice the normal fare using

some excuse about zones and doubles and something about having to get back to Main Street.

Clyde protested but gave up when a policeman on a black and white Indian motorcycle pulled up and told the cabbie to move on because they were shooting a movie scene and everyone had to clear the street.

Montana and Meyer was on the second floor. The hallways were mahogany paneled half way up the walls. The door to the office was massive and also of mahogany with simply the names Montana & Meyer stamped in brass for identification.

Clyde knocked and then entered into a very beautifully decorated outer office. All of the chairs were maroon leather, the tables and large receptionist desk were of very fine walnut and from behind the desk stepped a very pleasant looking well dressed young man.

"You must be Mr Montana." said Clyde and in quick bursts—"Glad ta meet with ya." "I didn't have no trouble finding this place"—"cab driver knowed just where to look"—"did you know they's makin some movie right outside yer place on the street?"—"Right nice place ya got here"—"Don't suppose ya got ah bathroom here where ah man can empty his bladder do ya?"

"Of course Mr Dodge just follow and I will show you the gentlemen's room." said the young man "And, I am not Mr Montana, I am the front receptionist—Mr Montana will be with you shortly after you satisfy your needs."

It was only then that Clyde realized how powerfully this young man was built and how serious the grey-steel eyes were which seemed to be dual searchlights moving and ever aware above the slightly bent nose and the fixed smile of his lips.

As soon as Clyde returned from the "gentlemen's

quarters" the receptionist led him through a door to another well appointed room which had five very busy, well endowed, lovely ladies setting at desks doing lawyer things—at least that's what Clyde thought them to be doing.

The redhead at the middle desk stood up and appeared to be almost as tall as Clyde and led him into yet another office where he was invited to have a seat by yet another very attractive mature lady who introduced herself as Mr Montana's assistant and assured him that the other parties were already with Mr Montana and that if he would take a seat he would be invited to join them shortly.

Clyde sat down and as he crossed his right leg over the left at the knee his white cotton socks glared back at the room over the lopsided tongues of his black low top mechanic brogans—the right shoelace revealed a knot—acknowledging the fact that it had outlived its time and had been pieced back together right at the second eyelet.

A buzzer buzzed and the lady picked up a phone—spoke quietly for a moment—replaced the receiver and invited Clyde "Right through here Mr Dodge."

She opened the door for him and said to those inside: "This is Mr Clyde Dodge, Mr Montana. Is there anything I can get for any of you folks?"

Clyde entered the door to be greeted by a gentleman who was six foot two, wide shoulders, large chest, sporting a black fuzzy neatly trimmed mustache and salt and pepper long wavy hair without a part. He was wearing a black silk suit, a white silk shirt with a black silk tie, black patent leather loafers and looked like he controlled at least something big.

"Good morning Mr Dodge—thanks for coming on such short notice—I am Mario Montana and am so happy that it was not necessary to be unpleasant."

"I believe you know everyone here." he said as first Uncle Louie came into the room, from an open alcove, followed by Trixie and then for the first time in almost fifteen years he gazed at Ada and the emotion of it kept him speechless as she led a man in a naval officers uniform through the door and the circle around him was complete.

"Oh! That's right, you don't know Commander Abner Plummer Pinkney, Medical Doctor, United States Naval Medical Corp."

Clyde at first thought that Abner, being a medical doctor, somehow had something to do with his amnesia stunt and he immediately said "About that amanesia thing, doctor, I never really had that, I only told some folks that I did so's I could get out'en that county jail but it didn't mean nothin." "An—an . . ."

As Trixie overrode him with "For Christ's sake Charlie shut up and sit down you self centered stupid bastard."

"Okay—easy" said Mr Montana "everyone sit down and let me lay out the information as believed to be true. This is not a deposition nor even a legal proceeding, as you can see, no stenographer is present and we will just talk things out as they come up." "Fair enough everyone?"

"Let me start up Mr Dodge—Lubeck by saying that Mr Benuto—whom you know—and if we were on record I would point out that he is indeed your brother-in-law by marriage—is that not correct Mr Dodge—Lubeck?" "As I started to say Mr Benuto is paying all of the fees for this mornings meeting so you don't have to worry about a thing."

"If I have the story straight—feel free to correct me any time you wish—I think I will just call you Charlie—it is Charlie and not Charles—right?"

229

"Well Charlie, as I understand it, you married Ada Slewter in 1926 and abandoned her as Mrs Ada Lubeck around Christmas time 1931 and had already abandoned her multiple times in between—is that fairly accurate Charlie?" "And, in addition, you left her with two boy children—one yet unborn at the time of abandonment and during the terrible depression times—to fend for herself and without proof, you have failed even until the present time to support her in any fashion and I find that appalling and believe any judge and any jury in the country would feel the same." "What can you say thus far?"

"Moving on—the matter before us today is very simple—Ada is terribly in love with Commander Pinkney here and wants to marry him so that he can adopt those boys and give them all something you never even considered—that is to say to be a husband and a father." "Only one thing stands in the way Charlie—and that is you." Louie and I go way back Charlie and I'm not so sure that his idea about how this should be settled shouldn't be seriously considered but we—being the civilized and good people we are—will not bring such a thought back to the table. Okay Charlie?" "Okay Louie?"

"Now Charlie as you can see, I am a very simple man living in a simple fashion and wishing to keep all dealings as simple as am I. Therefore, I have taken the liberty to draw up a divorce settlement which will be adjudicated in Nevada—where I am also allowed to go before the bar—not a gin mill bar Charlie—and which will be final six weeks from the time of you signing."

"So far so good Charlie?"

Clyde was too stupefied by this time to remember if his name was Charlie or Clyde or Charlie Clyde Lubeck or Clyde C. Dodge or just who the hell he was. He did, however, know that he might be in big trouble in a very short while because he, for certain, couldn't sign any divorce papers without talking to Efrom.

"My heads ah twist' in with all them words an I sure could use some aspirin." "I cain't rightfully say that what you say is wrong so I need ta call Efrom Lebowitz who is ah lawyer friend back home—do ya mind?"

"Just go right into that ante-room and pick up the phone and my assistant will connect you—she already knows the number."

When Clyde reached the number in Kansas City he was startled to hear a strange voice answering Efrom's phone— "Who is this?" Clyde asked.

"This is the ambulance driver—who are you and what do you want and if its something important like a bail bond or something you better find yourself some other mouthpiece cause this one just had a heart attack and died right here at his desk and we are taking his body to the morgue."

Clyde sat back in the chair—stunned for at least the fifth time and it wasn't even noon and he hadn't even had a drink. He simply didn't know what he should do but he certainly knew what he shouldn't do and that was to agree to sign his name on any paper that would eventually make it's way back east or for that matter even from this office.

He sat for what seemed too long and looked up to see Mr Montana open the door and ask "Are you okay Charlie?" "Can I get you something—you look like you just saw a ghost."

"No, I'm okay." said Clyde. "I jest need me ah drank ah water if y'all don't mind."

Mr Montana's assistant suddenly appeared with a glass of water and a cup of coffee which Clyde recognized immediately as being loaded with liquor of some sort. It was actually Courvoisier VSOP Cognac.

Clyde drank the water and carried the cup in one hand and the saucer in the other and for the first time faced and addressed the others in the room. It was as if he suddenly realized that he wasn't in the cat bird seat and that he had no place to run and something Knez had muttered recently about when you get in the water you got'ta swim with the ducks and it also dawned on him that he had never learned to swim.

"Ada—what is it you'r want' in me ta say?" "I'm pert near tha end ah tha rope an y'all can keep on makin sport with me but it don't change nothin an it cain't change nothin so come on back home with me an I'll make it right with ya—ya know that don't ya Ada?"

With that Ada spoke for the first time her voice barely above a whisper "Charlie Clyde Lubeck you are at least the most bumptious, miserable, pathetic, pitiful, deplorable, paltry, flawed, inferior mediocre misfit God ever created and why I didn't kill your futile, stupid, pointless backward ass almost fifteen years ago with that stick—and let me tell you, it still worries me and I do reparation for it often—the wrong being that I failed in fact to carry out the deed -you misologic bastard."

Uncle Louie got out of his chair and stood between Ada and Clyde and Mr Montana started to say something from where he was leaning on the edge of his desk when Trixie spoke first. "Charlie if you have ever completed a thought in your head I hope that you can follow what is going on. No one here at this time and place wish to ever see or give a second thought to anything which might be even slightly connected with you and let me assure you that Mr Montana is going to bring the wrath of God and all which that might entail right down on top of you. Ada and the gentleman you have until now ignored plan on getting married in four months and that will be exactly two and one-half months after the divorce and those boys are going to have a father and a mother and a life you can't seem to fathom—whether you are standing on the tracks or not. Do you get it Clyde?"

Abner suddenly stood up and without a word lifted Ada from her chair and headed her toward the door as she sobbed and clinched her fists and all two hundred ten pounds of him turned suddenly on his good leg and hit Clyde right on his nose with his size nine fist knocking him flat.

Uncle Louie said "Now you saw me hit him—now didn't you Mario?" and with that they all walked out.

Mr Montana walked over to his desk, lifted a pitcher of water and poured some over Clyde's head which brought him up with a start and a very sore mouth and nose.

On the way to a doctors office in a beautiful 1941 Cadillac Clyde said the first reasonable thing he had said in a long time "Mr Montana—when I sign them papers do they stay in Nevada or here in California an do they go any whur else?" "I mean do they git printed in other states?"

"Oh! You mean like in Missouri for instance?"

"Yea. In Missouri"

"Well Clyde that depends on how cooperative you continue to be. Today can be the end or the beginning—it is up to you—I am also a member of the bar in Missouri."

"Tell me somethin Mr Montana—you suppose y'all can make do fer me ta see those boys ah mine?" "That's what I really would be proud ta do. Ada of course won't never see fit ta allow it I suppose?"

"I can ask but not guarantee—do you know or really care anything about those boys?"

233

"Don't guess I ever thought much about it" blushed Clyde.

"The older boy Magnis is already successful you know—he is in his second year at the United States Naval Academy at Annapolis and in the top ten percent of his class." "Do you have any idea what that means Clyde?"

"Don't reckon I do." said Clyde

"Well, it means that he is just one hell of a bright young man and the younger one, Laurel, is even brighter, no one knows how intelligent he is as of yet." "Lets talk about you Clyde—I have authority to talk to you about anything you wish to talk about—the whole concern is that Ada can't marry Doctor Pinkney until you are dead, which would make her a widow, or until a divorce is final. Understand so far?"

"Yea."

"I have it worked out in my mind that you have something more than abandonment to be ashamed of in the past and can't go through with a divorce for fear it will dredge up what ever it is from the bottom of the swamp." "Am I close?"

"Maybe."

"What did your lawyer in K.C. say when you talked to him?"

"He died from ah heart attack jest afore I called. He probably couldn't help anyway cause he ain't knowed me that long." "Listen—if y'all can guarantee me noth'in goes beyond California or Nevada I might be will'in ta sign fer anything so long as it don't cost any money since I ain't got none much ta speak of." "An one more thang—I jest might like ta see that younger boy while I'm here in California—What did y'all say his name was?" "An one more thang—I ain't right sure he belongs ta me but I won't fight it." "Can

234

y'all guarantee me that?"

"You will of course need to make your own peace with Magnis since he is on the east coast and can pretty well speak his own mind but I believe I can make arrangements for you to spend a little time with Laurel if the lad agrees."

"Well here we are at the doctors office Clyde I'll go with you and make arrangements for his services—nothing out of pockct for you—you understand—and one more thing Clyde—my advice to you is not to cross swords with Louie Benuto ever again—he has lots of money but even longer arms—capish?" "I'll contact you tomorrow if I'm able to make arrangements for your meeting but this will take place only after you sign the necessary papers." "Blackmail ?" "Probably but who wants to contest it . Right?"

UNCLE LOUIE LOADED everyone into his car, found Vine Street, turned left on Sunset Boulevard, which somehow becomes Brooklyn Avenue, continued on until he passed Soto Street in East L.A. and found Kanter's Deli where they served the best pastrami and corned beef sandwiches in the world—and so it was.

Abner had never been to Kanter's so Ada ordered for him and introduced him to pickled hard boiled eggs. The conversation had been underway in the car and continued over the lunch and cheese cake.

"Can Mr Montana pull it off Louie?" "Charlie is dumb but sly like a weasel and can lie and connive and cry and he had the nerve to think that I might hold any feeling for him besides contempt which he is beneath." Ada conveyed.

"Easy now Ada." said Abner. "Besides my doing that dumb thing I did I believe everything went well." "I think Charlie will see his way clear to giving his approval. He doesn't have much ground to stand on from what Mr Montana says and I have no reason to believe he will want to stay any place close to L.A." "I certainly am happy I didn't break my hand—I haven't done anything dumb like that since high school days. It did feel pretty good though."

"Think you could use me in the ring Louie?"

Trixie filled in with "I been wanting to do just that very thing for longer than you could believe Abner and was thinking about it just when you stole my thunder." "I wonder why he didn't have some curiosity about the boys—I just can't imagine how anyone can be so detached and remote—oh! Hell Ada I shouldn't be running my mouth at a time like this—what if he wants to see Laurel ?"

Ada responded "Laurel can handle it okay—the little fart is smarter than all of us—well, excepting Abner here." "And besides, he just seems to take everything in stride, thinks about it and goes on doing what it is that he is doing." "Never seems to get rattled that kid—what do you think Abner?"

"Well" said Abner "I believe you are right. I think Laurel will just soak it all up and see right through any bull shit Charlie can come up with. I have run some pretty heavy situations which require logic and judgment past that kid and he is super on the uptake. I think he could twist Charlie any way he likes if necessary but I don't see him doing or saying anything mean or vindictive. He has simply accepted everything over the years in that pragmatic way he has. Not to worry." "Ada—I have to tell you, you are one special lady and how you raised those two to be what they are is remarkable." "Louie—thanks for everything you have been and all the support you and Trixie have given— Oh hell—here I am talking like I have a family claim or prerogative and I don't yet." "I guess I'm trying to protect what seems like the best thing that has happened to me."

Uncle Louie paid the bill and they headed south on Soto Street.

I got home from school just as they drove up and wondered where they had been and why they were dressed

237

up and Abner wanted to know what happened at school and to tell him the absolute truth about how things were going.

I was thirteen and some change, as Uncle Louie would call it, and second semester freshman in high school having more fun than I ever thought possible. I weighed 121 pounds and could stretch to five foot five inches and was the littlest and youngest kid in Stanford Park High. I had already played on the "Bee" football team but was more of a mascot than anything. I never broke any of my parts which was proclaimed a miracle by the coach. I had memorized every assignment of every position for every play in our book and the coach would occasionally ask: "Laurel—what's the right guard supposed to be doing on the last play?" "He didn't do it did he?" "When he comes out next time straighten him out OK?"

We had orange painted leather helmets which looked like something Jim Thorpe had used and more closely resembled pumpkins which had spent too long in the sun. I guess we didn't even know what a face mask was. Andy and Ernie were both playing first string. Andy was the left end and Ernie the right tackle. We played a single wing formation and there was no such thing as offensive and defensive units. You did it all. That is except for me. I was, believe it or not, the punter. Yea! I could actually punt that ball high enough to bring rain and far enough to be effective. It was all in the timing. I could put it out of bounds wherever the coach wanted it out.

I was gon'na try out for the track team later in the spring but didn't have any idea about what event I might like, except the shot put and had been at the library reading about track and field.

The next afternoon Ada and Trixie were having coffee at the breakfast table and I grabbed a piece of cheese from a plate when all of a sudden Trixie said that if it was okay with me that my father would be by to meet me in about an hour.

"Holy jumped up Jesus Christ." were the first words out of my mouth and which blew Abners prediction all to hell. "My father ?" "My what?"

Ada tried to control herself saying as evenly as possible "Laurel Hardy Lubeck since when are you allowed to talk like that—you sound more like your Uncle Louie every day and you apologize right this minute do you hear me?

I heard her but didn't know to whom I should apologize since Jesus wasn't present to hear it and Ada and Trixie had heard it at least two thousand times over the years but I managed to mutter "Well- I apologize Jesus. I'll try not to say that anymore." and started to follow up with "But I'll probably think it somewhere along the way." but thought better of it.

"I thought he was dead or something. Not Jesus—my father." "I told all my friends he died in the war. How come I have to see him now?"- I don't even know what he looks like—he never even ever wrote me a letter or anything—Miss Laura told me he was probably in Timbuktu and that's in West Africa—and Magnis told me he wasn't much and you never told me anything." "How long do I have to see him?" "I like Abner—is something wrong with Abner?" "I need to talk to Uncle Louie first."—and for the first time in a number of years I couldn't make a decision or figure what my next move would be—all I could think about was how this would affect what I had come to know as happiness and stability—"Why now ?" "Miss Laura told me that grown ups have a way of making wrong rules, laws and decisions and then when they don't work they try to cover things up and not tell the truth—she told me about a man named William Graham Sumner—he wrote things about sociology and one time said 'if a man is doing a good job of taking care of his own business he necessarily won't have time to take care of anyone else's business because minding one's own business is a full time job'—is he—my father—tending to a full time job ?"

"I don't know Laurel." whispered Ada sadly as she held me by my arms and looked me right in the eyes. "I don't want to influence you in any way Laurel. I want you to first understand that if you don't want to see him it will be perfectly okay and it won't happen."

Trixie joined in "I wouldn't blame you a bit if you refused Laurel and I know for sure your Uncle Louie wouldn't either."

Ada took over again "Talking with him will have no bearing on how our lives will continue to play out—he is here because he has to sign some papers so Abner and I can get married—I believe that would please you—but also know that your response will have no bearing on this." "You can make up your own mind after you meet as to whether you choose to have any relationship in the future— I can't be with you during this meeting because I am afraid I cannot maintain any objectivity relative to the whole matter and that wouldn't be good so Trixie and Uncle Louie will be with you so you know you will be safe" "Uncle Louie is coming in the driveway right now."

As Uncle Louie drove up a taxi pulled in behind him and as Ada hugged me I saw the reason she couldn't stay— running down her cheeks. She dashed out the back door and walked to the park—I guessed.

Uncle Louie walked Clyde to the door, told him to wait on the porch and came into the room and asked me how I felt about things so far. "I'll run him off right now if you want me to—and any time you say—even after we let him in the door. What say Laurel?"

"You know Uncle Louie—I'll bet he doesn't even know what a step-over-nose-hold is give you ten to one—deal?"

"Deal" said Uncle Louie and with that he opened the door and in walked the antithesis of victory, triumph or achievement. A regrettable excuse. A woody Guthrie—riding the rails through Oklahoma during the dust bowl—look alike. He had obviously had a bad night someplace and slept in his suit but at least had attempted to shave.

Hamartia—an error in development due to imperfect tissue combination—I had been reading the Tabers Medical Dictionary Abner had given to me—first came to mind.

"Well I swear—y'all must be Laurel." he said as he walked across the room toward me.

I said nothing—my composure had already drifted but I regained it and didn't respond with the flippant remark I had cooked up. I looked at Trixie and she said she thought she might go in the kitchen and make some coffee. Uncle Louie followed close behind and there I was alone with the flora of the seed of my existence and it sent shudders down my back.

"Here—I brung you this from Alyvaro Street—thought ya might jest like it." and he handed me a two inch long painted plaster figurine of a Mexican man with a yellow sombrero leading a grey burro—relief on the front and flat on the back and both ends—about one inch high—"That sure is some place ta go alright—they got a donkey whur y'all can climb up an get yer pitcher took wear'in a hat jest like that feller there is wear'in." pointing to the figurine. "I once owned some ponies at ah park an hired em out fer rides an done right nice as fur as money goes but ah got

241

tired do'in it an sold em ta this feller an ah guess he's ah still ah do'in it—makin money that is."

I got my first whiff of booze about the same time I smelled the bay rum after shave and the rancid odor of butyric acid being released from his shoes and couldn't decide which was the most offensive and when he acted like he wanted to come closer I retracted to the arm of an overstuffed chair and sat down.

"Why don't you have a seat over there—I believe Aunt Trixie is going to serve something pretty soon. Maybe you need to use the rest room or something?" "Maybe you need to tell me something about you—I don't even know your name really—Why do you need so many names?" "Did you get wounded in the war? Abner was wounded you know—had a carrier shot out from under him at the Coral Sea Battle—did you go to the Pacific or to Europe?"

"Y'all sure can ask questions fast enough—I cain't run em through my head cept one at ah time—now I never had no chance at go'in ta school like y'all did—we was mighty poor an had ta walk pert near ah mile ta school—didn't have nothin fancy. . . . but y'all couldn't understand be'in poor or nothin like that I reckon—gol dang it I never went ta thu army—I wus older than tha age limit ya understand—never had ta go . . . never needed ta go . . . "Clyde was staring off into space rubbing his fingers across his lips from side to side and slowly sat down in a straight chair as if in deep thought and then pulled the flaps of the coat pockets up and tried to put his hands in the coat pockets several times but couldn't because he hadn't taken the thread out which closed the pockets. Even today I don't know why they sew those pockets.

"I didn't mean to be impertinent or disrespectful sir— it's just that I don't know anything about you. I always thought of Uncle Louie as my father figure—he has really been good to me you know—he has really been good to all of us—without him I'm not sure we could have made it—and now we have Abner and I really love him and it seems to me that you are going to take it all away—and what is it that I couldn't understand about not having anything fancy or being poor?" I said very quietly.

"Now just a durn minute" said Clyde "Who said anythin bout takin away?" "I never said that. I ain't here ta take nothin away I'm here ta strait'in thangs out—ya see." "Ah jest needed ta strait'in thangs out—so ah come here ta California ta have my say so—jest strait'in thangs out."

"What is it that needs straightening out—I don't even know what to call you"

"Ya'll can call me daddy—that wud be real nice." Clyde gushed in.

"I'm gon'na have a hard time with that one sir—how about if I call you Mr Lubeck?" I sounded him out.

"How did y'all know about that name—yor mom been tell'in thangs bout me?"

"Great Scott Mr Lubeck my name is Laurel Hardy Lubeck and my mother has been married only once—to you I might add—so wouldn't you expect that my fathers name would be Lubeck? And my Mom has never even said one word for or against you that I have ever heard" "Magnis apparently had the same occurrence and circumstance but you will need to ask him just to satisfy your interrogative."

"Whur did y'all get them big words from—sounds ta me like yur getten sassy—are ya?"

"No sir—it's just the way I talk—I apologize if you were offended. I read a lot and things just seem to come easy."

"I thought y'all might ah had ah easy time of it." Clyde determined as he let out a great sigh.

"Well now—ah estimate thet y'all know I'm ah big shot—worked hard dur'in tha war—y'all recollect thet I was too old fer tha draft don't ya—well I met this feller an we pert near solved some big problems tha army had with airplane fuel tanks an got thangs ah go'in our way an ended up with ah great big wad ah money an then my lawyer wrote up these here Business Trust thangs an we put all that money in ta them an bought up apartment places an thangs all on account ah jest be'in able ta thank at tha right time." "Y'all able ta foller me okay youngster?"

"Would those be Massachusetts Trusts sir?" I asked surprised at what I had just heard.

"Ah reckon that's right—ah got so many thangs ah goin—cain't keep track—here, take ah look see at this here—it's ah certificate show'in some right important stuff." Clyde said as he pulled a paper from an envelope he had taken from his inside coat pocket and handed it over to me.

"Ah know it's a might complex fer someone young as y'all but when y'all grow up maybe business might jest mean more ta ya." he said as I scanned the embossed sheet once down and once up front and back before he pulled it away from me. "This here's tha key ta everthang ah been successful at." "Lot's ah hard work—yes sir."

I had become more relaxed now and realized that this was a more uncomfortable situation for him than for me as I asked him "Mr Lubeck would you like some coffee?" and as if by cue Trixie came in with a tray which held two cups of coffee and a bottle of Royal Crown Cola.

"Charlie—do you take your coffee black?" she asked. "Louie and Ada took off on a walk and will be back in a few minutes—have you had a good talk Laurel?" "He hasn't been rude has he Charlie?"

"No—we jest hit it off spankin clean—wish't I could'a done more than ah already done fer tha boy Trixie . . ."

But Trixie cut him off with "Spare us that Charlie— Louie said to tell you that Mr Montana will expect to hear from you by nine o'clock in the morning and that all the papers are ready for your signature and you will be free to go back to where ever—Ada doesn't want to say goodbye and I think you need to drink this coffee and I already called a cab—here it is now so drink up good old Charlie and bon voyage, farewell, aloha, arrivederci, auf wiedersehen, shalom and goodbye—if Laurel Hardy Lubeck decides someday to contact you he will—and if he does, it will be the most sensible thing that has ever happened to you—but don't hold your breath—fourteen years is a long time."

I had, by this time, taken my Royal Crown Cola and headed for the back yard and with that the Big Guy had opened and closed one more door in my life and I sat under the apricot tree singing Inka Dinka Doo and wondering how Jimmy Durante would behave in the same circumstance.

LATER ON IN 1946 Ada married Abner Plummer Pinkney and Magnis got to come home for the wedding. Abner was still in the navy and they had a military service in the chapel at the Naval Hospital. I thought it was the best and was surprised at how many friends attended. It wasn't lavish but it was fun.

Abner had decided that he would still be needed at the hospital for probably another year and was promoted to Captain. He was now the senior surgeon in a brand new field of reconstructive surgery and had been promised a teaching position at U.S.C. Medical School at anytime he decided to leave the navy and become a civilian.

None of this changed my life much except to say that I was a happy fella. We moved into a larger home on the other side of town but I still hung around with Wally, Andy,Ernie and Kip at school. Still talked thing over with Brenda fairly often and got put back on track.

Abner had long hours in surgery but managed to find time for his new family. He got me more and more interested in science and football. Ada took a job at the Mission Hospital learning office things and billing. She didn't want to throw the whole financial load on to Abner and he didn't protest. They were saving for a home and liked the Pasadena area but it was decided that we would stay in Stanford Park until I graduated from high school.

In June of 1948 Magnis graduated from The U. S. Naval Academy at Annapolis and we all gathered for the ceremony.

Trixie and Uncle Louie went to Pittsburgh on the way and Trixie got to see for the first time where Uncle Louie had grown up after his mother brought him to the States. She met some of his old buddies and heard them swap wild stories about who was the poorest, who was the toughest and who did what to whom. All those years gone by and they talked just like it was last week and the first liar didn't have a chance.

They arrived in Annapolis the same day as did Abner, Ada and I.

We took the train from L.A. to Baltimore and planned to visit D.C. after the graduation. And I was elated about going to the Smithsonian.

Magnis was in the top ten, got an award for playing with himself or something like that and the speeches bored me and I reverted to spit bubbles and mind games to pass the time and then began to snicker to my self thinking about why a navel orange is called a navel orange and then imagined a very small pit in a naval battleship enclosing a very small secondary battleship.

Abner leaned over and told me that we were hearing and seeing very serious stuff so I settled down and memorized the entire graduation program including the names of all 910 graduating midshipmen.

When they all threw their hats in the air my worry was how Magnis would retrieve his or if not had they all developed the same head size in which case it didn't matter except for cooties.

I made a mental note to ask Magnis about cooties.

Magnis got to come home on leave for a whole month and was then assigned to duty on board the USS Fred T. Berry (DD858) in the fire control division—the newest of the new and the lowest of the low—he was Mister Magnis Lubeck, Ensign, United States Navy.

Magnis floated around on the Berry for the next two years and for reasons unknown was transferred to a graduate doctorate program at Princeton where three years later he earned his PhD in Physics. He liked radar stuff a lot and wrote his thesis on some type of fire control guidance system which automatically aimed guns.

In 1949 I graduated from Stanford Park High still the youngest in my class but at least not the smallest. There were some girls who were shorter. I wouldn't be 17 until September and Abner had convinced me that I needed to go to UCLA and at least think about doing premed. I had been readily accepted and Uncle Louie had made all of the arrangements for financing this project.

I had been working at the arena and saved a few hundred dollars and in 1948 bought a tiny 1939 two passenger Bantam Roadster which was made someplace in Indiana and by then totally obsolete. It was great fun and got about 50 miles per gallon. The big problem was that my friends had realized that four or five of them could lift "The Rooster" and carry it places where it could not be driven— in or out. I learned to try to hide it when going to the movies because many times late at night I would find it sitting on the rear bumper leaned upward against a telephone pole or wedged between two other cars with zero clearance and on several occasions they carried it up the outside stairs of the school auditorium, turned it sideways to slip it through the Grecian pillars and deposited it in the alcove.

The radio disc jockeys had their hands full trying to keep all of the great renditions balanced—a brand new guy named Tony Bennett did his premier "Because of You" which had been in repose and going no place since its inception by Arthur Hammerstein and Dudley Wilkinson in 1940. I never seemed to get enough of Stan Kenton and sometime that year I saw this preeminent movie called "Words And Music" which was a biography of Richard Rodgers and Lorenz Hart—and featured just about everyone in show business who could sing or even pretend to sing—Lena Horne did "Where or When" and I fell for her. Frankie Layne had so many hits no one could keep track and these were arousing times.

I escorted CoCo to the senior prom. She was about five—eleven without shoes and I stretched five—seven with. I had been having a lot of fun over the past few months dating a cute gal named Georgie but something happened and she backed out and decided to go someplace else and I wasn't gon'na go but the guys set me up with CoCo and she was all thrilled because few ever asked her out since she was so tall and I was awed and scared and besides that didn't have the heart or the nerve to refuse.

Actually we had a great time and she didn't mind that I was a dancing klutz. She really was noticeable—a Rita Hayworth type face except for a very prominent nose, had a great body which she managed to hide while at school and which remained a secret from me for several years when one day I saw her pumping iron at "muscle beach" with some six foot four giant muscle bound bonzo—she had had a nose job and was gorgeous.

Abner, had now been discharged from the Navy and was teaching surgery at USC. They were buying a home in

Pasadena and off I went to Westwood leaving Stanford Park forever.

Uncle Louie decided to sell out his wrestling, boxing and other businesses and Trixie wanted to live close to San Luis Obispo so they bought 600 acres in the hills overlooking Pismo Beach because some underground gambling still existed at this quaint little sea side town and he still loved his card games and clam chowder. They never managed to build a home on the range because someone found oil and the whole area went bonkers and they of course profited enormously and then decided to settle down in San Luis Obispo and built a beautiful home.

Summer of 1950 and normalcy skidded off the road. I don't believe anyone alive then or now can explain what or why, but the Korean communists careened south from their northern enclave and comported themselves with such blunt, simple-minded, obtuse, dull witted behavior so as to cause others to strike them critically—causing dismemberment from which they still may never ever recover.

But, this story isn't about that terrible mostly forgotten "Police Action" . It is, however, about people and their lives—and deaths—and young people who died—for what and for why—If you were 18 or over you got drafted in 1950 and Ernie and Kip did just that and both died on Hill 800 better known as "Bunker Hill" on 18 May 1951. I never really got over the "why". And when I heard from the "Big Guy" his words came through the voice of Miss Laura—"It always works sometimes Laurel"—he, through she, was still looking after me.

Wally and Andy got drafted but neither ended up in Korea.

I went to school every day and sometimes heard

Tommy Edwards sing "It's All In The Game" and by the time I was old enough to be killed it was over and I could only wonder—just wonder—why—just why—even knowing the answer, the ignorance of war is just that . . . or is it just the ignorance of something man can never perceive . . .

I dated without much enthusiasm—had both platonic and atomic dates, none of which really exploded or imploded—thought daily of how Chancy must now look and what a date with her would be like—and—in June 1953 graduated from UCLA with a degree in biochemistry, a minor in psychology and in physiology and a scholarship at Stanford Medical School. I never did get to play football and don't remember having to study very hard to stay on the Deans List.

I sent a special graduation announcement and invitation to Charlie Clyde to attend my graduation but heard nothing in reply and actually felt a little sad and then humiliated—this was followed by a feeling of indifference. I had made a special effort to keep in touch with him after that ill fated primary encounter in 1946. I sent him several letters each year and occasionally would get a reply written exactly like he talked—"shur'nuffs, ah's" and "I been ah study'in on that very thang" and one time told me that he was "Thank'in bout makin tin funnels in this here factory I'm ah plannin ta build—lots ah money in them thangs—easy ta build an farmers all ah need'in em—kinda hi-tec stuff ya know" but had not had a reply now in over a year.

I would later learn that during this time he developed tuberculosis and was treated in a sanitarium in the high desert town of Silver City, New Mexico. Why New Mexico? I never found out. It just remained another unknown wrapped around this enigmatic character.

251

I was not yet 21 and looked a lot like the movie actor and dancer Donald O'Conner. This replication came in handy with meeting girls on campus but my dancing was still really dismal.

When I left Pasadena in mid August en route to Palo Alto I was driving a 1949 Willys—Overland Jeepster Convertible with a 4 cylinder Jeep engine and whitewall tires. I left a day earlier than originally planned just on a whim and was intoxicated with life and headed along Santa Monica Boulevard to Highway 1 past Malibu toward Ventura.

Passing through Oxnard gave me a thrill because this is where Uncle Louie, Trixie and I had eight or ten times turned west to go over to a little community called Hollywood By The Sea where there was a boardwalk and small permanent amusement park with mostly kiddie rides, hot dog stands and the usual assortment of midway huckster booths of chance and Uncle Louie knew everyone from his old days of wrestling on the carnival circuit. The three for a nickel rings really would fit over the square post but only if the trajectory was straight down and the bottom middle silver colored milk bottle was solid lead but even against those odds someone occasionally would get lucky and knock all five off of the pedestal and win a prize.

An old man everyone called "Captain" owned a "Rare Wonders of The World" exhibit—it was called an exhibit so he could collect donations instead of selling tickets thereby relieving him of tax consequences I suppose. Uncle Louie had know him for years and covertly conveyed money to supplement the meager donations.

All of the specimens were the work of some mentally deranged taxidermist no doubt still suffering from a powerful hallucinogenic hangover and unable to find his way back to the nervous hospital. There is no doubt that technically he did excellent work but an "Unlike South American Amazon Rain Forrest Parrot" which resembled a penguin? A five legged two headed cow with the udder bulging upwards from its back called an "Udderly Ridiculous PentaCowmadary."

But the one that I liked best was the restricted to "Adults Only" "No children Allowed" "Extinct Shuuuush Bird."

This resembled a very large rooster somehow reshaped like a Coca-Cola bottle with spread wings and a puffy blunted head at the small end and an array of feathers shaped into a target like nest at the other end and the whole thing acutely curved as if to indicate making a sharp right turn. A sign painted in Olde English block lettering detailed why this bird was extinct: "The Extinct Shuuuush Bird managed to work himself into a frenzy relative to every minor and trivial thing which entered his life and especially over things which he certainly had no control—He would then engage in the endless and mindless pursuit of chasing his own ass, until one day—flying in one of these never ending faster and faster, tighter and tighter concentric circles—he caught it and disappeared into his very own private portal leaving for posterity only a soft—silent— Shuuuush never to be seen again until now"

I turned off the main road and headed for this almost forgotten place and was pleased that some of it still existed although not as I remembered . The captain would—if still around—have to be over one-hundred years old and the whole place was shabby and seemingly headed for its own extinction and besides that, there is no real bona fide scientific evidence that a shuuuush bird had ever existed anyplace anyway except for a sub-species called

"Politicians" and I sat for a while reflecting on what the Old Captain and the deranged taxidermist must have somehow known and discussed.

Back on the road to Ventura—a left turn at the Ventura Hotel in those days would lead you down to the Ventura pier and an epicureans Eden—aptly named "Clam Chowder & Fish—Harry Short Owner." Clam chowder is not just clam chowder. Some joints should be ordered to be ashamed of what they call clam chowder. But this was the best up until this point in my life and besides that, they had real sourdough bread and brandy over ice which I could occasionally get by with ordering. I can still pass up most things for these three.

It was about two in the afternoon when I went in and found a seat looking out over the beach with the waves breaking on the sand. You know how you get when—what do the poets call it—rhapsodic premonition that good was about to happen. I was ready for almost anything—except for what actually ensued.

The first thing I saw was a pair of black and white Joyce saddle shoes with white bobby socks—because being the klutz I am I had already dropped my napkin and bent over to retrieve it. Then came beautiful calves protruding from a white skirt and which disappeared into the bobby socks. The rear of the skirt was featured just right and I realized that I was leering rather relentlessly at a waitress taking an order at the adjacent table.

"I'll be with you in a moment sir if you don't mind." were the notes which caused the rhapsody to become real.

When I became upright she turned toward me and all five foot nine of her came into focus topped off with long shoulder length shiny black hair and a face Roberta Flack would sing about almost twenty years later—adorned with two of the happiest and beautiful almond shaped eyes ever I have seen.

I didn't need to look at her name tag to realize that this was big time from "The Big Guy."

"Chancey !!" "My God!!" I blurted out "One of my prayers has just been answered."

"Oh excuse me sir. If you are in prayer I can come back" "Did I disturb some prophecy or an epiphany— I do apologize." "Can I get you something to drink?"

And with that I realized she didn't have the slightest idea who I was. So I told her.

"My God Laurel I would never have recognized you. You were a funny looking little guy with big ears—"

I cut her off with "Yea I know and now I'm a funny looking big guy with big ears and sometimes I wonder if there is anything between them and I've been in love with you Chancey Sekimora since the first day I laid eyes on you in that library twelve years ago and Great Scott you are without a doubt the most magnificent looking lady and Miss Laura was right and now is always and now is sometimes and . . . and. . . . tincture of time does heal most things and . . . and . . . and . . . she was right—we did meet again. . . . meet again. . . . and you don't understand anything I'm blabbering about and . . . and . . . or should I just run off of the west end of this pier? Or . . . or . . ." "My God Chancey what a day—I wasn't even gon'na leave until tomorrow and here you are here today and . . . and . . ."

"Wow! Laurel slow down—hold on a minute and I'll be right back and we can sit and talk. Okay?"

"Okay." was all I could say as I turned and watched her go and only then realized that I hadn't even stood up or shook her hand or anything else that had resembled politeness. I was so overcome with this encounter that I let

255

my imagination run amok and made at least a thousand assumptions—I was totally struck stupid and talking to myself out loud—for the entertainment of the spectators around me—"Need to think Laurel—need to be sophisticated Laurel—need to control that tic Laurel—need to be calm Laurel—can't blow twelve years Laurel—it always works sometimes Laurel and this better be that sometime."

She was walking toward the kitchen and as she disappeared behind swinging doors my heart felt like it dropped into my scrotum and panic took over for the second time in as many minutes emanating from fear that she would never come back.

The panic and fear was short lived because she walked out leading a very pleasant looking Japanese woman about fifty years old and introduced her as "My aunt; Mrs Onoko Short; Laurel." "Aunty and my Uncle Harry own this restaurant—I have been working here summers between semesters in school and if you had come by one day later you would have missed me because today is my last day for this summer."

My heart was again anatomically positioned and I said as I stood up "How wonderful to meet you and please excuse my lack of manners—I . . . I . . . I am completely overwhelmed with meeting up with Chancey after all of these years—I've been so much in love—Oh God I . . . I . . . well, as you can tell I . . . I . . . am thrilled to— Chancey—I have looked for you every day for the past twelve years in every crowd and places I knew you would never ever be and—is there someplace we can go to talk— everyone here is looking at the spectacle I've made of myself and I apologize for having embarrassed you and your aunt here in public—or anyplace else for that matter."

256

Chancey reached down and took me by my hand and started to lead me away from the table when she turned to the other customers and said "It's not everyday that someone as gallant and intrepid as Laurel Hardy Lubeck lets it be known that he has been in love with you for twelve years—and I didn't think he would even remember me." "What a goy."

"Back soon aunty—going for a walk." and as we turned to exit all of the customers clapped and at least one "A fine mess Ollie" followed us through the door.

We started walking along the pier and I couldn't take my eyes off of her and she never let go of my hand. Something magic was flowing as was something the scientific community would later recognize and call pheromones.

She occasionally glanced at me and then asked me to tell her everything about me. This I declined to do until first she told me about any obligations she might have with someone else.

"Well—when we were gathered up and sent away to the Gila River Relocation in Arizona I didn't think we would ever have a normal life again but strong faith instilled in me by my father and mother took care of that. We don't have enough time for a story of my life—suffice to say I am a free American without baggage or commitment—I am Sansei and I have to catch the train tomorrow to go back to school at Cal Berkeley where this time next year I will have my degree in psychology and hopefully on to medical school someplace and then into psychiatry. My mom, who was nisei, and a U.S. citizen died from a cancer about three years ago and my dad, also nisei, also a citizen, joined the 442nd Army Regimental Combat as a PFC, while we were in camp, even though he had a PhD in Chemistry, and was a hero and got medals and we have great pride in that fact. He has been teaching biochemistry at Stanford so I didn't choose to be an Indian and chose to be a Bear instead." "Mom and I moved to Oklahoma from the camp after dad left for the 442nd and lived with Aunty Onoko and uncle Harry in a little town called Enid—since Uncle Harry is Caucasian Aunty Onoko had no problem and when dad was discharged he found a teaching job at the high school in Grants Pass Oregon so that's where I finished high school." "When dad got the teaching position at Stanford we moved to Los Altos and there ever since. summers here with Aunt Onoko and Uncle Harry—he's Jewish and Aunt Onoko is Catholic—dad's a Mormon and I could probably be a pretty good Unitarian if need be. I date now and then but nothing serious. With dad living across the bay we enjoy a lot of weekends, dinner and a show in the city occasionally. He is well liked and gets to do a lot of private research in his lab. He was crushed the way he had to leave Cal Tech but all of that is behind us." "So now you."

She was still holding my hand and we were setting on a bench about half way out on the pier and I managed to tell my story with as much aplomb as possible. I told her that I had been unable to have any serious relationship because I kept believing in what Miss Laura had said that if something is meant to be it will happen and repeated that there was no earthly reason for me to leave one day early and if not for stopping at Hollywood By The Sea I would have been here on the pier before opening time and probably headed on up the coast without looking back.

"What time is your train leaving tomorrow and when do you need to be in Berkeley?" I asked.

"Why? You got something in mind ?" she responded

with an accompanying mischievous look.

"Yea—as a matter of fact I do—I don't need to be in Palo Alto for at least a couple of weeks so planned to spend a week or so with my aunt and uncle in San Luis Obispo and then a couple of days in Carmel, Monterey and Half Moon Bay then hit the campus." "But—what if you get off that train in San Luis—I pick you up at the station and we spend the day together maybe stay overnight—Trixie will love you and keep you safe I assure you—then I will drive you straight to Berkeley via a dad stop at Palo Alto of course." "My God Chancey listen how audacious I sound—I act like a fool sometimes—just can't help myself—Chancey will you marry me ?" I said as I laughed, tweaked and distorted my face and slapped myself gently across the mouth.

"Not right now I won't but keep asking as we get to know each other better—maybe on a monthly basis since I assume that with you being at Stanford and me a stone skip away we can spend lots of time doing exactly that—not skipping stones but seeing each other." "You would like that wouldn't you Laurel?" "Keep in mind that I do have to work part time since dad can't afford the whole thing—bless his heart—it's a good thing I have no siblings—and I do actually have to study to keep up my grades." "Gad, I know some folks at Cal who just look at something and remember it and never seem to have to study. I should be so lucky. Do have a 3.8 GPA though." "How is your GPA Laurel?" "Does it come easy or hard for you?" "I just thought of something, you will be taking bio-chem from my dad your first year at the farm—and if I get accepted next year so will I—damn, won't that be a howl?" "He'll probably flunk me." "And you—your GPA won't be worth a rice ball if he thinks you might have been mistreating his little girl." She had managed to say all of this with only two breaths, a mirthful twinkle in her eyes and this curled up at the corners of her mouth smile.

"Well, if you won't marry me right now will you at least get off that train in San Luis?" I begged lifting her hand to my lips.

"Not if you grovel but I might consider it if you lift me up and kiss me like I want you to."

And I did.

We walked back to the restaurant and once inside Aunty Onoko came running out of the kitchen to enquire about our need for some chowder which I accepted gratefully.

Chancey then announced to everyone in the restaurant —"Laurel Hardy Lubeck asked me to marry him but I don't think I will until later—maybe not next month either but without a doubt some month."

"Oh Chancy—you so funny—you never have changed." said a grinning Aunt Onoko.

Aunty Onoko was right—she still is and never has and I made it to San Luis Obispo about seven that evening and Trixie and I went out for dinner and the train stopped the next afternoon and before anyone could believe it I was starting my third year in medical school and Chancy her second and you talk about ingenuous, uninhibited, candid and trusting days—we grew together and we were.

IHAD DECIDED to keep Clyde informed about my progress in medical school and did so periodically. He wrote back one time—one line—"I jest had my gall bladder took out."

That was it, one line. Magnis was rising rapidly through the ranks and seemed to do everything right and was well liked and respected. There was no doubt in my mind that he would some day be an admiral. Clyde seemed to correspond occasionally with Magnis and even went back to the Boston Naval Shipyard one time to visit and they met someplace else later on.

He had now found another attorney. One who specialized in trusts and much like Efram, didn't mind walking close to the edge. Gerhardt Eros Trobler Geld, Esq.—better know around Kansas City as G.E.T. Geld.

Geld didn't try to fade Clyde with a cut of the action, he just charged high prices for his services and did a good job of it. All of the trusts Efram had organized were still water tight and simply needed to be "serviced." Everything in the trusts were "serviced" into negotiables as were all of the other assets including the real estate that could be rounded up and anything which had cash value was traded under the table at a discount in exchange for stock—General Electric,

General Motors, IBM, Standard Oil, Boeing, Westinghouse and several more Dow Jones big timers and a long shot with the funny name of Xerox. The shares were received in trust name and placed in a numbered trust account set up in Switzerland. Clyde was the trustee and had the prerogative to name successors. The corpus of the trust could not be touched and remained in perpetuity. A yearly annuity was to be released equal to twelve percent of the earned dividends. Nine percent to Clyde—which would be reportable as a consultant fee and therefore U.S.A. taxable and a three percent fee to service the trust. Sixty-eight percent of the earnings were to be reinvested in the stock from which it was earned and the remaining twenty percent was to be invested in cash-value Swiss insurance contracts.

Clyde didn't have a clue about how any of this worked—in fact he wasn't terribly sure where Switzerland was located—and didn't much care. A big concern was that Beryl might find out about all of this and he knew that then he would be in big trouble.

He had three farms but kept the smaller one—about 80 acres—separate from all this and lived in the little one bedroom farmhouse. His other major concern was that his water well kept getting contaminated and it cost almost one hundred dollars to get a proper filter system put in and an estimate of almost three hundred to install a septic system. Deja Vu. He was still using the outhouse and didn't even have indoor capability until Beryl refused to ever visit again until he did. The contractor had to build an entire new room and in one fell swoop Clyde had a bathtub with a shower, a sink, a flush toilet and a hot water heater in the same room. He bragged as if this equated with some original invention and secretly bemoaned the cost.

Shortly before this time he had stopped taking those

periodic trips to unknown parts and just settled down on the farm and gave up drinking for months at a time only to fall again under the wheels of his own limitations and impairments—binging for weeks and not even remembering how or where he obtained the juice, where he might have gone or even if he had gone since he would inevitably struggle out of the travail carrying his allotted consignment of penitence and remorse, and whatever else these tortured wretches conjure up, in the attempt to prove the rest of the world guilty of having caused this inadequate and ineffective progress through what normal folks call life. From all outward appearances he was a dismal failure.

In 1957 I sent him an invitation to attend my graduation from medical school and heard nothing. Not even a card. Everyone else in the family attended and I started my internship at Los Angeles County General Hospital. My main regret during this time was that I spent most of the year away from Chancey. She graduated from Stanford the following year.

In spring of 1959 something happened which is like so many other things in this enigma. Clyde and Beryl got married. They somehow found their way to Juarez, Mexico and crossed over the border on a day trip, got married by a Justice of The Peace and returned that evening to El Paso, Texas, stayed the night and the next morning headed back to Kansas City stopping only in Oklahoma City for a rest.

I had completed my first year of a pathology residency at L.A. County General and Chancey started a psychiatric residency at U.C.L.A. We both put in long hours but managed to have time to merge. We just grew together and long before it was popular to do such—moved in together.

One night in October 1959 Magnis called and asked me if I would like to join him in a trip to Kansas City to see

Clyde. He—Magnis not Clyde—was stationed in San Diego and was now a full commander and really looked elegant in his uniform. He taught secret stuff at a radar school and doubted that he would ever get back to sea—hence—doubted that he would ever make Chief of Naval Operations which had been his quest—since this position always went to those who plowed the waves.

I was certain that he would someday make admiral. He had a great marriage going which had produced two kids and our standing joke was that one of these days I would explain how these things happened.

We left on the Santa Fe Chief and had this great time together, mostly in the club car, just talking. I goaded him into talk about some medical things and a discussion about the description and model of DNA, which had been constructed by Crick and Watson in 1953, ensued. Magnis of course had little interest in anything that wasn't connected with electrons and RADAR imagery and would frequently comment "If it isn't working off of electricity it isn't happening."

I tried to explain how the entire body worked off of electricity and the "magic" of DNA. "What if the snake of the Caduceus or The Staff of Aesculapius is not a snake at all but rather the coiled helix of RNA ?" "What if the double coiled helix of The Staff of Hermes is a molecule of DNA." "How come I have to think of everything Magnis?" "Suppose the folks here on earth ten thousand—twenty thousand—thirty thousand years ago already knew more about medicine and RADAR and electrons and such than we will ever be able to know ?" "What if some folks came here from another galaxy about twenty thousand years ago and brought RNA and DNA with them?" "You need to think about these things Magnis. . . ."

We had never had a DNA discussion before but the extra galactical genetic material delivery system field had been plowed several times so he gave his usual: "I'm gon'na have you committed one of these days you silly shit. Maybe I can get Chancey to do it . You need to be kept away from normal folks although I concede that maybe someday someone will make a synthetic molecule of DNA and that will be exciting." "Maybe someone will build a synthetic electron. Did I ever tell you about when Tesla. . . ."

I cut him of with "Yea, yea, yea."

We went through what we might expect in Kansas City and did some planning and 36 hours later arrived in Kansas City.

I had great trepidation but big brother soothed this growing anxiety and at the end of the platform stood Charlie Clyde in his grey Dickies, stark skinny, almost bald, same black service station attendant bluchers, white socks, a black belt which was too long and the end hung down like a sad thing and the inevitable roll your own Bull Durham cigarette dangled from his lips.

He took a deep breath and began one of his spasmodic coughing spells which took several minutes and then extended his hand first to Magnis and then to me. He was rumpled but sober and that pleased us. I guessed I never would get used to that "nasal twang" voice as he said "Fellers, welcome ta K.C. we ain't very fancy here but thangs is ah look'in up an ah got lots ah stuff ta show y'all."

We got into his 1949 Chevy 2-door and took a strange circuitous route from the station out of Kansas City and on several occasions seemed to crisscross areas and several times slowed down—he seemed to be observing the

265

surroundings. He said nothing except that he was "jest a chek'in on somethin."

We finally made it out to the farm and I have to admit it was a beautiful setting. We pulled up in front of a small but nicely groomed farmhouse and were informed that he had "Jest bought this here place last week after I'd knowed y'all was ah cum'in." "This here only has twenty acres but it ties in ta tha rest ah tha land." "Our place is yonder down tha road. Y'all can see it from here." "We only got one small bedroom over yonder so y'all is ah gon'na stay here." "That seem okay ?"

We took our baggage inside and it turned out to be very homey and satisfactory.

"Now y'all make do here and when ya feel like it stroll on down tha lane an me an Beryl can get ta know ya."

We thanked him and he left.

"Wow Magnis—what do you think big brother?" "This isn't what I expected at all." "I think he really wants to make a good impression but doesn't know how to communicate it. What do you think?"

"At least he seems sober." "This is the first time for you since you were—how old—fourteen—fifteen ?" "I had that meeting back east a few years ago and one time last year up in Chicago." "Fairly unpleasant encounter—but mainly because we just don't seem to find a common level of discussion." "He is very aberrant and pretty shrewd—deceitful—cunning—in a way I can't explain. Kind of like 'I got a secret that you can't know'. . . . remember when I used to trick you when you were little by writing wrong things for you to memorize or changing words around after you said 'I got it' ?" "Quick now which is it, who or whom?" "You knew it wasn't right but that's the way it was presented and that's the way you remembered it."

266

"Something is just over the horizon and my radar mast isn't tall enough to spot it." "And by the way, I have never met Beryl—I understand they got married about six months ago in Mexico—I don't know what to expect—I talked to her on the phone a few weeks ago." "Let's wash up and head down the road Little Brother."

"How come you didn't wear your uniform?" "You really look good in it. If you want to someday I'll let you see me in my scrub clothes when they have lots of tissue sticking to them and if you 'be good' I'll let you hold some real human kidneys or a liver or some other exciting specimen without any gloves." "You never did show up for that autopsy meeting we had scheduled last month." "I was going to take you to lunch later—or have some liver pate' brought in to eat in the lab."

Magnis could never get used to anything that had to do with medicine, blood, body parts or suggestions thereof but I managed "pay back" whenever possible for all of the travails and kid misery he had put me through in the past. You have to take your shots when you can with a big brother.

We hiked down the dirt lane about a quarter of a mile and encountered a snarling dog at the door step of their little farmhouse and a rather troubled looking, skinny Marjorie Main type character slammed open the screen door and hit the dog with a piece of stove wood she had in her hand and without further greeting said "Come on in he won't bite ya." "I'm Beryl an I reckon we're kin now." "Laurel—I'm a nurse ya know?"

"Yes Maam" I replied "I do know that and am very pleased to be here." "May I call you Miss Beryl?"

"Yea, that'll be okay with me—and you must be Magnis—I seen you one time through tha winder when ya

267

was ah boy." "No reason ta look back at that ah reckon." "Hope ya both are hungry cause suppers wait' in."

Clyde showed us his meager surroundings and we sat down in the kitchen part of the living space to pork chops and mashed potatoes with iced tea followed up with a delicious chocolate pie. No one but people from the Ozarks would fry a fatty pork chop in a frying pan full of lard but what the hell, it was pretty good.

"I ain't learned ta cook real good yet but I'm ah learn' in." "Be'in ah nurse all these years didn't serve me well with domestic things ya know." "Clyde here he don't know nothin bout nothin cept he does like his pork chops so we have em most ever day." "Loves bacon an eggs ever mornin."

Clyde hadn't said a word during all of this and when we were finished he stood up and went into the bathroom which opened off of this kitchen combo and took a long time attending to his body habits ever so loudly. It was still light so he took us outside and we drove around his farm in a pickup truck. He had hired a sharecropper to do the farming and it was in good shape. We asked if we could take the two of them out to dinner at some nice place the next evening and he said okay.

He seemed to want to say something but couldn't get into it so we made small talk. Magnis and I had agreed that we would just troll along and see what would happen. We retired after saying good night to Beryl and walked back down the lane.

Next morning Magnis and I were having a second cup of coffee about six AM when Clyde drove up in the pickup and said that we were going fishing. On the way to a small lake we picked up some lunch material. I think we set a record for silence that day. Magnis and I didn't know what to talk about that would interest him and he apparently had the same problem. It is amazing how many Bull Durham cigarettes can be rolled from one of those little cloth bags.

Magnis made an attempt to open up something by asking Clyde how he had earned his living these past years. It seemed like a legit question to me but Clyde got his hackles up very quickly and said "Ain't none ah yor dammit business whut I done." and so much for that.

I asked if he had received the invitation to attend my graduation from med school and he replied "Yup."

I then asked if he knew what I was doing with my career and he answered "Nope—don't care."

Magnis asked if he knew anything about RADAR and he reacted "Yup—ah studied on it in ah magazine story."

I asked if someday he might again visit California and if so would he like to observe me doing an autopsy to which he replied: "Don't care ta do none ah that an don't care if California falls in tha ocean an sinks." "We cum here ta fish not ta jabber."

We left it at that and actually caught some Bass and gave them to an old timer at the bait shop.

Magnis had been told about a famous steak house, in Independence, and the four of us went out to dinner that night. We wore sport coats Clyde wore his Dickies. Beryl did her best but never the less looked like a makeover from a second hand store.

The first mistake was innocent but stupid on my part and I should have known better. I ordered a drink. A brandy, Magnis ordered a scotch. This triggered two water glasses of gin on the rocks for Beryl and Clyde. I should have ordered tea or coffee. Clyde asked about Magnis' family and how my love life was coming along and if I had a girl friend and I told him her name was Chancey

Sekimora.

Magnis and I had delicious steaks and Clyde and Beryl had five glasses of gin and got into a terrible, embarrassing loud argument about something she had whispered to him. Beryl walked out and took a taxi to the apartment she still maintained in Kansas City. Clyde took steak to the dog and Magnis and I left for home the next day—one day sooner than planned.

On the way to the station Clyde was still at least one sheet into the wind and all of a sudden turned to me in the back seat and blurted out "I'm ah guess' in y'all better jest gol-dammit know ah ain't ah hav'in no Jap girl fer ah daughter-in-law so y'all can jest make up yor mind ta that fact." "We done fought that dammit war with them people an I don't reckon ta spend no more time do'in that agin." "Ah don't reckon y'all give one gol-dammit thought ta how others in this here family might be ah takin that sort ah thang—did ya?" "It shur nuff ain't thoughtful see' in how we feel about that sort ah thang an if y'all go on with it I'm damn shur nuff tak'in ever thang back—ah mean ever thang—ever gol-dammit thang y'all hear' in me okay sonny boy?"

I had no idea what was to be taken back and the Alice In Wonderland statement "I can't have more—I've had none yet" crossed my mind for a quip but I managed to hold my tongue as Magnis reached over the seat and grabbed my knee and gave it a pat.

The trip back was sad but the brotherly seal we made was solid and healthy and we both knew we could move on with our lives.

Chancey and I married the next fall and it just got better and better. Her humor and her personality constantly astonished me and I had a perpetual case of the "happies."

Miss Laura was right.

It was a great wedding—everyone I knew seemed to show up—Magnis was best man—Aunty Onoko was Matron of honor. The band played the great Mack Gordon—Harry Warren song "At Last" instead of whatever is usual for the first dance—Doctor Sekimora danced with Ada and Abner danced with Trixie because Uncle Louie never learned to dance. Magnis danced with Hanna—the wife of his life. Uncle Harry insisted that Aunty Onoko stay seated in a chair while he danced around her with a black hat on his head while pretending to crush wine glasses with his heels.

Doctor Sekimora gave toasts and good happened.

Doctor Pinkney gave toasts and good happened.

Commander Lubeck gave toasts and good happened.

Uncle Louie gave a toast—"Holy jumped up Jesus Christ Laurel—you picked a hell of a good one."

I gave a toast to Chancey and laid a side pronouncement only the two of us could hear or would understand "It worked this time Miss Laura." and "Thanks Big Guy."

We didn't have time to go anyplace.

A PRIL 23,1979—a few minutes later.

Just as I got into the rented car to head back to Little Rock I recognized a couple of friendly faces through a windshield which was headed my way in the parking lot lining up drivers side to drivers side. The other driver came to a stop, the window rolled down and the huge military cap covered with gold things stuck out of the window followed by the forearm of a navy blue uniform with two gold stripes about three-quarters of an inch wide above a single very wide gold stripe which seemed to cover about two or three inches. Vice Admiral Magnis Lubeck tried to suppress a smirk without success and quipped: "We are just in time to be too late. Right?"

Chancey was in the passenger seat. I had left her at the airport in Little Rock to meet Magnis when we found out his plane was late and he didn't really want to come anyway. I knew she could talk him into it. She could talk him into anything. At least he showed up.

"Tell you what big brother—it's all over here except the shoveling and the truth is, I got here just as it was ending. Didn't see or hear a thing." "We need to do some paper and leg work so follow me over to the place they called home." "Who knows, could be interesting—maybe find some background about him and the name change thing—I'm pretty good at investigations—and you know that forensic pathology is the ultimate investigation—and Chancey is the best organizer ever."

As we drove to what had been Clyde's and Beryl's home these past six or seven years my mind raced with speculation about what we might find—and also what we might not find—we absolutely knew nothing.

The biggest mystery was why the name change—this had bothered both of us all of our lives and next in line was how he had lived all of these years without visible means of support. Beryl could never have earned enough to support both nor would she, or so I believed.

The small house was one of only two on this narrow dirt dead end and the closest neighbor was about three-hundred yards away and across the road. I estimated that it could not have a value of more than fifteen thousand even in these inflationary times.

The three of us went inside with the passkey I had been given by the mortician who claimed to be as much of a friend as either of them had. He had also told me that the only bank in town had some papers which we might need and to ask for a Mr Shrug.

We went inside and were overwhelmed by this musty mildew smell. Cheap heavy quilted drapes covered the three windows along the right side of the living room. The first door to the left was a closet filled with empty boxes and the second led to a bedroom which had evidently belonged to Beryl and the third opened to another small bedroom which had obviously belonged to Clyde and from this a terrible excuse for a bathroom with one corner stacked high with old newspapers and old shoes and clothes strewn all around.

"Where to start you guys?" "Where to start?" "Magnis. . . . the mortician said that a Mr Shrug over at that bank we passed coming in has some papers and perhaps some information." "How about if you start by going over there to talk with him. You know that admiral suit is pretty imposing and people who don't know you will be rightly impressed. If he starts to hesitate or not cooperate, tell him you are with the C.I.A. or Naval Intelligence or something and you are starting an investigation." "Tell him Clyde and Beryl were spies—what the hell for all we know they might have been." "Chancey and I will start looking through this place for anything important—she reads as fast as I do so we can go through a lot of stuff quickly." "Okay. . . . I figure we need to be here today but doubt tomorrow. . . . what do you think?"

He started off and we started in.

I began by going through what appeared to be Clyde's chest of drawers and found an odd assortment of buttons, coins, three pocket knives, two old Evans cigarette lighters, a cheap pocket watch with a cheaper chain, a metal hip flask, two broken lower dental plates, a shoe brush, a broken cigarette roller, a well worn brass cigarette case and a plastic toy Secret Decoder Badge.

Further search of the room revealed about a dozen sets of Dickies shirts and pants but no shoes, socks or underwear, and one necktie with palm trees which I recognized as the one he had worn when we met in 1946. No double-breasted grey suit—probably buried in it. Morticians use a clip-on tie for convenience—probably maroon. Several cardboard lettuce boxes were stacked in the closet which contained bank statements going back over twenty years ending as recently as February. I took these to the kitchen and asked Chancey to scan and log any glitches.

A smaller cardboard file drawer box contained tax returns which had been done by several different third party preparators dating back to 1947. These I took to the table and began my review.

"You finding anything Chancey?" "I found the tax returns going back to the forties—they might tell us something." "Why he changed his name may be deeper than what Ada knew about that brush with the law way back when. Who knows." "Magnis and I would certainly love to know something about his background and how he survived and from the looks of this place that's about all they did was survive." "Jesus how depressing—I wonder what they did for entertainment besides TV and booze?"

"Laurel—here's something interesting—how much do you think Beryl earned a year as an LVN at that TB hospital?"

"When?" I asked

"Say about 1955."

"Maybe three grand—probably got a buck and a quarter an hour—doctors averaged about twenty grand in 55 nationwide." I replied. "What did you find?"

"These earlier bank statements are from a small bank in Independence Missouri belonging to C.C. Dodge and look like they were done with a rubber stamp—month after month checks going to utilities, semi annual property tax payments—mundane things like that—with a balance of around four thousand and deposit entries generally equal to debits." "Then in1958 we see three times that amount and that has continued." "When did you say they got married?"

"Sometime in1959."

"Well, this was in. . . ." "Did she continue to work after

they married ?" "Clyde never worked did he?" "Where did he get money enough to keep a checking account." "Did he have a savings account?"

"Hey beautiful—I don't know. I only know that he was a full time conundrum." "Maybe this will take longer than two days—or maybe we won't find anything."

Scanning the tax returns revealed about the same pattern as the bank statements. Year after year simple uncomplicated tax returns with gross earnings five thousand give or take a few bucks and all listed as consulting fees and four canceled quarterly IRS checks made out as if they were quarterly estimates and not hand written but typed and without doubt signed C.C. Dodge by Charlie Clyde. "These were joint filings. Strange—why joint before 1959 ?"

In 1960 the gross consultant fees listed on the tax forms had more than tripled and by the time Clyde died had again almost quadrupled. Chancey started finding the same pattern on bank statements and then ran into one envelope which had nine savings account books from institutions scattered around Arkansas with thousands of dollars compounding. This was probably the result from the "Consultant Fee" entries on the tax forms.

So what—nothing wrong with that—he was allowed to have as many savings accounts as he pleased and all of the taxes had been paid. Getting this money out might be a glitch for us but we would cross that gap later. The tax forms had been filed timely up until Clyde's death last year. Beryl had not bothered for this past year and I made a mental note to get an extension for this.

"Where the hell did he get that money for those accounts?" "Enough time on these things—probably learned as much as we can for now." "Lets look through

Beryl's room before Magnis gets back and accuses us of not doing anything" Costume jewelry and cheap dresses and shoes all piled around, wrinkled and in disarray—that is everything except four perfectly white and ironed white nurse uniform dresses hanging side by side in the closet with a pair of perfectly polished nurse white shoes below.

Beryl evidently was one to keep scrapbooks and one in particular was like a diary going back to her teen years. Valentine cards, grade school papers, a letter of accommodation from some farmers group for growing a large eggplant, an add from a Little Rock newspaper recruiting Nursing Aids in Hot Springs and explaining how this could lead to further studies as an LVN or LPN, an undated newspaper article heading—Gun Fight in Hot Springs—her high school diploma from a Greenwood High School, location not revealed, but, most revealing, a Xerox copy of a Marriage Permit Application and Certification of Health—dated 11 January, 1933 between C.C. Dodge and Beryl McAdoo.

"Wow Chancey—look at this—Clyde and Beryl were going to get married in 1933—well he couldn't do that— they really took bigamy seriously in those days—a guy could get thrown in jail." "This might need a follow up." "I never knew her name was McAdoo." "Wait a minute, this doesn't look like Clyde's signature at all." "What's going on here. Isn't this sort of thing exciting?" "I hear Magnis— I hope he was successful."

"Hi little brother—you were right, the stars did come in handy. I decided that I would play it almost straight and identified myself as Vice Admiral Lubeck with Office of Naval Intelligence and oldest son of a deceased C.C. & B. Dodge and wished to claim any and all papers, access to any safety deposit boxes and any other information he might have in his possession." "He rolled right over and believe it or not he had a release ready and evidently Clyde had named me as a co-signer for any and all." "Could not have been easier and I believe that bank manager seemed relieved that I came for these things. He was nervous." "You are really going to be surprised at some of the contents so put that machine brain of yours to work." and with that he dumped the contents onto the table.

"Remember that farm we visited up by Independence?" "Well, it looks like we own it now. Probably grown in value—we also own this broken down house but, look at this." as he held up a sealed manila envelope with an actual sealing wax and signet impression still sealed and intact.

"From Zurich Switzerland—still sealed. Why in hell would Clyde have something like this?" It had been housed inside a certified manila folder addressed to C.C. Dodge, C/O G.E.T. Geld, Atty. 1701 Main Street, Kansas City, Missouri., postmarked 25 Sept. 1953., Zurich. The container envelope had been opened and resealed with scotch tape. The sealing wax of the envelope containing the contents had not been broken. "Lets open it at the bottom and leave the wax intact. Okay?"

"Sounds right to me—how about you Chancey ?"

"This looks like really big stuff and both of you know you are excited enough to pee down your legs. Right?" "Here let me do it." she said as she slit the envelope with her finger nail file and removed the contents.

A very official looking twenty three page document was covered by a letter which explained what was to be explained in the twenty three pages which were attached. The document noted that a trust numbered 22-9-1953-9632 existed in a special account in their establishment and named all of the stipulations which existed and many Swiss legal anointments. It further explained that a special certification-verification, which had been recorded and sealed in a special folder at the time of the trust being set up, must be duplicated in the presence of the trust officer of the securities company before any further disclosure would be made. This acted as validation and was needed even to make an enquiry about the trust.

Magnis let out a long slow breath—"Good God Laurel can you believe this. What—where -how. . . ."

I cut him off with "Chancey, see if that phone works and if so call information for someone named G.E.T. Geld in K.C. please?"

"Oh I almost forgot." said Magnis "I stopped and got some sandwiches and coffee on my way here." "Here Chancey—some coffee ?"

"Thanks Big Brother I am hungry and this is like some Sam Spade mystery. Maybe Sidney Greenstreet will come walking in."

"There is no listing for any Geld in Kansas City, Missouri, but here is the number of an Agnes Geld across the border in K.C. Kansas." reported Chancey after only a short time. "If she doesn't know G.E.T. maybe she knows Uncle Harry—you never know—Who names a kid G.E.T. Money anyway?"

I finished my sandwich, filled Magnis in on what we had found in the boxes, called Agnes Geld and was informed that indeed she had at one time been married to the "rotten bastard" and was happy to report that he died four years ago and good riddance. I asked about his practice of law and she told me that he had at least been a very smart lawyer who worked alone dealing only in trusts—made many trips to Europe and had left her well set up after the divorce but she knew no records or anyone else who would know. "He was one brainy, ingenious, resourceful, enterprising son of a bitch—I can tell you that." I thanked her and hung up.

"What else was in the safe deposit box Magnis?" "Any clues at all about past history with names or places?" said I with little expectation.

"Three more plain white letter size envelopes stuffed with one hundred dollar bills—about thirty thousand in all." posted Magnis followed by: "Well 'I swan' Laurel— how the hell are we going to account for all of this—I'm afraid of what we might find next." "How could Charlie Clyde accumulate this much wealth even living like the pauper—tight wad he must have been?" "Jesus—what if this is drug money or maybe it's from a robbery or worse yet counterfeit money—I am not aware that he ever worked a day in his life except that pony ride thing years ago he told me about and the few weeks he spent working at that metal company building air plane tanks and I know for sure he never made much on that share cropping deal he had up in Independence. This is about thirty thousand cash and in one hundred dollar bills."

"I'm really afraid of what we might uncover in that Swiss outfit after finding this much in this tiny burgh." I updated. "Let's consider that he felt that he had enough for subsistence, maintenance or survival coming in from those consulting fees listed on the tax forms, what ever their source might be—you know those were pretty tidy sums toward the end—and after paying tax he just stuck money where he thought it might be safe for a rainy day." "That could account for the cash and be consistent with his checking and savings accounts—I forgot to tell you, we found nine of them right here—not hidden or anything but not readily accessible either—some of the banks are miles from here and he could go to this local bank, click open his deposit box and extract a few bills from those envelopes." "I have no delusions that he got any closer to the IRS than he really had to so under the table probably suited him just fine." "I have already asked myself four hundred times in the last hour just who—or is it whom—would pay Charlie Clyde Lubeck Dodge a consulting fee—what could he do to earn it—the term consulting means to ask advice or opinion of—and G.E.T. Geld was an attorney specializing in trusts—do either of you believe Clyde knew something about trusts which he could peddle to Geld ?" "Or knew anything about anything worth placing in a trust ? And the answer is no." "Let me have another look at that trust agreement—something is churning—It's right here in my kidney." I said tapping my temple with my index finger.

Chancey had been holding this document like it was the Magna Charta and handed it to me with both hands.

"This says that a certification-verification has been recorded and needs to be duplicated." "You don't suppose the trustor in Zurich would let you just pop in over there and just start creating shot in the dark random chance combinations do you?" "I don't think so either." "Well 'I swan Magnis' I just got a message." I closed my eyes and started reading stuff I had in my storage boxes. "Hand me that pad and pencil will you Chancey?"

And she did.

I wrote the number 122125311 on the paper and handed it to Magnis and he just stared at it and said: "Right." "Now how in Sam Hill did you come up with that number you dingle berry?"

"Trust me folks that is the certification-verification." "I will bet everything on it because one morning in 1952—I was eating some Wheat Crunchies and had nothing else to peruse at the table except the box and learned that a secret decoder badge awaited me at the bottom of the box and instructions about how I could send secret messages using the special code." "Go look in the top drawer of Clyde's dresser and see if you can find the same things I found Magnis."

An immediate return with badge in hand only amplified the excitement.

"Using that very sophisticated plastic Wheat Crunchies cryptographic integer replacement equivalent machine—substitute the numeral one for the letter A and so forth and convert DODGE to a number."

"415475" Magnis reeled off almost instantly.

"Right." I responded. "But that isn't the answer." "My God Magnis you have forgotten everything we ever learned in those old Sherlock Holmes movies we used to see at the Lyric Theater. 'The power of observation my dear Watson'." "Let Chancey look at it you twit."

Magnis handed it to Chancey who immediately spotted the pencil scratches around the edge marking the randomly placed letters of the alphabet. "What does K-U-E-C-B-L spell?" Chancey blurted out before she felt embarrassment over not recognizing her married name.

"Well it doesn't spell Sekimora that's for sure." "Think about it folks—old G.E.T. Geld or a courier or anyone connected with him might have recognized that Clyde would likely use his name as part of the "password" but who could have known, besides us, that his real name was LUBECK?" "He probably thought that he would pass that secret on to you Magnis but just didn't get around to it or maybe there is a special clue around here someplace that we missed."

Magnis shuffled through the other unopened envelopes

from the deposit box and found another interesting legal appearing document from the same Swiss firm which turned out to be a copy of a Swiss Insurance Contract Certificate with a cover letter from G.E.T. Geld addressed to Clyde dated 5 May 1955 explaining the Contract Certificate. It indicated that from this parent contract other annuities would automatically be created from a "certain source known only to each of the parties."

"I am absolutely dumbfounded." said I. "Apparently this is tied into the trust and looks like a sophisticated insurance policy or policies." "I wonder what the value is and who the annuitant is."

Magnis just sat and shook his head back and forth mumbling "bizarre—astonishing -incredible—bizarre—astonishing— incredible—"

"Maybe Charlie Clyde was a savant." asserted Chancey "and no one ever knew." "Maybe he inherited a lot of money that no one ever knew about." "Maybe he found one of those bags full of money from the Great Brinks Robbery or dug up some loot buried by Jesse James—Jesse spent some time up around Independence I once read."

"Where did you put that scrapbook Chancey?"

"Right in front of you dummy." I answered for her.

"Magnis—take a look at this and tell me what I am thinking." I said as I handed him the undated newspaper clipping." "Do you remember Beryl saying that she had seen you once before—remember? That time we went to Independence" "How and when would she have seen you ?"

"I don't know—need to really think about that—how the hell do you remember things like that—maybe that time Trixie and Uncle Louie took me to K.C." "No, you are right, didn't she say something about seeing me from a window ?"

"Nope—what she really said was 'seen ya from ah winder—when you was ah boy'—that's what she said—now, where and when would that have been?"

"The time I saw him before the K.C. trip with Trixie was when he got arrested and the police drove me home after he had driven up to some boarding house and left me waiting in the car—must have been 1932—I don't remember you being around yet." "Something had happened and I later found out that he had been arrested on suspicion of stealing money from a bakery or some such act." assured Magnis. "A short time later he headed out to Kansas City and I guess the police didn't care."

I interrupted—"I'll bet we can find all of that in the newspaper morgue in Little Rock—what else can we learn here?" "We need to take that newspaper article and some of these papers and the scrapbook with us and run through the old issues in the morgue—it does not have a date on it but I am suspicious about when that might have happened. I just have a feeling that those gangsters in Hot Springs might lead us someplace." "We can put everything we need in one of these boxes to take with us and ask the mortician to make arrangements to ship everything else to a local storage facility but I doubt we will need it ever again."

We called the phone company and the local utility company requesting a shut down and headed to the morticians office. He gave us a realtors name and we headed south toward Little Rock in the two cars.

We found a hotel not far from downtown and after dinner Magnis guided us two blocks south to an old deserted three story brick building which was the first school he had attended.

The next morning on our way to the Arkansas

Democrat Newspaper office we drove down the street where Magnis had been born on the table—the table no longer existed—neither did the building.

All of the newspaper morgue was on microfiche and with Chancey and I scanning we made it through 1930 and 1931 with nothing of interest to our case but 1932 revealed the two small articles about Charlie Lubeck dated August 20th and 23rd -1932.

"This was just before I was born Magnis." "I thought that Charlie Clyde was in K.C. then." "He must have been one fast moving spurious critter." "I haven't seen a thing relating to that gangster shoot out though—hell, that could have been much later or even earlier—may have no meaning anyway."

"Remember Clyde had been to Hot Springs in his bread truck and Beryl had completed her training there—maybe it was written up in a Hot Springs newspaper and didn't get picked up here in Little Rock." said Chancey.

"Magnis—will you check with the librarian in charge here and see if they have files on any Hot Springs papers?"

He came back very quickly with the August 1932 microfiche and what we needed was right on the front page of the Hot Springs Geyser August 17 th, Monday morning edition with the heading: *ARMED ROBBERY—GUN FIGHT—Yesterday two armed men overwhelmed, robbed and killed a third man believed to be an armed courier delivering some private papers to a guest, who is believed to be a Chicago racketeer mob boss, vacationing at the famous Arlington Hotel. The messenger who was killed in the running gun battle was accompanied by a compatriot who was seriously wounded and not expected to live. Hot Springs has been considered an open town for many years and no reported illegal activity has knowingly occurred for a great while, as in the old west days, guns were supposed to be left at the city limits. The activity took place on Fountain Street outside the luxurious Arlington at 1:45 pm yesterday. The attackers escaped south, on foot, along the famous Grand Promenade carrying a large briefcase containing 'valuable documents.' It is believed that these two then entered the rear of the Fordyce Bathhouse but according to one witness three men exited the Fordyce onto Central Avenue in a hurry—and drove away in a car which headed south shortly after the gun shots were heard. The suspected getaway car was later found only three blocks away parked on Exchange Street and proved to be a Ford Sedan which had been stolen earlier in Little Rock. The suspected, intended recipient of the contents of the brief case, refused to identify himself or the nature of the documents contained in the briefcase and left the Arlington in a hurry with several bodyguards at his side shortly after the shooting. It is believed that the two perpetrators were wounded.*

The suspected mob boss was later identified as Benjamin "Tiny" Balano known for his dealing in stocks and investment securities. Authorities are searching for clues and anyone knowing the identity of the perpetrators or victims are asked to come forward.

"Great balls of fire" said I. "You don't suppose anyone we know was involved in anything like that do you?" "Lets take a look at any follow up stories the next few days."

Chancey worked the levers of the microfiche and found an almost identical story for August 19 and on the 20th: *COMPANION OF COURRIER DIES—The wounded bodyguard of the still unidentified courier who was killed in the shootout at the Arlington Hotel August 16, 1932 died last evening. He has been identified as Jacko Moretti, age*

33, Chicago, Ill., occupation listed as flower shop owner . No next of kin has been identified . Mr Moretti was in and out of a coma and a stenographer was constantly at his bedside taking notes when he periodically spoke some names and is reported to have revealed the contents of the stolen briefcase as being very valuable bonds .However, this is unconfirmed.

The story went on to tell about Hot Springs being free of this type of crime and perhaps it was time for the "City Fathers" to make the city uncomfortable for this kind of visitor. . . .

"You do see a problem here don't you folks?" Complained I.

"Certainly." Offered Magnis. "Tiny Balano got the hell out of town because he didn't want to be involved—ergo—if whatever took place or was about to take place was legal, why skip town?" "Right?"

"That's true but again my dear Watson you missed the obvious. Jesus Magnis The Marx Brothers could solve this one." "Check the dates you twit."

"You can't call an admiral a twit you retarded dim-wit, people will stare at me or make throat clearing sounds or wonder if I'm a fake admiral or something." muttered Magnis as he pretended to strike me over the head with a rolled up sheet of paper.

"Okay I won't call you a twit any more I'll ask Chancey to call you one." "Call him a twit Chancey—because Charlie Clyde didn't get hit on the head and robbed until the 19th according to those Little Rock newspaper clips." "The article about Charlie says he was robbed on the 19th but the shooting took place on Sunday the 16th and he would not have been delivering bread on a Sunday with his truck and police investigated him further on the 21st and

287

that must have been when you remember the police taking him away." "Right?" "We know that Charlie Clyde ended up with a lot of money that can't be accounted for." "Right?" "Right." "It was suspected that a third man joined the perpetrators in the escape." "Right?" "Who was that third man?" "I don't think it could have been Charlie Clyde." "Why did Beryl have need for reference to this fiasco in her scrap book?"

"Maybe she knew one of them." Volunteered Chancey. "She was a nurses aid and maybe one of the wounded came to her for help."

"Okay so far, but let me throw something up for grabs." "Magnis—you have heard the story about Charlie Clyde coming to L.A. right?" "Remember, I told you about our encounter when he tried to impress me with what a big shot he was ?" "He was very proud of a certificate he allowed me to hold and you know me, I read it—front and back—and it occurred to me just a few minutes ago that I still have it stored away.... 'Baldwin Pipeline Oil & Gas Transmission Corporation—30 Year Bearer Bond Certificate ' with some coupons attached and a ten-thousand dollar value." "A subsidiary of a Houston, Texas, company called East & West Petroleum." "I remember going to the library and looking it up in a securities manual." "East & West pumped oil and gas out of the East Texas oil fields and was later bought up by one of the big oil companies." "I even found out that a bearer bond certificate never has an official recording of ownership, the owner is the 'bearer' of the certificate—they didn't pay dividends or interest but you could clip the coupons and present them to the originating company. They were described as being just like gold only better and were issued for as long as thirty years." "I don't think they are legal anymore but we can find out."

"How the hell do you remember all of those things?" moaned Magnis "Does it relieve any pressure or anything like that when you expel some of it like you just did. I mean does your brain throb or squish or what."

To which Chancey replied: "He forgets birthdays, social functions, appointments and where he parks the car all the time." "Says he doesn't have to remember things like that because someone is sure to let him know about a birthday and he can always look for the car." "Duran T. is exactly like him only worse."

Duran T. Lubeck is nine years old and our only child.

"By the way Magnis did you open that other envelope you found in Charlie Clyde's lock box?"

"No but I have it right here."

Magnis opened it and you guessed it—one ten-thousand dollar Baldwin Pipeline Oil & Gas Transmission Corporation bearer bond certificate with four coupons still attached. Out dated of course.

"Tiny Balano was from Chicago as I recall. I have a friend who is also a forensic pathologist in Chicago and we talk often. He loves solving mysteries—kind of a hobby. I'm going to call and ask him to search and make copies of any Chicago Tribune microfiche stories relative to Balano and this Jacko Moretti and any cases of stolen stocks and bonds during that period." "Just might find something interesting—you can't trace these bearer certificates—it was said that if you had them you better look after them." "Now, how did Charlie Clyde get this?" "God, a short while ago our main concern was why he changed his name and now all of this and we are still without a clue."

Chancey had a great idea—she thought we ought to go have lunch and we did. She has never changed and is still

289

as beautiful as that day on the pier.

"How long to get to Hot Springs?" Magnis enquired.

"Hour and a half probably—never been there before have you?"

"No" said Magnis.

"See, I got you again." chuckled I. "You dummy, we went through Hot Springs on the way to L.A." "I can describe the Arlington Hotel to you—we spent about twenty minutes across the street waiting for Ada to do something so that makes you responsible for the cost of lunch."

"Shall we grab our things at the hotel? We probably have learned about as much as we can here. Maybe the ponies are running—they have a track you know." "Might be fun."

Three hours later we were in Hot Springs and checked into the Arlington Hotel and I tell you, those gangsters knew how to do it right—a really great place and food you couldn't believe and my description was exact.

Next morning we headed for the newspaper and indeed the morgue was on microfiche and easy to track.

Magnis had explained what it was that he wanted to do and it was clever. He asked the question—"Why did the robbers only drive several blocks and abandon the car?"

Chancey answered—"Because they had another car stashed and waiting in case someone could identify the escape car."

"Right" Magnis fired back "But something else occurred to me—I wonder if we can find old information such as phone numbers and addresses dating back that far. See where I'm going Dumbo?"

I did and told him for the forty-seven thousandth time in my life not to call me Dumbo or Sabu the Elephant Boy.

"I doubt that we can find school records since we don't even know the name of the school—but—most phone companies keep old phone books."

I headed for the local phone company and Chancey and Magnis started looking through the old papers for anything we had missed in Little Rock.

They turned up a story—August 18,1932 -*Two males, both approximately 30 years of age were found yesterday drowned in a car near Glenwood, Arkansas, both had sustained serious gun shot wounds which probably contributed to running off the road into the Caddo River. They are believed to be the armed robbers involved in the shoot out in Hot Springs on the 16th. No trace of identity and no evidence actually linking them to the crime was found. Authorities are still trying to determine if a third man was involved.*

It took me about an hour to do my assignment and I met them at the hotel and reported—"Guess who lived on Exchange Street folks?" "And guess what used to be on Exchange Street" "Beryl McAdoo and right across the street 'The Natureopathic School of Practical Nursing'—is this exciting or what?" "Did you two find anything?" and they told me.

"I managed a call to my friend Dave in Chicago and he already found some info on Balano for us. It seems that his big thing was dealing in hot securities. Didn't actually do the stealing, rather bought hot ones and apparently peddled them off later. Dave also found an article about a big heist from a Wall Street security firm in New York only a week before this incident down here." "Seems a Mr Jacko Moretti was a suspect in the action but not charged."

"Chancey—can you find that marriage application for Beryl and Clyde ?" asked Magnis. "I don't remember where that was taken out do you?"

"It's stamped Kansas City, Missouri." "Laurel says this is not Charlie Clyde Lubeck's signature—what do you think.?"

"I agree." replied Magnis. "I think we need to start a search for the name C.C.Dodge pre-1940 here in Arkansas and in Kansas and Missouri—you agree Laurel ?" "Why did Charlie Clyde come up with that name or start using it and how does it tie up with Beryl besides this application?"

I advised: "C.C. Dodge could well have been Charlie Clyde Lubeck except for that signature—our Charlie Clyde never developed writing skills beyond the third grade level and that signature was fairly sophisticated comparatively speaking. Let's get out of here and back to Little Rock and the capital building Department of Vital Statistics circa 1932 through 1940. Agreed?"

Back in Little Rock we launched a search—first through the birth records from 1890 through 1910 with no record of a C.C. Dodge being born. We found a birth certificate for Charlie Clyde Lubeck born Feb. 7,1904 and a death certificate for C.C. Dodge 1 July, 1977. Charlie Clyde Lubeck had in essence disappeared at least in Arkansas.

"Boy am I getting slow in the head—Holy Jumped up Jesus Christ. . . ."

Chancey cut me off with "You promised Ada you would stop saying that—remember?" "I'll need to report back to her about this you know."

"Chancey—not now—this is a serious thought—listen—Charlie Clyde died in 1977 and do you remember what Ada said when I told her about it ?"

"Yes I do—'It's about time that rotten bastard did something right—now I can collect on that insurance policy'—that's what she said." said Chancey. "You remember what happened later?"

Magnis chimed in "Yea, she came unglued when she found out that the policy had already been paid back in 1938."

"And what does that mean, when a policy is paid off?" I pretended annoyance with this line of reasoning. "It means that an insurance company has proof of some sort that the death of one of their clients has taken place—in other words—a death certificate. Otherwise no way will they pay off." "Do we find a death certificate here in Arkansas?" "No we don't so that means the insurance company got one from some other state—try Missouri maybe."

"You are now going to tell us we have to go to St. Louis—right?" moaned Magnis. "More records at the capital—and I wish I hadn't just said that don't I—I used to miss that on all the tests back in the sixth grade—it's Springfield isn't it?"

We caught a commuter flight to St Louis, rented a car and drove to Jefferson City where they keep the records, although Magnis wanted very badly for it to be Springfield, and very quickly found what we needed to know and headed west to Kansas City. It was almost dark when we reached the Central Cemetery and followed directions from the old timer on duty at Keeler Brothers Mortuary which had been listed on the death certificate.

Right in front of us stood a simple headstone:

C.C.Lubeck
4-4-1906
5-1-1938

"Who are you in there ?" quipped Chancey as she took

a picture.

The cause of death on the certificate had been: Primary Tubercular Meningitis. Secondary To:—Progressive and Miliary Pulmonary Tuberculosis

"No wonder Charlie Clyde didn't fight the divorce in 1946 and insisted on no notification in Missouri or Arkansas. He couldn't undergo any scrutiny—police wise or insurance company wise—and it just dawned on me. . . . no one has a picture of him or Beryl—and certainly no picture of this one" I said pointing toward the headstone.

"Give you one thousand to one odds that here lies C. C. Dodge—the real one—I need to make a phone call in the morning to Hot Springs—a nice lady at the phone company helped me find Beryl on Exchange Street." "I have a real strong hunch about something."

The next morning I made my call. Abigail Purvis at the Hot Springs Phone Company answered on the second ring, remembered me very well and assured me that my request would be no problem and to call her back in fifteen minutes which is exactly what I did.

"Doctor Lubeck I certainly hope that this helps—a certain C.C. Dodge, LPN had a listing at the same apartment house address as your Miss McAdoo back in 1932—now isn't that a coincidence ?"

"It certainly is Miss Purvis and I want to thank you once again and when I get home I will have my staff send you something more for your trouble."

"Oh Doctor Lubeck don't bother, that twenty covers everything real nice. Call me again sometime if I can be of service."

"This just makes the hair stand up on the back of my neck" I declared as I proceeded to inform Big Brother and the object of my affection about what I had learned.

"Wow—hair standing up!" shouted Chancey "That usually just means he is hungry or horny but now a third thing."

"Come on Chancey—this is still serious stuff—what if the real C.C. Dodge was the third man?" "What if his assignment was to drive the getaway car but then decided to abandon his task and loose himself in the Fordyce after hearing shots down the street only to meet his cronies coming out as planned. That would account for the witness who thought he saw three men but wasn't sure. He then drove south on Central Avenue—turned right on Court Street and right again onto Exchange Street drove up one block—parked and they split up—the two later found dead—drove off in a car they had parked earlier. They must have known and planned that it would be risky to try traveling the roads around Hot Springs carrying the briefcase so C.C.Dodge was assigned to hide it away for as long as it took to cool off. They certainly hadn't planned on getting shot. Dodge probably carried it up the street in a shopping bag or something. He knew Beryl, that's for sure, and if she was still living there probably put it in her room." What do you think so far ?" said I.

"Sounds great to me." said Magnis with Chancey nodding an affirmative.

"Okay—where does our Charlie Clyde fit in ?" "I think that he was in it from the beginning—remember, he may have been only a go-fer but he had to have known something because of what happened later. I think he was needed to haul the briefcase out of Hot Springs to Little Rock without suspicion in his bread truck—the police were not the only ones looking for the robbers—you have to believe that the fear of being caught first by Tiny Balano and his hoodlums was more frightening than the police and certain am I that they were checking things out."

"Go on Laurel—that is magnificent." praised Magnis.

"Okay—Clyde came into town in his usual manner on the 19th of August—made his rounds, delivered bread to the boarding house or apartment or whatever—some building right there might have housed the nurses aid school—we will never know because it no longer exists— at any rate, he went in with a full bread box and came out with an even fuller box and I don't mean brushes. He must have seen the newspaper headline about the two found in the Caddo River, finished his day and headed back to Little Rock—I believe he hid the briefcase somewhere in route and then faked his being robbed—or maybe he actually was coincidentally robbed—who knows."

"C.C. Dodge knew Beryl and they probably had a thing going—I just made that up folks—she probably didn't know anything about anything just relayed the instructions to Charlie Clyde—He probably had already been paid off for his part—the perpetrators—damn that's a big word for me—I suspect—frightened him at the beginning with a story about what happens to people who double cross. Anyway, Beryl was the person Charlie Clyde was visiting when you went with him Magnis. I believe Beryl went to Kansas City soon after and Charlie Clyde joined her. Sometime later when it was prudent to do so C.C. Dodge showed up in K.C.—knowing, of course, that his partners were dead and he was the big winner. He probably confronted Charlie Clyde about giving over the briefcase. Charlie Clyde, I suspect, told him he didn't have it because he got robbed on the way back from Hot Springs but I doubt that C.C.Dodge would have bought that and maybe settled down to play a watch and wait game until Charlie Clyde made a mistake by using some of the contents and then pounce on him—or maybe he did believe him and decided to lay low from the mob." "So far so good ?"

Magnis interjected "C.C. Dodge couldn't shoot him because the loot would then never be found and Charlie Clyde may have told him that he had arranged for a certain letter telling the details of Hot Springs to be sent to the F.B.I in case of his death or something else—I think I saw a scene like that in a movie—I didn't just make it up."

"That's exactly the way I see it plus I still doubt Beryl had a clue about much of it. Beryl had gotten a job at the T.B. hospital in K.C. and perhaps she paid more attention to C.C. than to Charlie Clyde who knows?" "Well, be that as it may, C.C. Dodge didn't dodge his fatality, however it came down, because someone buried him in 1938 as Charlie Clyde Lubeck and who—or is it whom—would that have been except our very own Charlie and Beryl McAdoo Dodge?"

We were having dinner that evening trying to figure out how to approach the Switzerland thing when Magnis said— "I have a hunch that Beryl and the original C.C. were married. In the morning lets check with Springcity or Jeffersonfield or what ever the head place is called and see about marriage—need to check Arkansas as well."

"It doesn't make any difference one way or the other." said Chancey. "But, knowing might wrap up some loose ends—just like this whole thing isn't a loose end." "I need to call the good old Doctor Sekimora tonight anyway to see how he is doing and he always has ways to find this sort of thing and besides it will make him feel useful." "He will know about a marriage before noon tomorrow." and he did.

Doctor Sekimora and I owned a rather substantial and successful incorporated pathology and automated clinical laboratory in Los Angeles and we did lots of business with a particular old-timer investment broker so, after he chatted and gave the marriage news to Chancey—the real C.C. Dodge and Beryl McAdoo had actually gotten married in Joplin, Missouri on the 27th of February 1933—I spoke to him and asked if he would call old Gerald Erskind and ask him a hypothetical question about how one would go about cashing in bearer bonds in the old days—and what if a street person found one lying on a park bench—how could he cash it—Seki was good at the "what if's" of life and promised information before we got home.

We were going to fly from K.C. to L.A. but first I needed to do one more important thing I had forgotten to do in the excitement of the past several days so like good soldiers—wups!—Magnis—I mean like good sailors—we climbed on board a commuter flight back to Little Rock— took a cab to 13th and Broadway.

I had not been here before but I instinctively found Row 17 and laid a red rose, which I had picked up from a vender at the airport, on Site Number 22 at this small Mt. Holly Cemetery.

"Hi Alice—It's me—Laurel—I'm sorry it took so long but as you can see I couldn't have made it without you. . . ." I pulled up my pant legs to my knees exposing well fitted, very expensive, over the calf socks with appropriate and proper adherence technique and application. . . . that is to say the soft wide rubber bands were properly in place and functioning. Chancey needed to lead me away cause something got in my eyes as I heard Alice—it was really Chancey—say "Thanks for coming my friend."

ABNER HAD RETIRED from practice and teaching and he and Ada had moved to Merced and were living at the beautiful vineyard which had now also become a winery and enjoyed life doing exactly what ever it was that pleased them at the moment. Duran T. and Dr Seki loved to visit them and Chancey and I got there as often as possible.

During the summer of 1978 Uncle Louie and Trixie both died in an auto crash on Highway 46 about five miles East of Shandon, California while on their way to Las Vegas. He was driving his latest toy which was a 1974—12 cylinder double six Daimler Sedan Vandem Plas. They did everything in style. The whole world showed up for the funeral service. We—Magnis and I were named as sole heirs to their substantial estate.

In July 1979 the Lubeck brothers, Vice Admiral Magnis C. and Doctor Laurel Hardy, entered the very old, distinguished looking yet small offices of Strausburger—Manheim & Company—Securities, Bonds & Trusts since 1882—Zurich, Switzerland.

We were surprised that the entire enterprise was no wider than fifteen feet and perhaps forty-five feet in depth which entertained a rather Spartan old fashioned office and one middle aged well dressed grim looking gentleman who inquired: "What business have you with Strausburger and Manheim gentlemen?"

Magnis was not in uniform but seemed to command more attention since all words were directed toward him.

We introduced ourselves and received no further acknowledgment that we were even present until we presented the 23 page document which included the numbered account and explained the death of our father—he simply shrugged his shoulders and shoved a three by five index card and an old fashioned ink pen across the desk and advised us to write the certification-verification on file.

We would only get one shot at this and the dilemma was whether Charlie Clyde had used C.C. Lubeck or just Lubeck. I opted for just Lubeck because Doctor Sekimora and I had put the decoder badge under black light, blue light, U.V light and a very high powered microscope which used a newly developed laser and by actually measuring the thickness of the pencil carbon deposited at each letter determined that the letter "C" had no more carbon present than the other letters and reasoned that if Charlie Clyde had spelled out C.C. Lubeck he would have marked the "C" three times therefore leaving a thicker deposit.

Magnis—being the physicist and engineer disagreed. He believed Charlie Clyde was so simple that he would just automatically assume that something this important needed to be formal so used the initials C.C.

I had previously told Magnis that he should make a wish or a prayer or what ever he was accustomed to doing when things started to get tense with his missiles and write the one which felt the best when the time came—and the time was now.

Just like the Oujie Board—something guided him to write the numbers 122125311.

He handed the card to the gentleman who asked us to have a seat on the small leather couch and disappeared down a spiral stairwell at the back of the room which up

300

until now had gone unnoticed.

We waited perhaps twenty minutes until he returned and said "Gentlemen you may come with me." He led us to the stairs and we were greeted by another well dressed demure gentleman standing on the stairs and who's head stuck barely above floor level. Almost comical.

Nothing could have prepared us for what was to come. When we reached the bottom of the spiral stairwell we were in one corner of a room about four times the size of the upper room and which contained desks with men in suits and—actually—some had green eye shades. No one looked up from work and we were escorted down another spiral staircase to what appeared to be a labyrinth many times larger than above. The walls were those of an underground fortress and one such wall contained four very large magnificent brass and steel walk in vaults.

One was opened and Mr What's His Name said: "Please choose one of our many alcoves and your portefeuille will be brought to you. Your account is up upgraded monthly and all is in order as you will see. All the time is yours, no one will disturb you. Your actual securities and certificates are not a part of this file but you will find a very accurate and up to date accounting since opening of the trust. None of these papers may be removed, photographed or copied. Please notice the surveillance camera and I assure you no hidden microphone is present so you may speak freely without risk of being overheard. Our only concern is the security of those things which have been placed in our trust."

This Mr What's His Name left us with a yellow three by five card with the number 122125311 and which, without doubt, had been printed by Charlie Clyde. A magnificent old fashioned wooden box which opened from the top held an elegant white parchment file folder with an identification number 22-9-1953-9632 embossed in gold. A cover folder inside the parchment contained a summation of every transaction from day one. Almost seven hundred thousand 1953 dollars worth of stock in General Electric, General Motors, Alcoa, IBM, DuPont, Boeing, Westinghouse, Xerox, Pacific Gas & Electric, Prudential Insurance and Occidental Life all paying dividends and compounding for more than 25 years. This was a trust into perpetuity and the value of the numbers were unbelievable.

Since we were not allowed to copy any thing—I got my copy machine going and filed it away.

When we finished going through this we signaled the sentinel that we were through and Mr What's His Name number 3 returned and placed each paper in its proper place. He then handed us a very thick walled letter sized parchment envelope and told us that inside we would find a yellow 3 X 5 card on which we should place a new certification-verification which would have to be duplicated before another opening of this file could be made. He once more left us alone.

Magnis invited me to come up with a number. I wrote on the card and placed it in the envelope. I called for assistance and handed it to the gentleman who sealed it with wax and a signet and placed it in the pouch just as he said he would.

When we reached the second level Mr What's His Name number 2 asked us where and to whom they might now forwarded dividends and we told him. He simply wrote it in a log book.

We were prepared to leave when he added "There is one more thing gentlemen. When we receive proof of death of the trustor where shall we forward the—I believe U.S.

tax free—insurance annuities ?" "I presume you will find them quite substantial—perhaps far beyond your expectations." "This trust was obviously conceived by a brilliant mind. One of our more successful accounts. Your benefactor must have been a genius to have thought so carefully and planned so well." "Good day and come as you please Gentlemen."

"Well 'I swan' Magnis   I suppose we can sort this out when we get home." said I as we walked out into the sunlight.

We were both numbed by what we had just been through and walked along the sidewalk in silence for most of two blocks before Magnis broke the magic—"Has it dawned on you as yet why he changed his name ?"

"Yeah, and you know Ada is gon'na want her six-hundred bucks don't you?" I quipped. "Plus interest."

"By the way dumbo." Said Magnis "What did you use for a new password?" "Probably some fifty digit number."

"How did you know ?"

"The....................number...........................is 92011223125192315181119191513520913519" "Can you remember it you twit?" and he screwed it up half way through giving out a groan.

"Well, 'them's the conditions that prevail', but, just in case you don't have your handy decoder badge with you." I pulled the plastic badge from my pocket with a grin.

"I didn't even use a number try—'It always works sometimes'."

The End